Bou

Lust Bites

Down and Dirty
Crude Oil
Beg Me
Afternoon Delight
Lust Bites: Vol 3
Lust Bites: Vol 2

Anthologies

Treble
Subspace
Bound to the Billionaire
Christmas Goes Camo

Single Titles

Summer Spice
Four Play
Carnal Caresses
Swingtime
Party of Three
All Jacked Up
Top or Bottom?

Unconditional Surrender

ISBN # 978-1-78686-124-5

©Copyright Desiree Holt 2017

Cover Art by Posh Gosh ©Copyright 2017

Interior text design by Claire Siemaszkiewicz

Totally Bound Publishing

Published in 2017 by Totally Bound Publishing, Newland House, The Point, Weaver Road, Lincoln, LN6 3QN, United Kingdom.

Strike Force

UNCONDITIONAL SURRENDER

DESIREE HOLT

Dedication

To all the men in Special Operations everywhere in the world—I wish you safety and hope you find your own happy endings.
And to Joseph Patrick Trainor, my go-to guy for all things military and law enforcement—thanks for your hours of endless patience answering my questions.

Prologue

The sound woke her, nothing more than a little squeak and so faint she was surprised she'd even heard it.

Maybe I'm imagining things. Dreaming. I'm so screwed up by this whole thing that anything is possible.

She pinched her eyes shut, tugged the covers up under her chin and tried to think of pleasant things.

There! She heard it again! A sound like the swishing of air or the rustling of fabric. Someone was in her room.

Her cell phone. She needed her cell phone. She reached out a hand and located it in the charger on her nightstand. Could she get to it? Very slowly, barely disturbing the covers, she eased her hand out and grabbed the phone. She had just lifted it from the cradle when fingers closed around her wrist and squeezed.

"We don't need anyone else here, my lovely."

The words were said in a whisper so low she barely heard it, but she definitely felt the pain in her wrist. He released her suddenly but before she could gather her wits, he slapped some kind of tape over her mouth and sat next to her. His hands stroked lightly over her body and nausea bubbled up inside her. She did her best to roll away from him, trying to avoid the groping hands and the disembodied voice.

"There's no place for you to go." The whisper chilled her blood. "You're all mine."

Without warning another man materialized beside her bed, his fist connecting with the intruder, again and again. She couldn't see who it was or what he was doing in her bedroom. She heard a loud grunt of pain, then a thud as a body fell to the floor. Who were they? How did they get there? Did — ?

She sat bolt upright in bed, shaking, her body covered

in sweat even as chills raced over her skin. Turning on the bedside light, she looked around wildly, heart thumping, relieved to see the room empty and nothing disturbed. A nightmare, but it had seemed so real. It had to be the cumulative effect of all the other incidents.

It was *him.* If only she knew who he was. She didn't know why he wouldn't leave her alone or even what he wanted with her. Would she ever be able to get away from him?

Chapter One

Slade Donovan, code name Shadow, moved silently into the room where the men on his Delta Force team waited. Tall and muscular, he was the essence of a warrior, his dark brown hair slightly shaggy with a gray thread or two showing here and there, and the expression on his chiseled face said *Bring it on.*

Lowering his gear bag to the floor, he dropped himself into an oversized armchair and pulled out his laptop. *First things first,* he told himself. Mission completed. Men all accounted for. Time to reconnect with the outside world. He turned on the machine and waited for everything to load.

He was more than grateful for the satellite setup at their base camp that allowed them all to communicate with the rest of the world. It was a great way to maintain contact with his 'brothers' in the many Spec Ops groups, not just on newsy items but on ways to do things better. He also kept in touch with the foreman of his ranch back in Texas and with the few friends he'd been close with for years.

While he waited for the computer to boot up, he glanced around the room at his men, the members of Team Charlie, sprawled out on the battered furniture, weary and battle-hardened. They still looked rode hard and put away wet, as the saying went in Texas. This last mission had sucked a lot out of them.

Just yesterday they had come down out of the Hindu Kush, the mountain chain that stretched from Afghanistan to Pakistan, tired, dirty and spent, although eminently satisfied. Despite the intel fuckup, the mission had been a success. One more terrorist cell destroyed, one more maniac blown to hell. And the troops fighting for the people of Afghanistan had one less bad guy — and his followers — to worry about.

Delta Force, the Army's top covert combat unit, had counterterrorism as its main focus and they performed their missions with cold single-mindedness. Like the one they had just completed.

Once they'd landed, they'd gone through debriefing, badly needed showers, a hot meal and fourteen hours of sleep. Now they were just hanging out, guzzling water and making plans for their imminent leave. They were facing ten days to let it all hang out, battle their demons and refresh.

"Damn, Shadow." Trey McIntyre, code name Storm and the team's demolitions and firearms expert, flopped onto the beat-up couch and looked over at him. "That last mission was a stone bitch."

Slade nodded agreement at Trey's comment. It had definitely been a shitstorm of epic proportions. Angry at the poor intel, at the danger it had put them all in, at the possibility the mission would fail, Slade had kept it all together. They'd regrouped, adjusted their plans and completed the assignment. But hellfire. He wanted to throttle everyone who had put this together.

"Fucking A," he agreed. "I told the captain the intel on this one sucked. You all pulled off a miracle and I'm damn proud of you all."

"No shit." Beau Williams made a rude noise.

With his sun-streaked light brown hair and green eyes, he looked like a typical surfer, fitting his code name. Surfer. Nothing could be further from the truth, though. Beau was their sniper, a job that required incredible focus and discipline.

The *ding* of a bell let Slade know his computer was now up and running.

When he clicked on the email icon, a flood of messages rolled into his inbox. As he scrolled through them, the subject of one caught his eye. He'd been searching for something he and his team could do together on their current downtime, something to work off the residual tension. Maybe this was it. Last time he'd talked them into it, they'd blown away the competition. Maybe he could coax them out to the ranch and get them to do it again. They might have plans or not, but they were all so drained after the last few ops he wanted them to recharge as a team where he could watch over them.

"Okay, you guys." The others looked over at him. "I've got something here that might interest you."

"What's up?" Beau stretched and yawned.

"Remember that shooting competition we took part in two years ago?" Slade glanced at his screen again. "The one held just south of my ranch?"

"Yeah." Marc Blanchard—code name Eagle—grunted. "We cleaned their clocks."

Beau grinned. "No shit. What about it?"

"There's another one scheduled for next week, right at the end of our leave. Handguns and long guns. Just like the last one." He paused. "I don't know what plans y'all might have, but how about hanging out at my ranch again and we'll go win a few more prizes?"

His spread was south of San Antonio, where he ran a small herd of cattle and kept horses he could ride fast enough and far enough to clear his mind. It had become his refuge, a place to heal after each mission and reconnect with humanity. He'd taken his team there a couple of times when they'd really needed to switch off from everything to pull themselves together again.

Beau sat forward, interest sparking in his eyes. "I can always use a chance to dazzle people with my skills. But, uh, Shadow? Besides the competition, will there also be women while we're there? That's *my* top priority."

Of course. Beau didn't care where or what as long as there were women.

"Did you notice a lack of them the last couple of times?"

Slade grinned. "Yes, there will be women."

"Then count me in."

"Me too," Trey echoed.

Marc was suspiciously silent. Still recovering from the disastrous end of an even more catastrophic marriage, bitterness had etched deep lines on his face and colored his entire personality.

Slade focused his gaze on him. "Marc? You in?"

The man was silent for so long Slade wasn't sure he planned to give him an answer. Then he gave a short, quick nod. "I'm in for the shooting. We'll see about the women."

Slade had discussed Marc's situation many times with Beau and Trey. They all worried that, when he had leave, the man just crawled into a hole for ten days and drank himself into oblivion. Still, he always showed up on time sober and sharp so Slade really had no cause to say anything to him. Yet. But he could still worry about him.

"And speaking of meeting women," Slade went on, "remember the JAG lawyer I introduced you to when you were at the ranch two years ago? Paul Hutton? Old friend of mine? We had dinner one night with him and his wife?"

"Is he providing the women?" Beau joked.

Slade chuckled. "Maybe. In a way, that is. He and his wife are having a party. If you all promise to clean up good and not pick your teeth in public, we're all invited."

"I'm guessing it will be a little different than the entertainment last time, right?" Trey winked.

Beau laughed. "I'd say that's a big Ten-Four."

Slade nodded. "No private sex club this time. We tried it at The Edge and you all passed on doing it again."

Beau nodded. "Not our cup of tea."

"I like my sex with no holds barred," Trey added, "but not with a lot of other people around. Call me simple, but I like my privacy."

"Is that so the rest of us can't see how inept a lover you are?" Beau teased. "Afraid your women will take a gander at us and leave you in the dust?"

"Ha ha ha. Very funny. As a matter of fact, I don't want *your* women to get jealous of my style."

"Whatever." Beau flapped a hand at him.

"But I think we're all agreed the club scene isn't for us, right?" Slade looked at each of them. "Speak up now and forever."

"Yes." Beau nodded. "Right."

Trey nodded his assent. Slade glanced at Marc Blanchard, who hadn't spoken a word. The man was in a very dark place and had been since the implosion of his marriage. Slade worried about him, a lot. He'd thought the visit to The Edge might have lit a spark in him, but Marc had disappeared into a private room with one of the subs and hadn't said a word about it afterward.

"Marc? You agree too?"

Marc just nodded.

"Okay, then. We'll head back to my ranch and make plans from there. Let me dig through my email and see if there's anything else on that might interest us."

Slade liked sex as much as the next man and had a healthy appetite for it. He lived by the motto—*We go abroad to vanquish and conquer for country. We come home and vanquish and conquer for us.* And why not? Tomorrow could be their last day on Earth.

Sometimes he wondered, though, if that would be the pattern forever. He was totally committed to Delta. It was his life. He had nothing left over to give to a relationship. Something he'd learned to live with. Sure, he'd seen others do it, but it required a mindset he didn't think he had. There were those who had retired from Delta Force, at least from active missions. They taught, trained others—any number of things. But could he do it? He was a warrior, after all. The leader of Delta Force Team Charlie. Up until now there hadn't been room for anything else. Could he ever adjust to a change?

But then, as he stared unseeing at the computer screen, *bam!* A memory popped into his mind. One that had been haunting him for five years. No matter how he tried, he couldn't get rid of it. He wasn't a man given to dreaming about women—except maybe for the occasional wet dream. But a trip to Chicago and a party with friends had ended in a night of the most spectacular sex with the most incredible woman he'd ever met. She had stunned him. Sucker-punched might be a better word. Blindsided him. Silky auburn hair, emerald green eyes and a body that had made his mouth water. Perfume that had tickled his senses, a low musical laugh and the satiny feel of her skin completed the package. She had been so put together on the outside, but wildness had sparkled in her eyes.

They'd come together as two strangers, looking for nothing more than the moment. A brief but explosively intense encounter. He'd wanted to wash away the devastation of his most recent mission and she had wanted—whatever she'd wanted. They hadn't spent a lot of time discussing it. In his hotel room they'd torn each other's clothes off in their haste to get naked. That first coming together had been hot and frantic and had blown his mind. He'd felt like a teenager on his first hot date.

Every moment of that night still haunted him, indelibly etched on his brain, on his senses. He couldn't forget her plump breasts tipped with rosy nipples, or the wet heat of her sex and the way it had clenched around him when she'd come. He swore he could still feel the satiny caress of her skin as she lay pressed against him, or the silken fall of her hair brushing his chest—and other parts of his body.

Underneath her proper exterior she'd been a hot, sensuous woman who'd liked her sex as rough as he did. It had been the best sex of his life, ever, hands down. He had definitely been up for more of it the next day. Worn out and replete, he'd vaguely remembered falling asleep with her in his arms, but when he'd awoken in the morning, she had been gone, leaving him with an unaccustomed emptiness. He'd asked his friends about her, but all they'd known was she'd come with some other people they'd invited. They hadn't recognized the name and apparently nobody else had known who Mandy Wheeler Baker was. Maybe she'd given him a fake name, just as he'd done to her. Women came and went in his life, and that was fine with him. The way he wanted it. He was married to Delta and had no plans to change that any time soon. But not even calling on all his personal discipline could get one time with that woman out of his mind. One night, for fuck's sake.

How was it possible that after five years he still remembered every erotic detail of those long hours? How many times had he replayed it over and over, like a video on constant rewind? She appeared in his dreams, as if taunting him, and his cock swelled and hardened every time. Other women hadn't been able to erase her from his mind. He was arrogant enough to wonder if she thought of him after all this time but pragmatic enough to know the chances they'd ever cross paths again were slim to none.

He wanted her with a hunger that ate at him. Worse than that, they'd made a connection. An emotional link. Whatever. He'd have thought with the passage of time that feeling would fade. Instead, it had just increased. Grown stronger. He couldn't get her out of his fucking mind. And if he did find her? What then? Where did they go from there?

"Hey, Slade." Trey's voice broke into his reverie. "You still with us? Where'd you wander off to?"

He shook himself back to the present, realizing with a start he'd zoned out right there in front of his men. Bad, bad, bad. "Yeah. I'm here."

"Good to know." Beau cocked an eyebrow. "You looked a million miles away."

"So we okay here? If nothing else, for ten days you'll get to eat terrific food, soak up some sun and not have to do a damn fucking thing."

Trey nodded. "I'm in."

The rest of them murmured their agreement, even Marc.

"Okay. Let's make some plane reservations. We'll fly into

San Antonio. Then I'll have the ranch chopper pick us up."

"Sounds okay to me," Beau agreed. "Let's rock and roll."

In less than twelve hours they were on their way out of Helmand Province, making a stop in Madrid to pick up a commercial flight to the States. Long hours after that they finally landed at San Antonio International Airport where Slade hustled them out of the door and down a long walkway to the private plane terminal. A gleaming black helo awaited them, a familiar figure leaning against it, arms folded across his chest, white teeth gleaming in a smile contrasting with his sun-darkened skin.

"Glad you're home, bro," he said, slapping Slade on the shoulder.

"Me too. Look at the bunch of ugly mugs I brought with me again."

"Hey, Teo!" Trey shook hands with the man. "Think you can put up with us again?"

"As long as the boss pays me extra." He winked. Teobaldo Rivera was the ranch foreman, fiercely loyal to Slade and excellent at his job.

Whenever Slade brought his team to the ranch with him, Teo always went out of his way to make sure they enjoyed themselves.

"Okay," he told them. "Let's get loaded up. The beer's chilling in the fridge and the steaks are thawing."

It was a tight fit for five oversized males, but Slade figured they could handle it for the short hop to the ranch. As soon as the chopper landed, they were out of the cabin. Slade shoved his hands in his pockets and looked around. He loved coming home to the ranch. It replaced the family he didn't have and the home he'd lost a long time ago. The sprawling ranch house off to his right rose two stories from the lawn around it, shaded by ancient oaks and maples. To the left stood the enormous barn that held his horses, any cattle that might need to be separated in an individual pen, and Teo's offices. Behind that nestled the building that housed all the ranch equipment, including the portable pens for branding. And beyond that, as far as he could see, the endless rolling pastures meeting the horizon of the blue Texas sky. Pastures that contained the small herd of cattle he nourished and bred and sold.

He inhaled the familiar scent of horses and hay and Texas sunshine and almost at once the tension riding him began to ease. He loved coming home to this place. He could regenerate, rest, ride his horses.

And there were always women to hook up with whenever he wanted, women he'd met over the years. Too bad none of them replaced the one he really wanted. He could almost see her here on the ranch, in jeans and boots, walking to meet him, two small figures hopping along beside her, filled with excitement. But he didn't know her real name, didn't know where to find her and no one seemed able to tell him. So all he had was the memory of the most incredible night of his life, a memory that plagued him whenever he opened his mind to it.

Fucking damn. He needed to find that woman or get over her. He was driving himself nuts.

While Teo went through his shutdown routine, he and his men unloaded their duffels and headed toward the house.

"Let's get inside," Slade told them, "and I'll get you all situated." He grinned. "Then we can crack open some cold ones."

The large ranch house had four guest rooms plus the master suite, a situation that worked out well for them. The air was still sun-warmed, even though the sun itself had dipped below the horizon, but a soft breeze added a cooling element. The air carried the heady aromas of hay and horseflesh and cattle, a mixture Slade loved more than any perfume. The spread was his haven, the place where he could put all the blackness of his missions behind him and feel like a normal person. If he ever did settle down, the woman would have to love it as much as he did —*if* being the operative word. Did the woman he'd dreamed about so much —?

Damn! He had to stop this. He was losing his grip here.

"I see Teo got the beer out?" he commented as he jogged down the stairs and out to the porch.

The men had dumped their gear in their respective rooms and were already out there waiting for him.

"Yeah," Trey joked. "We're trying to save you some, but you know how it goes."

Slade glanced around, realizing one of the team was absent. "Be right back," he told them.

Slade knocked on the door of the room Marc had dropped his things in. He'd wanted to give the man a moment to himself on the off chance he'd come on downstairs and join them, but it seemed he needed either prodding or dragging. Slade had hoped with such a peaceful setting, surrounded by the natural beauty of Texas ranchland, with a gorgeous sunset painting the sky, he'd feel relaxed. Maybe even looking forward to the ten days here. But nothing relaxed him anymore. While the rest of them kicked back and did whatever, Marc, the team's weapons and demolitions expert, often used his downtime in practice and refresher training. Considering the state of his personal life, Slade was glad the man was a disciplined soldier, committed to the job.

"Yeah?"

Slade pushed the door open. Marc stood at the window looking out at the scene below.

"Okay to come in?"

Marc shrugged. "It's your house."

"Hey, guy. That doesn't mean you can't have privacy."

If anyone asked Slade he'd say the man had too much privacy. Too much time to think about the dark place he couldn't seem to get out of. A place where the image of his naked wife, high on the drugs he hadn't known she was addicted to, was riding their equally naked neighbor and screaming with pleasure. He once told Slade, in a rare moment of confidence, he wished he could bleach his mind to erase that scene that played over and over like a video on a loop.

'That's what I got for letting my cock tell me what to do instead of listening to my brain.'

Slade knew some of the background. When Marc had met Ria, he'd been stunned by her beauty and swept away by her vivacious personality. Naturally quiet and introspective himself, he'd nevertheless been drawn to her at once. His total dedication to Delta Force had precluded any type of lasting relationship. Until then. She'd told him she loved him and had made him believe it. The sex had been unbelievable, so hot it had scorched the air around them. When he'd had leave time between missions, he hadn't been able to get home fast enough to immerse himself in his incredible wife. The fact that she had chosen him when, he was sure, she could have any man she'd wanted, was in itself an aphrodisiac.

Slade and the other team members had met her, at a dinner where he'd proudly showed her off. None of the team members, including Slade, had been too enthusiastic about her, but that hadn't bothered Marc.

"You're just jealous," he'd ground out.

Then the roof had fallen in and his life had come apart. The scene he'd walked in on had been bad enough. He'd managed to control his rage to not kill the guy when he'd tossed them out into the street. But when he'd realized she'd been high on drugs rather than alcohol, he'd done a thorough search of the house, including her personal belongings, and found baggies filled with multicolored pills.

He'd called Slade, because he'd been out of his mind. Insane. Especially when he'd learned she'd been doing that for a long time, both the drugs and screwing anything with a dick. He'd been torn between wanting to kill her and kill himself. Slade had talked him down off the ledge and waited while he'd packed his things—not too many, he traveled light—and had walked him out of the apartment and out of her life. He'd found him an attorney who had told Marc to do whatever was needed to get a divorce fast.

He'd asked Slade not to ever bring it up again and had spent the rest of his leave holed up in a motel room, trying not to drink himself to death.

Slade wasn't an emotional person, but his heart ached for Marc, so damaged by a selfish, insane woman. He often wondered if Marc would ever get back to the point where he wanted to rejoin the living.

Now Slade cleared his throat. "Heavy thoughts there, Eagle. Admiring the great view?"

Marc turned, his mouth stretched in an imitation of a smile. "Just giving my brain a rest. Give me five and I'll be right along."

"I'll hold you to it. Beer's cold, so come on down."

Swallowing a sigh, he left the room and headed downstairs. He could already hear the others on the back porch where he'd left them. Maybe, just maybe ten days at the ranch would be the first step toward Marc regaining his sanity and equilibrium.

* * * *

Slade watched Marc snag a beer from the cooler, pop the cap and move to the far side of the porch. As usual, close to the group but still separate. *Man.* The guy was going to implode if they didn't figure out how to get him some help pretty soon. Slade thought about telling him to move closer to the others but decided to keep his mouth shut. This was supposed to be a vacation. Downtime. If he wanted Marc to heal, he wouldn't accomplish it by giving him orders.

"You know"—Trey leaned back in the lounger he'd appropriated, staring off toward the horizon—"I can see why you like this place."

"Yeah?" Slade raised an eyebrow.

"I'm not sure I could take the peace and quiet in large doses," Trey added, "or too frequently. But right now? I have to say it's great."

"I actually think I might agree with him, shocking as that is." Beau took a long swallow of his beer and let his gaze travel lazily over the view that stretched from the house. "I can see why you love it here, Slade."

Some of the horses were in the corral, their coats glowing in the sunlight. Beside the first bar, two of the hands worked on the hay baler and from the far pasture, two hands who'd been riding fences trotted their horses back to the barn. It always reminded him of a painting he'd seen in a gallery in San Antonio that specialized in Western landscapes.

"Best tranquilizer in the world," he told the other men.

"So what's on the agenda now, Shadow? Riding horses or riding women?"

Slade considered each of them—lean, tan, hardened men, men he felt privileged to have on his team. They'd forged a bond that was unheard of in normal circumstances. He wouldn't trade it for anything.

"I'm thinking we should just hang out here tonight, try to get back to what passes for normal for us. Kick back. Drink some beer. Grill some steaks. Tomorrow night is the party I told you about."

"Is this the party your friend is giving?" Beau grinned. "And how clean do we have to get?"

"Clean enough to pass muster. Yes, this is the one. So pretty damn clean." He took his own swallow of beer.

"I know he's JAG now," Beau asked, "but was he ever Delta?"

Slade shook his head, irritated at the question. "No, we went in different directions. He loved the law and the fact he could be Army and still practice it. He had his law degree, applied for Judge Advocate Group and he's been with them ever since. Dumb luck for him he got assigned to Lackland here in San Antonio and he's been here ever since." Slade looked hard at each of them. "And he's done a damn fine job. He puts his ass on the line every day in a different way."

"Okay, okay." Beau held up his hands. "I didn't mean

anything by it. Any friend of yours and all that."

Trey took a sip of his cold beer. "Is this party for something special?"

"No. They just like to entertain. When he found out I'd be home for it, he insisted I come."

Beau lifted an eyebrow. "And us too?"

"Hard as it is to believe anyone would want your company," Slade teased. "But yes, he said to bring all you assholes."

Marc, who hadn't said a word up until now, shook his head. "I think I'll pass."

Slade leaned forward. "That's not an option, Marc. Even if you sit in the corner all night and glower at everyone, I'm getting your ass there, so just accept it." He unwound his tall body from the lounge chair. "Meanwhile, I think we could all use a shower. Then I'll throw those steaks on the grill. I don't know about you guys, but I've been waiting a long time for a decent meal. See you in an hour."

Chapter Two

"Want to join us, Kari? We're going out for a celebratory drink."

Kari Malone lifted her gaze from her desk to see Sasha Crew's petite form in her doorway. She couldn't think of anyone who appeared less like an assistant district attorney than this woman. Kari pushed her own thick auburn hair away from her face and rotated her stiff shoulders. The last day of a trial and the interminable wait for a verdict was always a strain. They'd barely gotten one before the clock ticked up to five o'clock.

"I don't think so," she answered. "Thanks, anyway."

"Oh, come on. You never want to go out with us." Sasha pouted. "I'm beginning to think you don't like us. You've had a tough week in court and I hear closing arguments are Monday morning. You need to unwind a little before you start to work on it."

"Right now I just want to soak in a tub and sip a chilled glass of wine."

"Maybe you could have that glass of wine with us? You turned us down so many times we're beginning to get a complex. Okay, okay." She laughed and held up her hands at the look on Kari's face. "But we'll be at Frankie's if you change your mind."

Kari watched the woman walk away, wondering if maybe she should have taken her up on the invite. People in the criminal district attorney's office saw her as a tightly controlled, focused woman in her business suits and sensible heels, with minimal makeup, her hair tamed into a tight French twist. Her entire life was the cases she tried.

I didn't used to be like this.

No, she didn't. She might be a tight-ass in the courtroom, even have a well-earned rep for it, but in her private life she used to be more open, more relaxed. Able to enjoy an evening out. But that was before—

Don't think about it.

She had been in San Antonio for three months now and still hesitated to venture out beyond her office, her apartment and the most necessary of errands. She'd turned down the opportunities for dates, earning herself some very unflattering nicknames. She didn't care. Danger lurked in every corner and shadow for her. All the pep talks she gave herself didn't seem to make any difference. The fear was always there. During the day, involved in her work, it wasn't so bad. But once she left the safety of her offices, she scurried home as fast as she could and triple locked her doors, worried that *he* had found her.

Just yesterday she'd checked in with Ross Delahunt, her old boss, state's attorney for Cook County, to see if anything was happening.

"A lot of people are asking where you went to in such a hurry," he'd told her.

"And what do you tell them?" *Please, not that I'm here.*

"That you're taking some time off and doing some traveling. That I'm hoping you'll decide to come back but you insisted you needed a change of scenery."

"And people buy that?" Would they really believe that was the truth?

"The business with your stalker wasn't any secret," he'd reminded her, "so it's not so farfetched."

"I can't believe we couldn't find out who he was."

"Whoever he is, he's one smart bastard," Ross had commented.

If only she knew who *he* was, the nameless, faceless man who had tormented her so intently in Chicago she'd been forced to flee half a continent away. Last night she'd had the dream again, had been so shaken by it that she'd had to work hard to pull herself together for court.

"Kari?"

She looked up to see her boss, Bexar County Criminal District Attorney Kip Reyes, standing in her doorway.

"Sir?"

He laughed. "You can actually call me Kip after hours. You don't get your pay docked or a black mark on your record."

She forced herself to relax. He wasn't coming on to her. Not even a little. He might be a dark-haired, dark-eyed, sexy Latino, with a runner's body that made women drool, but Kip Reyes was happily married to one of the sharpest, nicest women Kari had ever met. Straying wasn't even on his horizon. She forced herself to draw in a breath and let it out slowly. "Okay. *Kip.*"

"Better." He braced himself on the doorjamb. "Closing arguments in your case on Monday, right?"

She nodded. "I'm going to work on it this weekend." *Because I never go anywhere or do anything anyway.*

"Listen, Natalie and I are going to a friend's tonight. Nothing special. Just kind of a casual Friday night get-together. You remember meeting Paul Hutton the other day, right?"

She frowned. "The JAG colonel?"

"Right. Anyway, he and his wife are having a little informal gathering at their place and Nat and I think you should drop in."

Anticipation coursed through her, until she remembered this was a different party, different state, different city, different people. The last time she'd allowed herself to be talked into a party she'd spent the most incredible night of her life, one she still had erotic dreams about. She had never dreamed sex could be that great or that hot or that off the charts. Too bad Sam—if that had even been his real name—had disappeared off the face of the earth.

Now, with the fearful twist her life had taken two years ago, she stayed away from events like this. Or, in fact, any events at all.

"I can't imagine he'd be happy with you inviting guests to his party."

Kip laughed. "As a matter of fact, after he met you and learned you were new to town, he suggested I pass along the invite."

"Oh. Well." She shuffled a few more papers. "Um, thanks, Kip, but I think I'm just going to go home, soak in a tub and drink wine."

"The glamorous life of a prosecutor," he joked. "Right?"

She managed a little smile. "If the public only knew."

"Okay, I'm playing my trump card. Natalie's worried about you, says you keep to yourself too much. And when Nat's worried, I try to make that go away."

Kari stared at him. "She's worried about me? She barely knows me."

"Listen." He shook his head. "I swear my wife has psychic powers. The last visit to my office she told me, *Kip, that woman needs taking care of. Take care of her.*"

Kari couldn't help herself. She burst out laughing. "She definitely has your number."

"No kidding." His face sobered. "Listen, Kari. I know where you're coming from. I know what chased you to San Antonio and I promised Ross I'd keep an eye on you. Which I'm doing. I wouldn't urge you to venture out anyplace I didn't think was safe for you. This is a private party, everyone's vetted and there's nothing to worry about. Natalie and I will be there so you always have backup." He gave her a reassuring wink. "So can you do us both a favor and say yes?"

She chewed her lip, trying to figure out how to do this without offending Kip, who was a great boss and a great guy. And someone who had gone out of his way to keep her situation private while providing her a secure work environment, and to make her feel welcome. But go to a party? She thought she deserved a medal for going to *work* every day.

"You don't have to stay long," he added in a soft voice. "But I do think it would do you some good to see something besides this office, the courthouse and your apartment."

The last thing in the world she wanted to do was go to a party with people she didn't know. On the other hand, what could be safer than being with a prosecuting attorney and a JAG officer? Okay, she owed Kip something. She could manage a half hour or so to satisfy him. What could it hurt?

"Okay." She swallowed. "I'll go. Give me the address and I'll plug it into my GPS."

"Great." Relief washed over his face. He took a business card from his shirt pocket and handed it to her. "On the chance I could get you to say yes I wrote everything down for you. You've got my cell number if you need it."

She stuck the card in the pocket of her skirt. "What time is this shindig, anyway?"

"Seven o'clock." He glanced at his watch. "It's five-thirty now. Does that give you enough time to do whatever you need to before then?"

"Yes. Of course." Time to shower and change into fresh clothes. Wash off the burdens of the day.

Find some courage.

"Good. See you there." He started to leave then turned back. "I think you'll have a good time, Kari. And you'll met some new people, expand your horizons beyond this office."

She didn't want to tell him she needed to keep her horizons as narrow as possible. The narrower the safer. San Antonio had been a clean start for her. At least she hoped so. But only if she was very cautious, very careful and wasn't very visible beyond the courtroom.

What a hell of a way to live.

Signing off on her computer, she then closed everything down, gathered her purse and took the elevator down to the parking garage. She always made sure to ride with others. Her parking space was near the elevator so in minutes she slipped into it and was heading out of the garage.

Driving to her apartment she had second and third and even fourth thoughts about doing this.

For the past two years she'd lived a very compartmentalized life, first in Chicago then here in San Antonio. Before the move her social life had disintegrated to zero, but even then *he'd* found ways to torment her. More and more ways.

At first she'd thought someone had been playing a joke on her. Maybe one of the other attorneys who'd teased her about her lack of a social life. She hadn't dated much at that point and had lost interest in parties and Friday night happy hours.

How did you compete with a dream?

So she'd figured one of the wise-asses had decided to have a little fun. First a card had arrived, taped to her front door, professing great admiration and affection. It had been unsigned except for the drawing of a heart. Then a flower had appeared on her desk at the end of a hectic trial. One flower. A peony. No card. No one had known where it had come from. At least that's what they'd all said. She'd looked up its meaning, hoping that would point her in the right direction. Romance and an omen of good fortune. Anyone could have sent her congratulations. But romance?

Next had come a gardenia. One of the legal assistants had told her it meant secret love. That had given her an uneasy feeling. Who the hell had been in love with her? She'd barely dated anymore, measuring every man against the memory of a phantom. Then a cactus flower had been delivered and she'd freaked out when she'd discovered it meant lust. The whole thing hadn't been funny to her any longer, so she'd gone to Ross Delahunt. He'd tried to find out where the flowers had come from, but none of the florists remembered who'd ordered them. Only that they'd been paid for in cash.

Kari had kept hoping it would stop. Anyway, flowers were just harmless, right? Until the hang-up calls had started on both her landline at home and her cell phone. Until she'd gotten the feeling someone had been watching her. Following her. Until computer-generated notes had begun appearing in her mailbox, notes that left no question what had been in the mind of the writer.

Until someone had broken into her condo while she'd been at work, placed all her lingerie carefully on her bed then, as evidenced by the imprint, lain down on top of it. The police had found no trace of whoever it had been. Of course. Her stalker had developed stealth into an art form. Her nerves had been raw and she'd found it increasingly difficult to concentrate on her cases.

She'd had an alarm system installed, but somehow her follower had managed to bypass it one night. When she'd awoken to a shadowy figure in her bedroom, just standing there, obviously watching her, she'd lost it, screaming her head off. That must have startled him, because he'd fled at once. But that had been the end for Kari.

Ross had taken it all very seriously. The first thing they'd thought of was someone she had successfully prosecuted who might now be free and carrying a grudge. He'd had one of his admins check the whereabouts of everyone on that list, but they'd all still been in prison. Anyway, to her this hadn't felt like someone out to hurt her. More like someone who was secretly obsessed with her. But why hadn't he come out of the closet, so to speak? Why not approach her in a normal manner?

"Because unfortunately," Ross had said, "he's got a twisted mind. He might be a high-profile person who for a number of reasons can't approach you in person. Or maybe he's married and this is the only way he can act on his feelings for you."

"Great," she'd groaned. "So I'm going to be his secret obsession forever? Ross, I don't know how much more of this I can take."

"It has to be someone with easy access to the offices," he'd commented. "Someone whose appearance wouldn't be cause for alarm."

"But that could be dozens of people," she'd protested.

They'd checked all the attorneys who had appeared against her, but that had seemed to be a dead end too. Ross had his top investigator interview them and these were men who could read people. They'd told him there was nothing to find. Not even a twitch from any of them.

When she'd finally hit the breaking point, she was more than grateful to him for reaching out to his contacts and finding her this position here. No announcement had been made in Chicago, no farewell parties, nothing. No fanfare at all. She'd managed to slip out of her job and the city unnoticed without, she hoped, a trace. She just wondered how much longer she'd have to live like this.

"He's off the grid, Kari," Ross had told her last time she'd asked. "Everyone's got feelers out for him but you know how good he is at being invisible."

Yes, she did. Even when he'd tormented her, he'd been like a wraith in the night.

"We don't even know what the hell he looks like," she'd protested.

"Tell me about it." Her boss's voice had been filled with frustration. "That's the damndest part of it."

"He's like a ghost," she'd told him. "How does he leave all these things and no one sees him? Get to my house? Find my information without anyone knowing it?"

"You and I both know that devious people can accomplish devious things. I can at least tell you no one out of the ordinary seems to be nosing around to find you and for damn sure none of us are telling anyone where you went."

"But what if it's someone who wouldn't raise any red flags? Someone so commonplace no one thinks of him for this?"

"Then we need to examine all your options and decide what's best for you."

Hence the move to San Antonio.

Shake it off. It's been months. He's probably given up by this time.

If only.

Making a conscious effort to redirect her thoughts, her mind wandered to the upcoming evening. She'd never been much for parties—oh, wait, Kip had said gathering—even before her life had imploded. The one she'd attended five years ago had given her the most memorable night of her life. Too bad she'd run like a scared little girl, not willing to mess up her career plans. Look where that had gotten her—chased out of Chicago by a relentless stalker and wondering every day since then if she'd ever again see the man who still lived in her dreams.

The image of her incredible lover had never left her. He had a tall, muscular, lean body…a warrior's body. Thick hair the color of melted chocolate and hazel eyes with flecks of brown in them. A square-jawed angular face with high cheekbones and a tan that she somehow didn't think came from hanging out at a beach. The image of him was like a photograph permanently etched on her brain cells. The instant they'd touched, something powerful had passed between them. Every time she thought of him since then her breasts had ached, her nipples tightened and the walls of her pussy thrummed with need. How was that possible after just one night five long years ago?

Because he is so much more than any man I met before or since.

What would he say if he knew her situation? Of course, she'd never have a chance to find out. She'd managed to deep-six that possibility. The chances she'd ever find him again were less than slim to none, but she did wonder if he ever thought of her the way she thought about him.

Stop it, Kari. Enough already.

* * * *

"I'm always impressed with the size of this place." Beau reined in his mount next to Slade's. "I can see why you like coming home to it."

They'd stopped at the little creek running by a stand of trees. Teo had packed thick sandwiches and ice-cold beer for them in their saddlebags and Slade figured they needed the break right about now. He took a moment to draw in a deep breath, relishing the blend of grass and hay and horseflesh and yes, even sweat.

"Thanks, Big Boss." Trey swung down from his saddle and stood there rubbing his ass. "I think I'll need a cushion to sit down after this."

"Maybe your ass needs toughening up," Beau teased.

Trey flipped him off and everyone laughed.

Lunch was a leisurely meal, just relaxing by the water. There wasn't even a lot of discussion. Slade talked about the ranch, how they moved the cattle around, what he hoped to do with it once he left Delta Force. They shot the breeze and bullshitted until all the food and drink were gone. Then they headed back to the ranch to give themselves time to clean up before driving into the city.

"You're really into this, aren't you," Beau commented as they slowed their horses. "I see it every time we come here."

"Working on the ranch or even just riding always helps clear out my mind," Slade answered Beau. "No matter how dark it is inside my brain and soul after some of our missions, a few hours on horseback seems to let in the sunshine."

"You're right." Beau inhaled the scent-laden air and let his breath out slowly. "I ought to take you up on your invitation to visit more often. This place is great."

"You know you're welcome any time, buddy."

"So tell me about the party tonight. Dinner? No dinner? Large group? Small?"

"From what Paul said, a buffet dinner, casual, and I'm guessing about thirty people. They've got a large home in Alamo Heights with a big yard and plenty of room for people to mingle."

Marc drew up next to them. "And what if I don't feel like mingling? I'm considering not going at all."

Slade studied the man, the tight lines of his face and the darkness in his eyes. He could just as easily tell him to stay home, but Marc needed someone to yank him back from the abyss he was teetering on the edge of.

"If I have to give an order as your commanding officer," he told him, "I will. I know what you've been dealing with is soul-sucking, but I won't let you destroy yourself over it. If you do, your ex-wife wins, and I'm not about to let that happen. So no, you won't be staying home tonight."

"Are you sure there'll be women there tonight?" Trey joked.

"Yes, but they may be a little too high-class for you." Slade edged his horse closer. "And you'll need to shower first."

"Seriously. Are we allowed to troll the population if there are single women? We'll behave, big brother. Word of honor." Trey crossed his heart.

"If I had a brain, I'd leave you guys at home. But tonight you'll start learning how to act civilized again."

They unsaddled and stabled their horses then walked up to the house.

Slade knew the women the Huttons invited would be nice, attractive, intelligent. That was their circle of friends. But the one he wanted wouldn't be there. He'd had a long, dry stretch as far as women were concerned, what with all the back-to-back missions. In some of the foreign cities where they'd been, he'd tried to find someone who could excite him. It never worked. Despite their experience and sexual expertise, they'd left him wanting. He'd finally stopped searching, instead spending the nights in his hotel rooms dreaming about a woman he'd never have. His fantasies were so real, so erotic, he often woke up gripping his cock, working it until he finally found some relief.

Sometimes he actually regretted the trip he'd taken to Chicago. Oh, he'd been happy to see his friends again. He didn't get to Chicago often enough. The party they'd taken him to had been a great way to relieve the stress of his job as a Delta Force Team Leader. And the woman. Yes, the damn woman. The electricity that had sizzled between them the moment they'd bumped into each other at the bar had been enough to light up all Chicago.

He didn't remember exactly how it had happened but one minute they'd been jammed into a crowd and the next they'd been in a darkened hotel room, having the most incredible and inventive sex of his entire life. He could still see the teasing smile on her face, the sparkle in her eyes, the silken fall of her hair that later in the dark had curtained the two of them as she'd ridden him to completion.

The things they'd said to each other, done to each other, their exploration of each other's bodies had taken him to a plateau he'd never reached before. And they'd talked. Oh, not about their real lives, but about things they enjoyed, things they loved to do, things that were both funny and sad. He'd never realized how just whispering to someone in the dark could be so erotic.

The next morning when he'd woken up, she'd been gone. If there hadn't been lingering traces of her perfume on the sheets and his body, he might have convinced himself he'd imagined the whole thing. What good did it do to meet a woman you connected with so suddenly and so intensely if you never saw her again? One would think with his mental discipline he could just have put her out of his mind and move on, but no amount of effort on his part had made that happen.

He'd dreamed about her more nights than he could count, always waking up with his cock so hard that his only relief came from his good right hand.

He swallowed a sigh. Maybe tonight he could go in with a different attitude and find someone who really excited him. Someone who could replace the phantom image that haunted him constantly. Lord knew he was definitely ready for it.

Chapter Three

Slade wondered how long he'd have to stick around the party. He didn't want to be rude to his friends, but he realized he'd lost the party spirit somewhere along the way. He had to make sure his guys were taken care of, though. They knew no one here and he wasn't sure how comfortable they'd feel with this crowd. They'd come in one vehicle although Teo was always on standby.

He spotted Beau Williams leaning against the living room wall, nursing his beer and people-watching. Slade moved over to stand next to him.

"Trolling the crowd?" he joked, knowing it was one of Beau's favorite pastimes.

"Actually got my eye on something interesting."

Slade cocked an eyebrow. "Already?"

"You know me. It's in my genes. Anyway, I've been watching this interesting little byplay going on over there." He nodded toward where a bartender was serving drinks.

Slade glanced at the spot Beau had indicated. Three people—two men and a woman—were engaged in what could only be called a heated discussion. Maybe even an argument. The woman wasn't his type. These days hardly anyone was. He could see, however, why she'd caught Beau's eye. Her blonde hair was pulled back in a ponytail that swayed as she moved her head. Her skin was lightly tan and the silk blouse and slacks she wore hugged the curves of a mouth-watering figure. Her eyes were framed with thick dark lashes that gave her face a dramatic look. She was smiling, but neither of the men were.

"I think I should check this out." Beau pushed himself

away from the wall. "She might need some help."

"Just don't get into a hassle with any of the guests," Slade warned. "I don't know who these guys are. They might be someone important to Paul."

"I promise to behave." Beau headed toward the bar.

Slade was right behind him. *Just in case,* he told himself.

Beau stood at the end of the drink line closest to the trio, facing the woman. When she glanced over at him, he grinned and winked.

"Looks like you might need some help here," he teased.

She smiled back. "With these guys? *Pfft.*" She flipped a hand in the air.

"Do you mind?" The speaker, a man in tan slacks and a dark brown silk sport shirt that appeared tailored to fit his husky body, glared at him. "This is a private conversation."

"Oh, come on, Barry," the woman teased. "Maybe we can get a fresh point of view here."

Beau held up one hand. "I'm just an innocent bystander."

Barry, Mr. Hostility, ran his hand over his thinning dark-brown hair and glared at him. "I told you, butt out."

"Barry, for Christ's sake." The other man's eyes widened. "Maybe *you're* the one who shouldn't be out in public."

"Barry." The woman's voice was soft yet firm. "Not cool being rude to the guests." She smiled over at Beau. "Sorry about that, Mr…?"

"Williams. Beau Williams." He held out his hand. "I'm actually a guest of a guest."

"A party crasher?" Barry still had a belligerent tone to his voice.

Beau just looked at him, his face expressionless. "I was invited. I came with a friend."

"See, Barry?" The woman gave him a snarky grin. "Learn to keep your mouth shut."

Slade was doing his best to swallow a laugh as he watched Beau do his 'I'm just a guy' routine.

But Barry had obviously visited the bar too many times already. "I don't know you. I know everyone who's anyone in this town."

The woman burst out laughing. "Oh, my God. Did you really just say that?"

"Barry," his friend snapped. "Will you for chrissake tone it down? Paul will throw your ass out." He turned to Beau and held out his hand. "Norm Leyden. Nice to meet you."

Beau shook hands with the man. "Ditto."

Slade decided it wouldn't hurt to introduce himself too. Just in case, although he wasn't sure of just in case what.

"Slade Donovan." He grinned. "I'm the guest that he's a guest of."

The woman smiled at them both, a dimple flashing in her cheek.

Shit! Beau's a goner!

"Megan Welles. Nice to meet you."

"Oh, is this a fucking tea party now?" Barry sneered.

What a jackass, Slade couldn't help thinking.

Megan gave the idiot a glare as if he were something distasteful. "You'll have to excuse Barry. He can't seem to find his manners anymore."

"What is this?" Barry growled. "You're not my mother. I think I need another drink."

He tried to shoulder his way past Beau. In doing so he bumped into Megan and jarred the glass in his hand, splashing what little was left of his drink onto her blouse.

"Oh! Damn it anyway, Barry." She tried to brush off the moisture with her fingers. "The last thing you need is another drink."

"I'll get a fucking drink if I want one."

Norm Leyden grabbed his elbow and tugged him away from the bar. "Megan's right. You've had enough." He looked at Beau and Slade. "Sorry about this. I'll get my so-called friend out of here. Come on, asshole, before you embarrass all of us."

Megan had grabbed a handful of napkins from the bar and was trying to blot the liquid. Slade swallowed a smile at the expression on Beau's face, as if he wanted to pat her blouse dry himself.

"There." She squinted down at herself. "I guess that's the best I can do."

"It's fine." Beau grinned. "Of course, I could help you if you like."

Slade bit back a grin of his own.

She gave Beau an 'in your dreams' look and patted her blouse one last time. "Damn it all, anyway. I keep forgetting Barry's got such a short fuse."

"What's his problem, anyway?" Slade asked, wondering if he and Beau should take the guy out back and punch his lights out.

"He's a sports attorney." She said the words with a little sneer in her voice.

"Is it sports you don't like?" Beau asked the question with a half-smile on his lips. "All sports in general or just one in particular?"

Her lips curved in a tiny smile. "I love sports. It's just some of the athletes I can't hack."

Beau cocked an eyebrow. "And Barry objects to that? Aren't you entitled to your own opinion?"

She laughed, a tinkling musical sound. "That's not it, exactly. He doesn't like it when I criticize any of his clients, but he knows I always tell it like it is."

Beau moved an inch closer. "Are you in the business too?"

"You might say." This time her grin was real. "I'm a reporter for Yahoo! Sports."

"No kidding?" Beau's eyes widened. "So what was Barry the douchebag's problem this time? One of his clients on the hot seat?"

"Barry the douchebag? I like the name. Very appropriate." She sighed. "Like I said, he gets his shorts in a wad when I criticize his clients. He's unhappy because I recently wrote a couple of columns criticizing the lack of personal responsibility in a lot of today's athletes. I named a few examples, some of them his clients."

She took a sip of her drink then ran the tip of her tongue

over her lower lip, catching a stray drop.

Slade wondered just how much longer Beau was going to stand there making small talk before he steered Megan Welles to a dark corner. He'd never seen any one strike faster or more smoothly than Surfer. He felt like an interloper, but it always fascinated him to see Beau work his magic.

"I agree with you on the lack of responsibility." Beau nodded. "It seems to grow and expand more each year."

"I told him if he didn't want to see their names in my columns, he should teach them how to behave."

"No wonder he was unhappy." Beau chuckled. "I don't mean to sound chauvinistic, but isn't it unusual for a sports reporter to be female?"

Slade, still eavesdropping, had to bite his tongue to hold back the laughter. He wanted to tell Beau that for a babe magnet he could use some smoother lines. He waited for Megan Welles to haul off and smack him.

She stiffened. "Hmmm. Isn't that a little narrow-minded of you?"

"I apologize. I'm just a knuckle-dragging male who spends too much of his time in the company of other males. And no one else."

She tilted her head and interest flared in her eyes. "Yeah? What do you do?"

"What's that saying? I'd tell you, but then I'd have to kill you?"

Her eyes widened. "For real?"

He laughed again. "How about we get a couple of fresh drinks and take this conversation someplace away from this mob scene? Maybe I'll even share some of my secrets with you."

Okay, Slade thought. *At last.* He'd been beginning to wonder when Beau would make his move.

She nodded. "Sounds good to me. I always wanted to have drinks with a spy, or whatever you are."

"Name your poison."

"Scotch and soda."

"Ahh. A woman after my own heart. Right this way." He cupped Megan's elbow and directed her toward the bar. As he passed Slade, he winked.

Slade nearly choked on a laugh. Whatever the woman drank, Beau would have said the same thing. He'd honed his approach to perfection. Slade had wondered what would happen when one day Beau met a woman who knocked him off his feet. And it was bound to happen. The law of averages. He watched the two of them walk away with their drinks, Beau's arm draped casually over Megan's shoulder.

"I see lover boy has scored again. He sure didn't waste any time."

Slade turned to see Trey behind him. "And as smooth as I've ever seen him do it."

"Want a little side bet that says he doesn't sleep at the ranch tonight?"

Slade threw back his head and laughed. "No takers." He studied Trey. "How about you?"

"Don't you know I never tell my secrets?" He winked. "Anyway, I only came over here because I'm thirsty."

But Slade noted that he carried two drinks away with him. He didn't think the man was *that* thirsty. *Interesting,* he told himself. Very interesting.

* * * *

Kari's apartment was located in as secure a place she could find and still afford, just north of downtown, in a multistory building. A house would have made her feel too exposed and a building with a locked outer door or one with a doorman would have stretched her budget too much. But this had turned out to be a very good second best.

The master bath had been one of the selling points. It had both an enormous shower and a whirlpool tub, to satisfy whatever her mood happened to be. Today she needed the luxury of a hot bath, something to relax the tension she seemed to always carry with her. She sank into the scented bathwater up to her neck, hair piled on her head out of the way, bubbles teasing at her chin. The heated water soothed her tired muscles and she felt them relax. She hoped the bath would wash away the troubles dogging her and the memory she could not seem to rid herself of. Today's trial closure had been tense, the accused a violent, vicious abuser. Just looking at him in the courtroom had made her stomach knot. But she'd done well, gotten her guilty verdict and she knew the judge would hand down the maximum sentence.

But that wasn't what made her tense. No, the thought of socializing with a group of people she didn't know made every muscle in her body twitch and every nerve fire. Once upon a time, she'd loved get-togethers like this. Then her life had fallen apart and had become one long nightmare. She tried to tell herself it was like falling off a horse. You just had to get back in the saddle and move forward.

Easier said than done.

If only the man she'd had awesome sex with that time could be there. Whoever he was. And wherever he happened to be. She'd had dreams about him now for five years, the occurrences much more frequent in the past year or so. Sometimes, as she struggled with the shadow that had been cast over her life, only those memories kept her sane.

She leaned back against the tub pillow, closed her eyes and slipped into a dreamlike state.

"Are you comfortable?"

Comfortable? She was lying on the bed, naked, her hands gripping the headboard, legs spread wide. He hinted he might tie her hands to the polished spokes. The idea of it, the image of it, made the inner walls of her pussy flutter with spasms. He kneeled over her, his thighs bracketing her body. She was so stimulated that the pulse in her core throbbed and she ached with unfulfilled need.

She wet her lips and nodded. "As comfortable as I can be."

"I like you like this. I can see every bit of your wet pink flesh,

41

your hot channel just waiting for my fingers or my tongue. And maybe, if you are a very good girl, my cock." He smiled down at her, white teeth flashing in his tan face. It was a hungry smile, one that signaled he'd like to eat her right up.

Oh, yes, please, she wanted to tell him. Do it now.

His long, thick shaft was at eye level, so swollen the head was a dark purple and a tiny bead of fluid sat at its slit.

"Open your mouth," he commanded. "And don't move your hands."

Kari opened as wide as she could, a shivery sensation racing through her as he placed his cock on her lower lip and slid it slowly onto the surface of her tongue. She closed her lips around him, his girth stretching them with its thickness. His taste was all male, musky and hot. She moved her tongue against his shaft as much as she could within the space available and when she looked up at him, his lips curved in an erotic smile.

"I want you to suck me." His voice was thick and husky. "But don't make me come. If you are very, very good, I'll come inside you, bring you to orgasm that way."

Her pulse accelerated at the thought. To feel that thick cock inside her, plunging into her…

Water splashed in her face, waking her from her fantasy, and Kari realized she'd almost slipped beneath the surface of the bathwater. But, Lord, dreaming about her ghost warrior had wiped everything else from her mind. And a warrior was what he'd been, indeed. His body might have been carved from rock, as hard and lean as it had been. A thin white scar had run from his left shoulder to the nipple, while below his rib cage on the right had been two round healed holes that she was sure had come from bullets. His entire demeanor had spoken of the total alpha male, someone in control at all times. She wondered what it would be like to get beneath the surface. To shred that control. To…

He was the only man she'd ever lost all measure of control with. A craving for rough sex she hadn't even known she harbored had surged to the surface and she'd given herself over to anything and everything. Nothing—not the binding of her hands to the headboard, not the blindfold that had made every sensation so much more intense—had changed the intensity of her response. Had it been because it had been so anonymous? Because no names had been exchanged? Was that why the prim-and-proper assistant prosecutor had behaved like a wild woman? Yet, every time she thought about it, she craved it again.

Kari gave herself a mental shake. She'd never find him now so she might as well stop dreaming about him. Right now she wanted to make sure she enjoyed the evening ahead, so she'd better concentrate on the here and now instead of the once and gone.

She didn't know if it was the thrill of winning a tough case in court or the satisfaction of a job well done, but a tiny kick of excited anticipation danced through her system. As if something special was waiting for her. She certainly hoped so. And despite her unknown stalker hovering over her like a dark shadow, she still would have loved to have a man in her life. The right man, of course.

What a paradox. I'm afraid to go out, but I want a relationship? Who the hell would put up with me?

She longed for someone who could respect her for the strong person she was in public and still love her for her softer side. A man who could fill the empty spaces in her life. Someone with whom she could let down her guard. Someone who knew her outer bitch was only for court. Someone she could trust. She was tired of lusting after a man she'd never see again.

She'd watched the men and women she worked with find happiness with others and had to tamp down the little spears of jealousy. She wanted what they had, but no one had come along who appealed to her that way.

Except her phantom lover.

Five years was a long time to dream about a man she'd only spent one night with. Maybe she needed to have her head examined.

She guessed she'd just have to banish him from her thoughts. If he hadn't come looking for her in Chicago, she for sure wasn't going to find him in San Antonio.

Dressed in cream slacks and a purple blouse, her hair loose around her shoulders, she took one last glimpse at herself in the mirror and decided she'd do. Alamo Heights, where the Huttons lived, was about a twenty-minute drive for her. She figured to spend an hour at the party at the most. Then she could be home by eight-thirty, safe behind her triple-locked doors.

Okay. Let's get this over with.

Stop it, Kari. You're going to a party, not an execution.

She found the Hutton home with no problem. Parking took a little more ingenuity, but she finally found a spot at the end of the block. Damn! All these cars meant a lot of people. She wasn't sure she was ready for this. Inhaling, she let her breath out slowly and walked up to the front door.

A two-story gray stone with definite Spanish influence, like many of the homes in the Alamo Heights area, it was fronted by a neatly mowed lawn and equally well-tended shrubbery. A giant pin oak tree stood gracefully just to the left of the walkway to the porch.

A note had been tacked to the carved wood front door, telling people to just come on in. She opened it and stepped into a large foyer with a terrazzo floor and a unique brass chandelier hanging from the high ceiling. People were spilling into it from the open living room on the right. What she could see of the furniture had a Spanish flavor to the style. She wondered if the framed pictures on the walls were originals or really good reproductions. How much money did a JAG attorney make, anyway?

Kip must have been watching for her, though, because as soon as she entered the house he shouldered his way through the mob of people and came over to her.

"I was afraid you'd chicken out." He gave her a reassuring grin. "I'm glad you didn't."

"Kari!" Natalie Reyes broke away from the group she was with and hurried over to her, wrapping her in a hug. "I am so glad you came. We were afraid you might change your mind at the last minute."

"I nearly did," Kari admitted. "I still don't understand why you were so insistent I show up tonight."

Nat threw a graceful arm around Kari. "Because if you spend all your time with my cutthroat husband in those dreary offices, your wonderful spirit that I see hiding there will dry up and blow away."

She wanted to tell Natalie that the spirit had dried up a long time ago. Instead, she forced a smile.

"Thank you for caring."

"Come say hello to the hosts. Then we'll get you something to drink."

Paul and Melinda Hutton were standing together by the fireplace, chatting with a few people. Kari tried to hold back, unwilling to break into a conversation.

"I can say hi later," she told Natalie.

"Nonsense. This will just take a second. They said to be sure and bring you over when you got here."

Kari frowned. "But they hardly know me."

"And now they can get to know you better. Come on."

Paul Hutton, tall, dark, with a hint of gray in his hair, reminded her a lot of her boss. She could see why they got along so well. Melinda was a stark contrast, a petite blonde with a warm smile.

"We're so happy you could make it." She squeezed Kari's hand. "Please help yourself to food and drink. Lord knows Paul made sure we had plenty."

"Thank you. And thanks for including me."

"Kip raves about your work," Paul told her. "We owe it to him to make sure you stick around."

The compliment gave her a warm feeling. With nothing else in her life now except her work, it was important she make a solid place for herself. She didn't want to have to pull up sticks and move again.

"Thank you very much for that," she told Melinda.

"Let's get you something to drink." Natalie tugged her to a corner of the vast great room where a bartender was working at a makeshift setup in the corner. "What's your poison?"

"I'll have a beer and the lady will have an amaretto on the rocks."

The deep voice, so vivid from her dreams, jolted her and froze her in place. Her nipples hardened and her breath felt trapped in her throat. Her pulse throbbed with a heavy beat in the walls of her suddenly wet pussy. Words deserted her and she stood there, immobile, trying to find something to say. A kaleidoscope of erotic images flashed through her brain, one after the other, teasing and tantalizing her.

Stunned, she peeped over at Natalie whose eyes widened in surprise.

"I, uh, wasn't aware you two knew each other." The woman smiled. "Kari, you've been keeping secrets."

Kari's breath was trapped in her throat. She clasped her hands together to still their shaking before she turned to look at the man behind her. Oh, Lordy. He looked even better in real life than he did in her memory. The lines in his face were a little deeper, but his body was just as lean and muscular as she remembered. He stood tall and tan, the sculpted muscles of his body evident even beneath the collared shirt and dress slacks that fit him so well they could have been tailored for him. How many nights had she lain in bed since that one time, remembering the feel of him beneath her hands, the hardness of muscle, the softness of the hair on his chest, the swollen thickness of his cock?

Just staring at him now and remembering all that took her breath away.

"I—" She couldn't form words. What was he doing here? How had he come to be at this party? Was she dreaming him? But no, when she inhaled, that remembered scent of earth and clean air tickled her nostrils.

Natalie glanced from one to the other. "I take it you two

know each other?"

"Uh, we— That is—" Kari stammered.

"We've met." Slade's voice, thick and warm, rolled over her.

Kari looked at him, mesmerized by the flare of heat in his hazel eyes that had turned more of a dark gold. His dark-brown hair seemed shaggier than the last time she'd seen him, although it was apparent he'd made an effort to tame it. She had to stop herself from reaching up to let it sift through her fingers. She had to fight a desire to run her hands over every inch of him.

"Kari, I think you're in good hands." Natalie grinned at them. "I'm sure you two won't mind if I excuse myself. I see someone signaling for me."

Kari wasn't even aware of the woman leaving. All she could see was the tower of testosterone standing beside her. He received their drinks from the bartender and put hers in her hands. Her fingers closed over the glass automatically and she took a sip. The smooth drink coasted its way down her throat, easing her edgy nerves.

"I see you haven't changed your drink preference since I last saw you, Mandy Wheeler Baker. Or whatever your name is."

She nearly choked on her drink, her hand shaking so she almost dropped the glass. A few drops spilled over the edge. A lean, tan hand took her drink, wiped the glass and her hand with some bar napkins and handed the glass back to her.

She stared at him, a face she'd dreamed about for so many nights yet never expected to see again. One that obliterated the faces of other men she'd met since then. "Uh, yes, it's me."

"And I'm guessing your name's not Mandy Baker Wheeler."

The lopsided grin he gave her sent heat rushing through her.

"I, um, I mean…" God, she sounded like a blithering idiot.

"Maybe we should sit down." He paused. "Outside."

He took her free hand, his fingers burning themselves into her skin, and towed her easily through the crowd, through the open sliding doors out to a patio adorned with appropriate furniture. She went with him, unresisting, still shocked to see him here, of all places, and after all this time. When they reached an umbrella table set in one corner, he pulled out a chair and gestured for her to sit. Her legs were shaking so much she collapsed into it. Her heart raced and she had trouble catching her breath. *He was here!* She wanted to pinch herself to make sure she wasn't dreaming. Her nipples tingled as she remembered the hot wet feel of his mouth on them, and the walls of her sex clenched with immediate need. She knew her panties were soaked, for sure.

Then he was sitting across from her in the other chair in all his masculine awesomeness. She stared at him, at the hazel eyes that looked as if he wanted to devour her and the thick dark-brown hair she wanted to run her fingers through. His face, as hard and sculpted as she remembered, showed slight signs of having aged—deeper lines at the eyes and the corners of his mouth—but was otherwise still the same one that haunted her dreams.

She wet her lips. "I… You… That is…" Her tongue wanted to stick to the roof of her mouth and her brain had become nonfunctional.

"Yeah. Me too." He grinned.

A wave of heat almost melted her panties. He was staring at her with such a penetrating gaze she was sure he could see right through her.

"W-Where did you come from? I mean… No, wait." She took a healthy swallow of her drink while she tried to pull together her scattered thoughts. "I didn't mean that the way it sounded."

"I know." He studied her face, maybe seeking any changes, as she had with him. "I was just as stunned to see you standing there. I had to look twice to make sure it was you."

"It's me." *God, could I sound any more inane? Stupid?*

Silence stretched between them, heavy with sexual memories.

"Are you friends with the Huttons?" he asked at last.

Kari shook her head. "No. My boss is. Kip Reyes." Her laugh was shaky.

"Oh? Are you—? Do you—?"

She laughed, aware that he was trying to figure out a way to ask her what she did for the county prosecutor. Was she clerical or legal or what. "I'll put you out of your misery. I'm an assistant prosecutor in Bexar County."

He leaned forward, arms folded and resting on the small tabletop. "But you lived in Chicago when I met you. Or were you visiting, like I was?"

"No, I was living there." She shrugged. "I moved. Recently. I live in San Antonio now."

One corner of his mouth tipped up in a grin. "Lucky for me."

She tightened her grip on the glass, unable to tear her gaze away from his. "And you?" she asked. "Are you visiting here?"

He shook his head and quirked a grin. "I live in the area too. Go figure, right?"

She licked a drop of amaretto from her lower lip. "So what's your real name, or is it a big secret?"

His gaze lasered her and she wondered if he was trying to see inside her head before answering her. "I'll tell you mine if you tell me yours."

She felt warmth creep up her cheeks. "Fair enough. Kari Malone."

He held out a hand, palm open. "Slade. Slade Donovan."

God! Even his name had an erotic sound to it. With only the slightest hesitation, she put her hand in his. "Nice to meet you, Slade Donovan."

He squeezed her hand and left it tingling from the contact. She felt rough callouses on his palm and wondered what he'd done to earn them.

"Same here, Kari Malone."

"Saving the good stuff for yourself, Slade?"

She jerked her head sideways at the man who had ambled up to the table. She didn't think Slade had noticed him, either, until he'd spoken. He was tall, like Slade, only leaner and with longish blond hair. He winked at her, his smile cocky.

"Did you leave your manners inside?" Slade demanded. He had a slight edge to his voice.

"Just wanted to make sure I got an introduction."

"Fine. Kari Malone, meet Beau Williams. He's just about to go back inside for another drink. Right, Beau?" He looked past the man. "What happened to Megan? She dump you already?"

"Ha ha. She's in the powder room."

"Well, then. I'm sure you need to be inside when she comes out." Slade's tone was pointed.

"Oh, uh, sure. Nice meeting you, Kari Malone." They heard him chuckling as he walked back inside.

"A friend?" she asked.

"He's, uh, visiting me for a while."

"Oh." That startled her. "Don't you need to spend time with him? I shouldn't be monopolizing your time."

"Beau is very good at taking care of himself." Slade took a swallow of his drink. "He's visiting, but we don't live in each other's pockets. He'll be just fine." He turned his attention back to her. "I tried to find you, but not having your name made it very difficult, as you can imagine." He cocked his head. "Did you look for me at all, Kari? Ask about me?"

"I—" She bit her lower lip. "I was going to, but then I figured I should wait and see what you did."

He laughed, a low, rumbling sound. "We certainly put ourselves behind the eight ball."

"Man, Surfer was right. You skimmed the cream right off the top."

This time Kari could actually see Slade tense. "You guys are itching for trouble," he said between clenched teeth.

The new man, darker than Beau, held out his hand to Kari. "Trey McIntyre."

She looked at Slade. "I gather these are your friends?"

"Not for much longer, if they don't get out of my business. I believe he was just about to go back inside and get himself a drink. Right, Trey?"

"Oh, uh, yeah. That's right. Nice meeting you, Kari."

"And could you guys kindly stay out of my face?" Slade was joking, but not. "They're some of the, uh, men that I work with. They think it's a lot of fun to give me a hard time."

"Really? What kind of work do you do?"

"Government work." The words were clipped and gave the definite impression no more explanation would be forthcoming. Maybe he worked in a hush-hush office of some kind. No, not an office. This was a man who did dangerous, physical things.

"So I'm gathering you still live here, right? Are you friends with Lt. Col. Hutton?"

He nodded. "We grew up together."

"Are you also an attorney?" She frowned. "Is that what you do for the government? I don't remember hearing your name mentioned, although I've only been in town a few months."

"No." A faraway look came into his eyes. "Actually, I'm in the Army."

"Oh!"

What did she say after that? She sure couldn't ask the usual career questions. He obviously wasn't sharing anything about where he went or why.

"Are you here with someone?" he asked.

She shook her head. "N-No. You?" She swallowed back the fear that had almost prevented her from coming here tonight. She hoped none of that showed on her face.

His mouth curved in that slow, sexy smile that never left

her dreams. "Now I am." He still held her hand in his, his thumb caressing her palm. "Are you done with this party? How about if we get out of here? Go someplace private."

The seductive tone in his voice sent the butterflies in her stomach into a wild jitterbug.

"Private?" The look he gave her had her nearly climaxing where she sat. "You don't think the host and hostess would be offended?"

Not to mention what on earth Kip and Natalie would say. She had to be crazy to even consider it. God! She hadn't even been on a date in forever.

Then he gave that sexy laugh again and she knew what her answer would be. "Paul and I have known each other a long time. He'll understand."

Kari nibbled on her lower lip again. "I don't want them to think—"

Slade shook his head. "I'll take care of it. I'll just tell him we're old friends who reconnected." He gave her that same hungry look. "We are, aren't we? Right?"

"Yes. Yes, we are."

He was still stroking his thumb back and forth on her palm. "What about you? What will your boss say?"

"Um, hmm." She took a swallow of her drink. Yes. How should she handle this? "I'll, uh, just do the same thing. Tell them I met an old friend and we're going out for coffee. Or a drink."

Slade's laugh this time was full-blown. "And you really think they'll believe that?"

"No, but that's my story and I'm sticking to it." She wasn't about to let him get away a second time.

"My friends and I came together. I don't want to leave them without transportation." He paused.

"I have a car." She almost couldn't get the words out. Was she really doing this?

"Then let me go leave my keys with one of the idiots you met. Where's your car? If you feel more comfortable with us leaving separately, I'll meet you there in ten minutes."

Quaking inside, Kari managed to slip out of the house unnoticed. She knew her boss would have a boatload of questions for her Monday, but she'd worry about it then.

She waited for him at her car. When he walked up to her, she drew in a breath, calming a sudden attack of nerves. "Was your friend okay with you leaving? Did he ask any questions?"

He shook his head. "He just listened to me, nodded and grinned. And don't worry, he's not a gossip, nor is his wife. This is just between us. For right now."

For right now? Does he already have plans to take this further? We hardly even know each other.

"It's all good, Kari." He reached for her hand. "I promise."

"What did you tell your friends?" Maybe they should have taken out an ad in the paper, or online.

He pulled her close to him, his free hand stroking her back in a reassuring gesture.

"It's fine. I mean it. We don't get all up in each other's grills about stuff. They don't ask questions and I'll only tell them whatever you want me to." He slid his hand around to cup her chin. "I hope we're going to have more than this one night, Kari. I *want* this to be more than that. And I'll only tell them whatever you want. But I have just ten days of leave and I want to spend as much of it with you as I can." The look he gave her scorched her clear to the soles of her feet.

"O-Okay." Only ten days? What would she do after that? *First things first, Kari.* "Come on, then."

"This first." He tilted her chin up and brushed a kiss lighter than a butterfly's wings over her lips.

The contact was so electric her nerve endings sizzled. The heat rushing through her had little to do with the temperature of the night and everything to do with her level of expectation about what was ahead.

One thought etched itself on her brain.

At last!

Chapter Four

Slade waited while Kari unlocked her apartment door, then followed her inside.

"This will just take a second," she tossed at him. She closed the front door, the snick of the lock loud in the little foyer, and fiddled with two other locks. "Don't go anywhere."

As if!

"No worries there," he assured her. He just hoped he could control himself while she did whatever her routine was. He shoved his hands into his pockets to keep himself from grabbing her and pulling her into his arms, wanting to touch her again, to feel her soft skin, to inhale her heady perfume. Was it possible to make up for five years in one night?

He was still trying to conceal his shock at finding the woman who had haunted him for five years at this party tonight. What were the odds? If he strung together all the circumstances on both sides that had brought them together in this time and place, he'd definitely have to believe fate had a big hand in things.

He hadn't wanted to admit to himself just how tightly wound he'd been, waiting to hear what she would say. Would she take him home with her or suddenly decide it was a bad idea? He couldn't remember ever being so nervous waiting for a woman to give him an answer. Once he'd been selected for Delta Force, his social life had been confined to bar hook-ups and women he met in other casual situations. He was afraid the few social niceties he'd learned ages ago might have faded away.

He'd had to restrain himself from slugging down the

entire glass of Jack Daniel's at the party. Until he actually saw Kari Malone again he hadn't realized just how much she'd come to mean to him in such a short time. Hadn't even thought something like this could be possible. He was the original love 'em and leave 'em man, convinced that as a member of Delta Force he wasn't relationship material. Kari Malone had put a crack in the wall he kept around himself. Was he crazy to want this to go forward? To see if it could lead to something more? Probably, but he didn't seem to be able to stop himself.

A prosecutor! Who'd have thought it? But he could tell at once she had brains, a self-assurance that was nothing like the hard edge he'd found in so many women. They either had a streak of dependency or a type of grittiness that irritated him.

But Kari was...Kari. A unique treasure. He'd never believed in fate before, but he was sure that was what had brought them together in the first place. Neither of them had been looking for more than a night of off-the-charts sex. But now? A different story.

He'd felt a little guilty, leaving the way he had, but Beau had already had some woman cornered. When he'd left the car keys with Trey, the man had just stared at him then glanced at his watch as if to say, *Fifteen minutes and you've already scored?* He wanted to tell Trey it wasn't what he thought, but he was in no mood to share his thoughts.

"I have to say," he'd drawled, "you've got damn good taste."

Slade had wanted to tell him it was a lot more than that, but he'd had no intention of discussing this—whatever *this* was—with any of his men. At least not right at that moment.

"Just keep an eye on Marc, will you?"

"Oh, hey, on that front, Trey said Marc is sitting outside talking to some woman."

Slade had felt his eyebrows rise almost to his hairline. "Are you shitting me?"

"Not a bit." Beau had grinned. "Maybe he's coming out

of his shell."

"That would be a godsend. And even more reason to keep an eye on things with him."

"Count on it, Shadow," Beau had assured him.

But Slade had already been heading out of there. He knew they would have given him a raft of shit if he hadn't given them *the look*, the one they all referred to as *Fuck up and you die.*

So here he was, still shocked that he'd found his mystery woman in a very unexpected place. And that just catching sight of her had the same electrifying effect as it had five years ago. At first he'd thought he was imagining it. That he'd been thinking about her so much lately he'd projected her onto some other woman. When he'd realized it was in fact her, it had taken him two full minutes to get his shit together enough to approach her. What if she'd forgotten all about him? What if she was there with someone else? The relief he'd felt when the answer to both those questions was no was so overwhelming it'd almost brought him to his knees.

On the drive here the images of what the evening could hold had run through his mind and straight to his cock. Last time he'd gone at her like the horniest man in the world, one who hadn't had a woman in years. This time he needed to find some control. Needed to dig for his famous finesse.

Shit, Donovan. Get it together. You aren't twenty-five years old anymore.

He'd been with a lot of women, probably more than he wanted to admit. He might have unleashed his sexual needs with them, but never his emotions. But this woman? Even after that one night together he knew she could undo him.

Slade realized he knew nothing about her beyond the fact that he was obsessed with getting her into bed. He'd never before been interested in anything else with the women he bedded — didn't care what movies they liked or what books they read or if they liked chocolate or vanilla ice cream. So why was he so fixated on learning everything he could about Kari? That smacked of something long-term. Something Slade He didn't even know if he could sustain that.

Sure, he'd had that tiny little twinge that he might have been missing out on something. But that's all it was—a twinge. So where did he go from here with Kari? To settle down he had to be able to handle a committed relationship. For too many years that relationship for him had been with the Army and Delta Force. Was he too old to change?

One thing was very clear to him. When he looked at Kari, the memory of the dirt and grime and cold of Afghanistan, the hot, dry desert of Iraq, the tension of the missions, the long years of battles faded away completely as if a healing shower had washed over him. Could he take a chance on something here, something longer than these ten days?

He'd been so busy standing there having a conversation with himself he hadn't paid all that much attention to what Kari was doing, but now it registered. The three locks on the front door—a key lock, a deadbolt and a chain. And next to it on the wall a small white object that looked like an entry-point alarm with a small button she pinched. She moved around the apartment, doing something with the sliding glass door that led out to a small balcony. Then she disappeared into what he assumed was the bedroom area and was back in seconds.

What the hell?

"Kari?" He pulled her into his arms, her body so soft and pliant against his hard one. "Is something wrong here?"

If he hadn't been paying close attention, he might have missed the edge of strain in the smile she gave him. It was gone so fast he wondered if he'd imagined it. But there was her security routine, which had to mean something. He hoped being trained to be suspicious of everything didn't have him seeing skeletons where there were none.

"No, something's right." She cupped his cheeks with her soft hands, the light floral scent of her perfume invading him and kicking his hormones and pheromones into overdrive.

"Wait." He wrapped his fingers lightly around her wrists. As much as he wanted to strip her naked and plunge himself into her mouthwatering body, he wanted answers first. "I asked you a question. Is there something going on you want to tell me about? Are you having trouble with someone?"

"What?" She frowned. "Oh, you mean because of the alarms? I live alone, Slade. A girl can't be too careful." Her full lips curved in a smile that went straight to his groin. "Okay?"

He sensed there was more to it than she was telling him, but tonight he wasn't about to push it. Tonight was all about them. About reconnecting. If she had a problem with someone, well, he'd be here all night and would take care of anything that came up.

"Okay." He parked it in the back of his mind and focused on her mouth that was scant inches from his. So kissable. So tempting.

She ran her tongue over her lower lip and all stops were gone. Cupping her head to anchor her in place, he brushed his mouth over hers, feeling the softness. He sketched the outline with the tip of his tongue over and over in soft and teasing strokes. When he traced the closed seam with light pressure, she opened for him at once and he swept inside.

God, she tasted like seven kinds of sin, just as he'd remembered. Every molecule in his body went on high alert, his blood rushing right to his cock, which swelled at once. Sliding one hand down the line of her back, he then cupped one nicely rounded cheek of her ass, pulling her tight against him until her breasts were pressed hard into his chest and his thick shaft imprinted itself on the swell of her mound.

Slow, he told himself. *Take it slow. Make it good for her this time.*

The last time they'd been together, he'd gone at her like a hungry animal. He wasn't feeling much different now, with all the pent-up desire and need stored in him, but he wanted her to enjoy every second. He also remembered that she liked rough sex. Was it the anonymity that had knocked down all restraint and barriers? Would it be the same way tonight? God, he hoped so.

He licked at the inside of her mouth, tasting her, coaxing her tongue to dance with his. Electricity sizzled through him, straight to his dick and his balls. Somehow he dragged himself back from the edge, reminding himself again this was for her.

He trailed his lips along her jawline and peppered her neck with tiny nips and kisses. When he lightly closed his teeth over the tender spot where neck and shoulder joined, she shuddered in his arms and a soft moan drifted from her mouth.

"We need a bed," he murmured in her ear, doing his best not to strip her naked where they stood.

"Lucky we have one." Her voice sounded as shaky as he felt.

He scooped her up in his arms and let her direct him to her bedroom. On the way she kicked off her shoes. If only he could divest her of her clothes that easily, but then he might miss something. Just inside her bedroom she reached out to flip a wall switch and a bedside lamp came on, bathing the room in a warm glow. Slade set Kari on her bare feet next to the bed and let his eyes drink their fill of her.

Silky masses of auburn hair cascaded down to her shoulders, calling attention to the way her thin silk blouse draped over her softly swelling breasts. The rich cotton of her slacks molded over her hips and down the long legs that he wanted to feel wrapped around him. His need to see her naked was so fierce his hands shook as he unfastened one tiny button after another. Why did women wear clothes that took forever to remove? Were they determined to drive men insane?

No, just me. I hope I didn't leave all my self-control out on the battlefield.

She was scarcely breathing while he undressed her, but

the rapid beat of her pulse at the hollow of her throat told him she was as aroused as he was. He slid the garment down her arms, yanked the tails from her slacks and tossed the garment to the side. His eyes widened at the flimsy lace bra that held her plump breasts. Without the additional layer of her blouse, the darkness of her nipples was blatantly evident. He gave in to temptation, lowered his head and closed his lips around one taut bud, fabric and all. When he sucked it hard, a gasp escaped her mouth and she clutched at his biceps, head tilted back.

His cock throbbed with renewed force, demanding attention.

Jesus!

He'd forgotten how just touching her made him hungry and needy, and he sucked harder, finally releasing the nipple and moving to the other one. By the time he'd had his fill, both pebbled tips were hard and swollen, just like his cock. Needing to see them without any covering, he released the clasp of her bra and tossed it aside with the blouse. Holding the luscious creamy mounds of her breasts in his palms, he trailed his tongue across the upper swell. Out of nowhere he wondered what they'd look like with tiny rings dangling from them. He'd been with women who pierced their nipples. They told him it made them ultra-sensitive and more responsive. Maybe he could—

Slow down, asshole. One thing at a time.

Her skin was satiny smooth and the scent she used, something with vanilla and flowers, invaded his senses. He laid a string of kisses in the valley between her breasts and on down until he reached the waistband of her slacks. He had to see the rest of her. Now. Right now. And taste every inch of her. Jesus! Was he some horny teenager about to have sex for the first time? No woman had ever done this to him, ever made him feel this way. Trembling with impatience, he opened the button on her slacks and tugged on the tab of the zipper. He wanted to rip off the rest of her clothes and plunge himself into her, but he forced himself to go slow, easing her slacks down her toned legs and urging her to kick them to the side. That left her quivering in his arms in just the tiniest lace bikini he had ever seen.

Holy fucking shit!

Every bit of moisture in his mouth dried up at the sight.

Some might think her body less than perfect but for Slade—now, as it had been five years ago—it was exactly what he wanted…full and soft and way too tempting. He restrained himself from unzipping his fly and reaching in to grab his shaft.

Control, control, control.

He kneeled almost in reverence, skimming her curves with his hands. Leaning slightly forward he pressed a kiss to her navel, running the edge of his tongue around the ridged flesh. She shivered in his grasp so he did it again. But then, drawn by the scent of her musk, he trailed his tongue down across her belly to the narrow band of lace at the top of her panties, where he dragged it back and forth. Then he pressed his face to her mound and inhaled deeply.

Taking the top band of her panties in his teeth, he tugged the scrap of fabric slowly down her legs and coaxed her to step out of them. At the sight of her naked cunt covered with soft auburn curls, his cock flexed behind the fabric of his pants.

God!

He wanted to do everything with her. *To* her. He wanted to control her, to bend her to his will. He remembered in sharp detail the few light bondage games they'd played that night. Would she be up for them again? He'd tried BDSM, but he'd discovered that while he wasn't a full-out Dom, there were some aspects he really enjoyed and he wanted to draw her into them. He had discovered they meant a lot more when he had a real connection to the other person. Did he have one with her? And how far could he push her?

One step at a time. This time there'll be a tomorrow.

He looked up at her as he kneeled between her legs. "Do something for me."

He heard the breath escaping her lips. Her cheeks were flushed and her eyes gleamed. She ran the tip of her tongue over her lower lip, making it gleam in the lamplight.

Fuck! He wanted to bite it and suck it into his mouth.

"D-Do what?"

He had to struggle to remember what he wanted her to do. "Hold your breasts and rub your thumbs over your nipples."

For a long moment she hesitated. Then, her eyes on him, she lifted her hands, cupped her gorgeous breasts in her palms and stroked her thumbs lightly over the distended tips.

"Like this?" Her voice was breathless.

"Yes, like that." He almost growled the words.

God, the sight of her touching herself had his cock hardening even more, if that were possible. The ache in his balls was growing and he'd hardly begun to do all the things with her he wanted to.

Eyes still on her, he nudged her thighs apart and slipped his hand between. Wet! She was soaking wet. He lifted his hand to his mouth and licked the drops of her juice from his fingers. She tasted like seven kinds of sin and he wanted every one of them. In truth, what he really wanted was to lay her down and fuck her until neither of them could breathe.

Slow, he told himself once more. *This time take it nice and slow.* He didn't plan to disappear out of her life again. He wasn't sure how good she'd be with someone who was gone for months at a time, but maybe they could figure out a way…

One thing at a time.

And the one thing right now was to take an even greater taste of her. He spread the lips of her pussy with his thumbs, inhaled the incredible scent and lapped the length of her slit with his tongue. She tasted so damn good he did it again, and again. When she shook in his grip, he rose to his feet, sliding his hands up the length of her body and molding them around her own hands that were still holding her breasts.

The deep rose nipples were so tempting he had to pause to bite each one. Then he yanked back the covers and placed Kari gently on the bed, legs wide apart, knees bent, the lips of her cunt gleaming.

Let's see just how far we can take you.

He loved the way she trembled with expectation, despite her obvious effort to maintain control. Praying for strength, he kneeled between her thighs and went back to work on her She was gorgeous spread out like that, her labia a pretty shade of pink and swollen with need and her clit begging for his attention.

He traced the length of her slit over and over, opening her wide to give him full access. She thrust her hips at him, silently begging for more, begging for him to fill her. In answer he thrust his tongue inside her hot, wet, slick channel, fucking her with only that again and again.

"Oh! Oh! Oh!" Her soft little cries were like erotic whispers to him.

He increased his pressure on her lips, careful not to take her past the point where it became only pain with no pleasure. Their one night together might have happened five years ago, but there were many things about it he still remembered, things that had replayed in his mind nonstop.

She'd been a wild woman that night, open to anything he'd wanted. There had been no boundaries. He wanted that again with her, and more.

She made a small sound of protest when he slid his tongue from her heated, slippery clasp. But then he placed his lips over her clit and took it in his teeth, biting down gently. She detonated, her orgasm so explosive she writhed beneath him, crying out for more, begging for him to fill her with his tongue, his fingers, his cock. He finally slid two fingers inside her, feeling her inner walls grasp them as spasms shook her.

When the tension in her body eased, he began anew,

licking every inch of her skin. Trailing his tongue up the inside of her thighs and tracing the line where hip and thigh were joined. He slipped his hands along her ribcage until he reached her nipples, tweaking them hard enough with his fingertips to elicit a groan from her. But he caught the nuance of the sound. It wasn't a groan of agony but of pleasurable pain. He slid one hand down her hip and thigh and over to her core, easing two fingers into her slick channel. And slick it was, wetter than before.

Oh, yeah. She got off on this.

He moved his free hand to her cunt, seeking and finding her clit and pinching that swollen nub, hard. She gasped, her hips rising from the bed yet at the same time her inner walls clutched hard at his fingers. He did it again. And again.

"Slade!" His name was a cry bursting from her throat as she tried to press down on his hand.

"Come for me," he urged, his voice thick with lust. "Come on, Kari. You can do it some more. Pinch those nipples like you did before."

Damn if it wasn't the hottest thing he'd seen in a long time. He kept his eyes on her, watching her torment her nipples while he did the same to her clit, moving his fingers steadily in and out of her. This time she came even harder, bearing down on his hand, throwing her head back and crying out her release. He drove her to completion, the look of utter pleasure on her face making his balls ache with need.

She came down from the erotic high very slowly. Her fingers rested on her nipples, just touching them, while Slade stroked the inside of her sex and licked her moisture from the lips. He wanted to lick his own lips to capture every drop of the flavor. It was only with great reluctance that he slid his fingers from inside her and pushed himself to his knees. As Kari watched him from beneath half-lowered lids, her cheeks flushed with pleasure, he lapped every bit of her cream from his fingers, sucking the tips into his mouth.

Fuck!

He was afraid he'd come just from that taste of her alone. He was far from a novice where women were concerned. He'd had his share and probably someone else's. He'd experimented with all kinds of erotic activities, but never, ever in his life had he been turned on the way he was with this woman, and he hadn't even been inside her yet.

"S-Slade?"

"Yeah, sugar?"

"I want you."

His laugh was low and guttural. "You have me."

"I mean, I want you inside me."

He'd hoped to hold off longer, to give her more orgasms before finally taking her completely, but her words snapped his control. In seconds he was off the bed, digging in his pants for his wallet and the condoms he'd stashed there with the hope that he'd get lucky. Damn! Lucky didn't begin to even touch this.

Then he was back between her thighs, condom in place. From the moment they'd walked inside her apartment he'd been determined not to fall on her like a starving maniac this time, but to take it slow and easy. To give her the maximum amount of pleasure. But fucking damn, it sure was hard. He took a moment to center himself, pulling in the frayed edges of his control so it wouldn't be over before it had started. Then, with agonizing slowness, he eased himself into the hot clasp of her pussy, her liquid bathing him, her muscles clamping down on him.

"Look at me," he rasped. "Watch me, Kari."

She opened her eyes and stared at him with irises darkened to a deep forest green, little flecks of gold dancing in them. Slade braced himself on either side of her and began the slow, erotic glide in and out of her body, her inner muscles clutching at him with a fierce grip. Beneath him she shivered with anticipation. He gritted his teeth, forcing himself to go slowly, to maintain a steady pace, to not rush this.

But she had other ideas.

"Harder," she urged him, hands clutching at his arms. "Do it harder, Slade. Just like before."

The first time he'd been inside her, he'd slammed into her so hard it had shaken them both. He remembered now how it had aroused her. He wanted to go slow this time, to make it last, but she was making it impossible. She wound her legs around him, crossing her ankles at the small of his back and pulling him tight to her body.

Oh, fucking damn!

The hot wet clutch of her inner walls milked his engorged cock, each movement dragging on it. And all his good intentions disappeared in a puff of invisible smoke. He drove into her time and again, slamming hard, rocking her, and she stayed with him thrust for thrust.

"Yes," she breathed in a raspy voice. "Yes. Like that. More. Harder."

He rode her, every drag and thrust sending sharp spikes of fire through his body. He was on the edge, his orgasm rising up from deep inside his body. The muscles at the base of his spine tightened and his balls drew up. Sliding one hand between them, he found her clit and pinched it between thumb and forefinger. Hard.

"Oh, God!" she screamed.

Every muscle in his body tightened as his control finally snapped. They climaxed together, bodies shaking with the intensity of it. His shaft pulsed inside her heat as he spurted again and again, until there was nothing left. He had emptied every bit of himself inside her. He leaned forward, catching his weight on his forearms, and studied her face. Her creamy skin was flushed with pleasure, her eyes slumberous. He wished he had a camera to capture her just like this, just at this moment.

He brushed his mouth lightly over hers, then did it once more. Even that soft contact sent shards of pleasure stabbing through him. A shattering release had barely taken the edge off his need for her. Being with her transported him, cleansed him, washed away the clinging shroud of death and destruction that he faced. With her he could tuck away his battlefield persona and pull out the humanity he kept hidden away to do his job. It both amazed and scared him. Could their briefest of encounters have worked all this magic on him? It hardly seemed real.

"I wonder if I'll ever get enough of you." The words were out of his mouth before he realized it.

Her eyes widened. "Slade?"

Had he scared her off? Damn.

"Just tuck that away in a corner of your mind, okay?" Another light kiss. "Our night is just getting started."

He eased himself from her body to deal with the condom. Then he was back beside her, pulling her against him, her head nuzzled into the side of his neck. Sliding his hands beneath her, he stroked her back, tracing the length of her spine with his fingertips before dancing lower to follow the nicely rounded curve of her ass. With a lazy stroke he slipped them into that hot cleft, tracing its length, stopping briefly to press fingertips against the hot puckered little opening. God, he remembered the unbelievable feeling of his cock in that hot, dark tunnel, her screams as he'd dragged his cock slowly in and out, reaching hard for the control she robbed him of so easily. He squeezed one of the plump cheeks and she sighed, arching her hips for him, the curls covering her mound feathery soft against his renewing cock.

He needed to take it easy, not go at her as if he were a sex-starved maniac. This time he wanted to draw everything out, make sure every moment gave her maximum pleasure. Maybe it was the desire to imprint himself on her so no other man would measure up. Whatever the reason, he had ten days to see where this went, ten nights for them to enjoy each other. He planned to spend as much of it with her as he could. Get to know her. They had a connection, and that scared the shit out of him. Men in his line of work were death to relationships, in more ways than one. He'd have to make sure she knew that.

But not now. No, not yet. After this leave he'd figure out what to do next.

"I never thought I'd see you again." Kari murmured the words into the crook of his neck, her breath a soft puff of a breeze as she spoke.

"Same goes." He slid one hand up the soft arch of her thigh and around to her mouthwatering buttocks again.

"Do you believe in fate?" she asked.

He gave a short, rough laugh. "I didn't think I did, but I may have to re-examine that position. Because if it wasn't fate that brought us to both parties five years apart, I don't know what it was."

"I don't even know anything about you." She wiggled against him as he continued to smooth his hand over her curves.

"I could say the same." He had to concentrate on what he was saying, because her reaction to his caresses was lighting a fire in his own body again. His cock, so recently depleted, was making its demand for attention known once more in what had to be the quickest recovery in his history.

"No, you know I'm an assistant prosecuting attorney for Bexar County. You might not know it's for the criminal trial division."

"I'm impressed." And he was. She had to be sharp, intelligent and fearless to have won a spot on that staff. "Is that what you did in Chicago?"

She wriggled against him, distracting him for the moment. Maybe he should hold off on the conversation until later. His body was certainly voting for that. But she was more than just a warm body to him. His interest was piqued and he had to satisfy it.

"Yes."

"What made you move to San Antonio?" He wanted to find out what forces of the universe had brought them together again. Was it his imagination, or had she tensed beneath his touch? "Kari?" he prompted when she didn't answer.

"I needed a change of scenery." She kept her face buried in his skin. "Change of direction. A change in…everything. I, uh, heard about the opening here and applied for it."

He sensed there was a lot more to it than that but he also knew this wasn't the time to push it.

"I've never seen you in court, but I'm guessing they're damn lucky to get you."

She finally looked up at him and the corners of her full mouth turned up in a smile. "Thank you for saying that, but I think you might be biased."

"One of these days I'll get to see you do your thing, though." He tucked a finger under her chin and tilted up her face. "Would that be okay with you?"

"I think I'd like that." She squirmed in his arms, her thighs bumping into his ever-swelling erection.

She pushed herself up slightly. "Okay, you told me you're Army. Are you stationed here? At one of the local bases?"

"Not exactly. I'm based at Fort Bragg. In North Carolina."

"Oh." She wrinkled her forehead. "Are you in some kind of special unit or something?"

"You could say that." He rubbed his jaw. "I'm Delta. Delta Force." He didn't usually tell that to the women he was with. Of course, the kind of women he'd chosen to be with weren't the type he'd trust with anything more than his name.

"So…a warrior."

"But with drawbacks." He locked his gaze with hers. "I'm here for ten days this time, Kari. I'd like to spend as much time with you as I can."

She frowned. "What about the guys that are with you?"

"I'll work it out. Besides, I can spend time with them during the day when you're working." He traced the outline of her mouth with his finger. "But the nights belong to me. That work for you?"

Heat flared in her eyes, a hungry look that made his erection swell to the point of pain. Jesus. He'd never get enough of this woman.

She ran her tongue over her bottom lip. "Yes. It does."

He'd figure out how to handle it with his men. Meanwhile, he had other things on his mind.

"Kari?"

"Uh-huh?" Her words were soft and languorous.

"I don't suppose you keep any lengths of rope around here, so where do I find your scarves?"

Chapter Five

The man sat in his apartment, staring out of the window at the vista of downtown Chicago but not seeing it at all. In front of him his laptop sat open, the screen showing nothing at the moment. He lifted the rocks glass with his favorite Scotch splashed over ice and took a slow sip. Only the satisfying burn of the liquor coursing through his system allowed him to rein in his frustration.

Where was that fucking little bitch? Where in the hell could she have gone? She'd disappeared like so much smoke in the air without a trace. He'd tried every legal site listed. He'd looked for legal journals and publications. Then, frustrated, he'd gone to every search engine he could think of with no results. Putting her name into them only brought up references to Chicago or her professional bio. Like him she had graduated from Northwestern and from Stanford Law School. She had become a bright shining star in the Cook County State's Attorney's office under Ross Delahunt. There was plenty of press on the cases she'd tried and her spectacular record of success.

He had watched her in the courtroom and seen the brilliance of her behavior first-hand. Juries were fascinated by her. She was always well-prepared when she tried a case, her evidence right on the money. Her interrogation of witnesses often had them squirming and her summations were nothing less than genius. He had admired her from a distance, until that no had longer satisfied him. No, he had to express his feelings. Carefully, he'd told himself. *Don't want to scare her off.* He didn't know if she was in a relationship or not. She was obviously a very private person. Nothing of that kind had turned up on his research and he couldn't exactly ask people without raising eyebrows. Either way, however, he wanted to ease her into one with him.

But nothing had worked. He'd managed to find out that she had not been impressed with his gifts. In fact, as the process had worn on, he'd heard she was actually afraid. She and Delahunt had called the police, for fuck's sake. And all he had wanted was to woo her, to show her he cared so that when he revealed himself, she'd be happy about it.

Perhaps he shouldn't have broken into her apartment. But if he couldn't touch her, he could at least touch her personal things. That, however, had tripped some kind of switch with her. Then breaking in at night, well, it had seemed he'd scared her to death. The next thing he'd known, she'd slip off the radar completely.

She had to be working somewhere, he reasoned. She wasn't independently wealthy. But how could she just disappear as if she'd never existed? It didn't seem possible.

He rose and went to his bedroom, opened one of the small top drawers in his dresser and took out the piece of silk. Her panties. He'd taken them from her apartment the first time he'd broken in. They were a pale lavender, bikini-style, edged with a narrow band of dark purple lace. Whenever he held them in his hands he imagined them on her body, the lace resting just above her mound, the rest of it covering her pussy. He wondered if she waxed. God, he'd give anything to see her bare, all that soft pink skin his for the tasting and touching.

Now he lay on his bed, on top of the covers. He took off his shoes but left on his clothes. Very carefully he unzipped his fly and took out his cock. He rubbed the silken garment over it, becoming instantly excited.

He closed his eyes and began to stroke himself, visualizing his love as if she were standing there before him. He moved his hand faster and faster, stroking himself harder, until he erupted, spilling his juice all over his hand. When he could move again, he lifted her silk panties, the feel of the fabric soft in his hands. He used them to clean himself, the delicate material so arousing against his skin he was afraid his cock would harden again. Finished at last, he rinsed them in his sink. He'd dry them and put them back so he would have them to use again.

Chapter Six

Kari opened her eyes to full sunlight slanting in through the windows and the warm body of a man curled around her. She couldn't remember the last time that had happened. In Chicago she'd been too busy for far too long building her career as a prosecutor and establishing herself to be distracted by relationships. Then for the past two years she'd been so on edge because of her unknown stalker she had stopped bringing anyone home with her, even for a few hours. Or going to someone else's place.

Of course, if she were honest, the real reason was the one night with her then unknown lover. After that night, no man had been able to measure up. Hadn't been able to make her body react as it had with him. Hadn't been able to haunt her dreams. The stalker had just turned out to be an excuse she told herself.

If she'd never seen Slade again, would she have continued to walk away from every other man?

She smiled to herself. Good thing she didn't have to.

And good thing she'd moved hundreds of miles away from her phantom stalker. Army or not, Slade Donovan would not want to be bothered with a woman who had some crazy after her, disrupting her life. He wasn't looking for that kind of entanglement. Of course, she didn't know what kind he *was* looking for, so—

"I can smell your brain burning from here."

The deep Texas drawl sent shivers through her and woke up every hormone in her system.

"I'm not sure I have any energy left in any part of my body to burn," she teased.

"I'll bet I could stir some up." Slade brushed her hair away from her face and nipped the shell of her ear.

That sent plenty of burn through her body, especially right *there* between her thighs. She squeezed them together, trying to still the insistent throbbing that had blossomed the moment he'd touched her.

"Do you have someplace to be today?"

When she tensed, every muscle in her body tightening, he slid his hand around and pulled her even closer to him. She could feel the soft curls of hair from his chest imprinting themselves on her back, the hard wall of muscle, the muscular thighs and, of course, most of all, an erection she was sure would win awards. *That* was a memory that hadn't faded. In fact, it was even better than she remembered.

"I was planning to spend it with you. I just need to call my guys first and make sure they're set for the day." His low voiced came from against her shoulder. He licked the outer shell of her ear before dropping his mouth to nip at the tender place where her neck and shoulder met. "I guess I should have asked. Do you have things to do?"

If she did, she was wiping them from her calendar. "No. I'm good."

"Yes, you are." His deep voice rumbled. "Very good, as a matter of fact."

He slid his hand down over the swell of her stomach to her mound, slipping one finger between the lips of her cunt and sliding it lightly over her clit. The inner throbbing increased in intensity.

"Oh." The word escaped on a soft puff of air.

She was more aware of the touch of him this morning, more conscious of everything. His fingers were strong, masculine and slightly calloused from whatever he did for the Army. The sensation of them abrading her skin with such an intimate touch sent shivers racing through her.

Slade kept up a slow, gliding movement, adding another finger and rubbing on either side of her hot nub. She began to move her hips back and forth but Slade pressed his hand hard against her wet flesh, holding her still.

"I think you need to learn about following orders." His voice was thick with lust.

He turned her over, arranging her on her stomach, sliding a pillow beneath her. If she was hot before, she was burning up now.

"This good?" He bent down and put his lips close to her ear. "We did this in Chicago. You good to go again?"

She nodded, so turned on she couldn't speak. She remembered every bit of that night in vivid living color. Slade told her about a BDSM club he'd been to, said much of it wasn't for him, but some things? Damn! They just turned him on. When he'd shown her, they'd turned her on too. She'd felt the imprint of his hand on her ass for weeks after the redness had faded away, the sensation making her so hot when she'd gotten home she'd yanked her vibrator out of her nightstand drawer and turned it on even before she'd been fully undressed.

"Better," he growled. "Much better. Remember. No movement."

She gave a deliberate wiggle, knowing the response it would elicit. Sure enough, he brought one hand down and slapped one cheek of her ass. In an instant lust exploded inside her, her pussy vibrated and she wriggled back against him.

"I said stay completely still. Maybe you need more of a reminder of who's in charge here. Close your eyes. Close your eyes and cross your wrists over your head."

The next thing she felt was the softness of the silk scarf binding her wrists together. She wished she could see herself lying naked on the bed, eyes closed, hands restrained. The image increased the intensity of the spasms in her pussy. She wet her lips as she waited for the next slap. God! Whoever knew she'd be so responsive to spanking and restraints. Maybe part of it was Slade's tone of voice, the one she thought he must use commanding his men.

Give me orders. Tell me what to do.

As if he'd read her thoughts, he said, "No matter what I do, don't move. Understand?"

She nodded.

He nudged her thighs apart with his hands, exposing her pussy. The spanking began again and, moisture flooded her as need shot through her. One cheek, then the other, just hard enough to sting and create a pleasant burn that spread to her thighs. When he stopped, she had to press her lips together to not beg him to give her more.

Leaving her wrists bound, he eased her back onto her side so she was once more lying against him, cradled by his big body.

"Such beautiful skin," he murmured. "Such a gorgeous shade of red. Your body tells me how much you like that."

He smoothed his palm over the hot skin of her ass, a light stroke before sliding his fingers into the crevice between her cheeks. She felt the tips of his fingers coasting up and down *there*, each time brushing over the puckered entrance. She clenched her buttocks, trying to hold it in place, but he gave a short, self-satisfied chuckle.

"Don't worry. You'll get plenty of attention here before this weekend is over."

He moved his hand with unerring accuracy, finding her clit and stroking her with a steady rhythm, again and again, sinking his fingers into the wet flesh on either side of it. She wanted to rock into his hand, but he wouldn't let her. When he removed that hand, she cried out in protest, feeling its loss with acute awareness. But in the next minute he lifted her leg over his so she was wide open for him, ready for him.

With infinite care he returned to her pulsing flesh, positioning his hand so as he thrust his fingers in and out of her, his thumb brushed her clit over and over again. And while his hand worked its magic, he licked her ear and the side of her neck, trailed kisses on her shoulder and whispered erotic things to her.

"God, you are so fucking wet." His voice was hoarse

and thick with lust. "I love the feel of you, the slick walls clamping down on my fingers like this. Next time it will be my cock. When you grip my cock, I can hardly hang on to my control."

"Oh, God." The words came out like a sibilant whisper as her body's response grew in intensity.

"Feel this?" He pressed his hips into the cheeks of her buttock, his long, thick cock nudging into the hot crevice.

"Yes." She tried to wriggle against him yet he kept her solidly in place with just the pressure of his hand.

"Before this weekend is over I am going to fuck you back here again, fuck you in every part of your body. I'm going to lick your oh so sweet wet flesh until you come on my tongue, and make you come one more time with my fingers. Then I'm going to fuck you once more, just in case you have one ounce of strength left."

His words licked at her nerve endings, pushing her higher and higher. Her climax was coiled low in her body, slowly unwinding as his fingers and his mouth worked their magic. She wanted to squeeze her legs together, but he was determined to hold them open, her release dangling just out of her reach. Her entire body thrummed with need, her breasts heavy and aching, her nipples so hard they were almost painful.

Then, finally, *finally* he thrust his fingers deep inside her, working her, rubbing, his thumb strumming her swollen clit. And she exploded, her body shuddering with her release. She was still caught up in the aftershocks when Slade shifted, grabbed one of the condoms left on the nightstand, rolled it on and positioned himself between her thighs. Her pulse still beating wildly, he grabbed his thick shaft in one hand, placed the head of it at her opening and drove into her with one smooth slide.

He paused, bracing himself on his hands and looking into her eyes.

"Okay?" he asked.

She nodded, temporarily robbed of speech.

"Then hang on." His voice was thick with desire and need.

He drove in and out of her, sliding back until only the tip was inside then thrusting hard. He loved slowly at first, so slowly she tried to signal him to hurry with her body. But Slade seemed determined to set the pace and keep to it. She couldn't believe how ready she was again, how her body was hungry for his after the earth-shattering release.

The heat from his body surrounded her, along with his intoxicating male scent. Slowly, inexorably. He began to take her up that erotic climb once more. His cock filling her, the thickness of it dragging against the hot sweet spot with each movement in and out.

His breathing increased and so did the pace. Kari wrapped her legs around him, digging her heels into the small of his back to lock herself as tightly to him as possible. Everything fell away except the intensity of the moment and the feel of him inside her. Every muscle in her body tightened with anticipation. It only took him to growl, "Now!" in her ear to tip her over the line.

The orgasm swept over her, gripping her like an erotic fist and shaking her in a whirlwind of sensation. The muscles of her sex clenched and clenched, grasping Slade's hot erection and milking him. She felt every throb and pulse inside her as he emptied himself into the thin latex sheath. And when he sealed his mouth to hers, his tongue driving inside and mimicking the movement of his cock, she was completely undone.

She had no idea how long they lay there like that, her legs still locking his body to hers, their sweat-slicked skin barely cooled by the ceiling fan. Slade broke the kiss and lifted his head slightly, brushing her damp hair back from her forehead. For a long moment their gazes locked and held. Kari would have given a week's salary to know what was going on in his head right then. Was he disappointed? Had the reality not been as good as the memory? Was he satisfied now and any minute he'd get up, thank her and head on out?

"I'd ask you what you're thinking," he drawled, "but I'm not sure I want to know the answer."

"W-What do you mean?"

Did he think she was going to be too clingy? Make a scene? Whatever?

"If you're gonna tell me that the fantasy was better than the reality, I'm not sure I want to hear it." He touched his lips over hers in a light caress.

Kari smiled at him. "Since you brought it up, I was thinking just the opposite."

"Yeah?" He arched an eyebrow.

"I was wondering if, um…" Damn. She was probably going to sound like she was in college. "I mean, now that we unexpectedly got together again if *you* were disappointed." She paused. "In me, I mean."

He cupped her head in his large, warm hands, his lips curving in a smile. "No, I wasn't disappointed. Just the opposite."

She ran her tongue over her lower lip. "Is that the answer?"

He laughed, a soft chuckle. "The answer is, it was way better than I remembered, and I didn't think that was possible." He paused. "How about you?"

She exhaled a breath of relief. "Oh, yes. For me too."

Then the smile disappeared from his face and a serious expression replaced it. "Listen, Kari, I—"

Her stomach knotted with tension and her breath felt trapped in her throat. Whatever this was, she was sure she didn't want to hear it.

She touched his lips with the tips of her fingers. "Don't say anything. You've said all I needed to hear."

"You have no idea what I was going to say," he objected.

"How about the fact that you have a job to do for the Army. That you're away for long stretches, that you've made a commitment and you can't afford distractions and you don't want me to have expectations."

When he didn't answer her for what seemed like the

longest minute of her life, she wasn't sure if that was good or bad.

"You're right. That's the speech I usually give," he said at last. "I won't lie to you, Kari. I haven't lived like a monk. When I'm on leave between…assignments, I enjoy female company with no commitments. And yes, the Army is my major focus. But—"

"That's why I—"

"But," he continued, "there's something different here. I don't know." Another light kiss. "I want it to be different. I just don't know if after all this time I can change."

She forced herself to speak in a soft, calm voice. If all they had was this time, she didn't want to ruin it. "I'm not asking you to change, Slade. I'm not asking for anything right now except to be with you."

He stroked a thumb over her cheek. "Here's the deal. I've got ten days leave and I want to spend as much with you as I can. I know you have to work and I have a couple of things the guys and I are doing. But the rest of it I want to be with you. Can we do that? Live in the here and now? See how it plays out?"

"Of course." She wanted that, too, even if it was all she'd ever have of him.

"I've never made a connection with a woman like this before," he went on. "I gotta say it again, though. Relationships aren't always so good for men like me. We live in danger, Kari. The thought of leaving you with sadness and pain is more than I want to deal with. I've seen it destroy others. I don't want that to happen to us."

"So what are you saying? That you want us to be together whenever you're in town, but you can't offer more than that?" If she was truthful to herself about it, the whole thing with her stalker had left her emotionally shaky too. Maybe she didn't have more than this to give.

She looked hard into his eyes, as if some mysterious answer might be written there. What she saw was much better than she expected. Take a chance? Okay. Yes. She could do this. She'd have to do this if she wanted anything with Slade. And part of him was better than none of him. Maybe, as things went along…

"I don't know what I'm saying, and that's the fucking truth."

"We all have challenges, Slade." Like her, with her stalker. She certainly had no intention of putting that on the table. Not when she'd moved more than a thousand miles to get away from him. "I'm with you. Let's have fun, see how we are with each other. All that good stuff. Nothing heavier than that. Just one day at a time."

He didn't say anything, just wrapped his arms more tightly around her. Then he gave her one of his smiles that made every erogenous zone in her body throb like a bass drum.

"Let's do it, then." He eased his body from hers and headed to the bathroom to dispose of the condom.

"Hey," he called. "This is a damn fancy shower you've got here."

"It's one of the things that sold me on the place," she told him as she pushed her own body out of bed.

"Are you going to come shower with me?"

"Only if you promise to feed me afterward so I can keep up my energy," she teased, heading for the bathroom.

It was a lazy, relaxing shower, what they both needed after the intense night of lovemaking. *No, of sex,* she told herself. *Remember. No promises here, no commitments. So it's just sex.*

But damn good sex!

"Have you had much chance to check out the places on the Riverwalk?" Slade asked as he stuck his feet into his shoes. "There are some really good restaurants."

"Not really." Kari knew it was the jewel of the city and a top tourist attraction, with its colorful mixture of shops and restaurants on either side of the very narrow San Antonio River. "I've been invited to join people from work for lunch and dinner, but I've usually been too busy."

And too nervous to be out in strange crowds. She wanted to go there, but even with a group she hadn't felt safe. Maybe that would change if she was with Slade. Besides, *he*—whoever *he* was—couldn't follow her there, right? How would he find out where she'd gone?

"Then how about lunch at Casa Rio? It's the original restaurant on the Riverwalk and still one of my favorite places."

Kari had been such a social hermit since arriving in the city. Work and home and that was it. She knew it was silly to think her stalker had followed her here. How would she even recognize him? But the fear was always there, so she did what she could to feel safe. All those locks and alarms at the apartment. An open parking space, one without cover for someone to lurk. Taking different routes home all the time.

I'm nuts, that's what I am. And I have the man of my dreams here who makes love like a champion and wants to spend time with me. I can't ruin it.

"Sounds good to me."

"Let me touch base with my guys. I should have checked to make sure they got home okay but…" He smiled. "I was a little busy."

"I'm surprised they haven't already called a bunch of times."

"They might have, but I turned my phone off."

She was surprised he'd done that, surprised and pleased. It meant he'd intended from the beginning for her to be his entire focus.

"And yeah, look at this." He held up his phone. The screen was filled with a list of missed calls. "They nearly blew up my phone."

He opened the sliding door to her balcony and stepped outside to make his calls. Kari busied herself straightening up the already neat apartment, mostly in the vicinity of the living room. She tried not to pay attention to his conversation with his friends, tried not to listen in but she couldn't help it. She wanted to know what he said to them. The snatches of conversation she did catch didn't tell her a whole lot.

"...meant to call...get home okay... Yeah, sorry... Teo will... Yeah? No kidding? What about...?"

Then indistinguishable mumbling that she was too embarrassed to try to eavesdrop on. Finally he turned and slipped the phone back into his pocket.

"Everything okay?" God. She hoped he didn't have to leave.

"Yeah." He gave her that slow grin she was fast becoming used to, the one that curled her toes and made her sex throb with need. "Believe it or not, two of my guys each met someone at the party who tickled their interests."

"Wow. They work fast."

"Not as fast as me." He brushed a kiss over her lips. "They assured me they behaved in a most appropriate manner."

Kari burst out laughing. "Does that mean none of them scored? I'm not sure I believe that."

He grinned. "I expect they were on their best behavior, trying to make a favorable impression and not embarrass me." His face sobered. "Beau said even Marc, our lone ranger, was talking to some woman for a long time."

"Is that strange? I didn't think any of you guys were shy."

"Marc's been going through a really dark time in his life." Slade shook his head. "I want to help him but I don't know how."

"Sometimes there isn't anything you can do."

"I'm not ready to throw in the towel yet." He ran his hand over his face. "Apparently Trey ended up with the woman he met at the party."

"Really?" Kari cocked an eyebrow. "They really are fast workers."

"All except Marc. He's the one who needs it the most."

"So he didn't go home with anyone last night?"

"No. I guess he called and had Teo come pick him up." He frowned. "I don't know which way to turn with him."

It really was none of her business, but she could tell he was upset about it.

"Can you share what the problem is? Maybe I can help."

He shook his head. "First he has to want help and right now he doesn't." He blew out a breath. "He had a wreck of a marriage and the divorce was even worse."

"What on earth happened to him?"

Slade leaned back, a hard look on his face. "Marc has never been a ladies' man, womanizer, skirt chaser, whatever you want to call them. He's always been a little dark and introspective. Ria came into his life like a flame licking a moth and dazzled him. Before he knew it, they were married and settled into a small house that he always hurried back to."

"Doesn't sound too bad so far."

"That's just the beginning. We all met her at dinner and every one of us wanted to tell Marc to get rid of her as fast as possible." clenched his fists. "There was something wild and unstable about her and we all smelled trouble."

"But Marc was in love and didn't want to hear any of it," she guessed.

He nodded. "Until the day he came home on leave a day early, walked into his house and found her naked in bed with the next-door neighbor in the middle of some very hot sex." He paused. "And high as a kite."

"She was drunk?"

"No. High on drugs. He threw the guy out of the house and confronted Ria, only to find out she was a long-time addict and that man was only one of her playmates."

"Ohmigod!" Kari felt cold. "How awful for him."

"I always thank the Lord he called me that night. I came over and got him out of there and into a hotel. I wanted to bring him back to the ranch with me, but he didn't want to be around anyone. I think he only called me so I could stop him from killing her."

"Holy crap, Slade."

"No kidding. After that we couldn't reach him. We can't

seem to pull him out of the pit he's dug himself into."

"Wow. That sucks." She took his hand. "If you like, maybe I can offer some suggestions. But I really don't want to intrude."

"Trust me." He snorted. "If there comes a time I think you can help, I'll grab you so fast your feet won't touch the floor."

"Does this mean you have to go back to the ranch?"

Slade shook his head then squeezed her hand and smiled. "Beau and Trey have plans for today and Teo, my foreman, is keeping an eye on Marc."

"Oh good. So we're still a go?"

"Yeah." He grinned. "Come on. Let's hit the Riverwalk."

Chapter Seven

Kari sat back in her chair and sipped the icy-cold margarita. A soft breeze brushed against her skin and ruffled the hem of her skirt. Slade had convinced her to sit at one of the outside tables rather than inside the restaurant. She didn't want to tell him how very exposed this made her feel, so she'd forced a smile and let the server lead them to a table right at the edge of the narrow body of water. Shops and restaurants lined the stone walkway on both riversides. The stores were heavy on Texas and Spanish items, although there were some exclusive dress shops sprinkled in. Windows were filled with a kaleidoscope of displays and ancient trees lined the street like sentinels guarding the treasures.

The narrow walk for foot traffic ran between the two rows of tables and the restaurant itself. The crowds on the path were so thick she was surprised people didn't keep bumping into them. A wrought-iron fence separated the outside eating area from the water, where ducks bobbed playfully. All the tables sat under canvas umbrellas of vibrant, colorful stripes and mariachi music filled the air. Under ideal circumstances she would be completely relaxed, enjoying the ambience and the company of the man across from her. But it was hard not to look at every passing stranger — and there were tons of them — and wonder if one of them was *him*. If *he'd* found her.

She knew it was the residual fear gripping her. In the three months since she'd been in San Antonio, there hadn't been any hint of her stalker. Nothing to make her believe he'd somehow found out where she'd gone to and followed her. She reminded herself that Ross Delahunt had assured her they'd had no one out of the ordinary back in Chicago asking about her or anyone showing unusual interest.

Still, she couldn't shake the feeling that whoever this was, he was far from finished with her.

She did her best not to look over her shoulder every minute or scan the crowds around them. She didn't know if it was Slade's commanding presence or the excellent margaritas but the tension that almost always gripped her eased at last until she found herself actually enjoying herself. The people she worked with had been right when they'd kept recommending she get out more. The margaritas were crisply chilled with just the right bite of tequila. It all combined to ease the tension that had become a part of who she was.

She stared over the rim of her glass at her companion. She thought she could probably look at him forever, with his tall warrior's body and the dark hair she still itched to run her fingers through. The eyes that darkened to almost black when they were making love. When he was buried deep inside her. The smile that turned his face from a hard mask to one of warmth. Although he was every inch the alpha male, from his posture to his constant air of readiness, he was easy to be with, an unexpected bonus.

As the drinks worked their magic and she slowly relaxed, he coaxed her into conversations about movies they liked and hated. Television shows. Even whether a chocolate bar was better with nuts or without. When he told her he ate them with nuts because they had nutritional value, she burst out laughing.

"Why can't you just say because you like them better?"

He gave her a mock stern look. "My body is a temple and I must worship at it. Nuts are beneficial."

That set off another fit of laughing. "And the chocolate?"

He wrinkled his forehead. "I think that's supposed to soothe my jangled nerves."

She tossed a tortilla chip at him. "You are so full of it."

Kari was surprised to realize she could be so relaxed with him, so at ease. The tension slowly slipped from her body, allowing her to breathe and smile.

"This is nice," she told him.

He lifted his eyebrows. "This what?"

"Sitting here like this." She gestured with her hand. "Having lunch. Talking, about everything and nothing."

"Don't you usually do something like this?"

She shrugged. "Not usually." *Not since something evil seeped into my life.*

The Riverwalk itself was filled with Saturday crowds, the usual mixture of residents, convention-goers and tourists. The river itself wasn't more than a few feet wide, meandering through downtown San Antonio with cobblestone walkways on either side. Bright awnings and signs combined with live music and the sightseeing boats that cruised slowly up and down the river lent a festive air to the entire environment. Kari was sorry she'd waited so long to enjoy it but glad that her first visit was with Slade. If they didn't have anything beyond these ten days, at least she'd have a mental memory book to hold tight.

Just as she found herself relaxing even more, someone jostled her elbow.

"Oh, sorry."

She looked up to see a man staring down at her. He was tall, nearly as tall as Slade, with hazel eyes and close-cropped brown hair sprinkled with gray. Without realizing it she hitched her chair a little closer to the railing and away from the man.

"You know, you remind me of someone." He studied her face, looking for — what?

"I don't believe we know each other." Kari was proud of the fact that she kept her voice calm.

He shook his head. "No, you're right. I was mistaken. I just thought— Sorry to bother you."

He moved away, heading down the walkway and under one of the bridge arches. Kari clenched her fists in her lap as she stared after him, willing her heart rate to slow down. He hadn't looked familiar to her at all, but then she didn't know if her stalker was someone she knew or a complete stranger who'd seen her around the courtrooms or anywhere else in Chicago and had become fixated with her.

Oh, please, don't let whoever it is have found me out and followed me here.

"Kari?" Slade's deep voice cut into her thoughts. "You okay?"

She blinked and forced a smile. "Yes, fine. That man just startled me."

"For a minute there he acted as if he knew you?"

She shook her head. "He was mistaken. People tell me I have a very common face."

He laughed. "I wouldn't say it's common at all. Anyway, that's the one problem with eating outside like this. People don't pay attention to where they walk and on the weekends the walkways are jammed."

"It's okay," she assured him. "Like I said, he just surprised me for a minute."

"I thought you said we could play by ourselves today, Dad."

Kari stared at the man who'd stopped at their table. *Not another one. Please.* Then she realized the tall, tan, muscular blond man looked familiar.

"You following us around?" Slade joked. "I thought it was supposed to be the other way around." He turned to Kari. "Kari Malone, meet Beau Williams. You might remember him from the party. He was one of my so-called friends who thought it would be fun to hassle me."

She realized the words might be a little harsh but the tone was relaxed and joking, so she smiled at the man.

"Nice to meet you again."

"Same here. I'm glad to see the old man found someone with class for a change."

Kari felt heat creep up her cheeks but Slade just winked at her. She looked at the woman with Beau. Tall, with cornflower blonde hair in a ponytail, clear hazel eyes and a dimple when she smiled that Kari would kill for.

"Kari, this is Megan Welles," Beau said.

"Nice to meet you, Megan."

"Slade met her at the party."

"Sure did." Slade winked at her. "How's the asshole doing these days?"

Megan threw back her head and laughed. "Being his usual asshole self. Thanks to both of you for jumping in the way you did." She turned to Kari. "Barry is someone you never want to meet. He's a sports attorney but one who gives the profession a bad name. Beau and Slade were treated to his obnoxious personality when we met." She shifted to glance at Slade again. "I'm really sorry for that."

He shrugged. "No biggie"

"Besides," Beau added, "if not for that we might never have met."

She grinned at him. "There is that."

Kari saw the unmistakable flash of heat between them and thought, *Uh-huh. Beau looks like he could be a ladies' man, but I think this lady has a fire that's consuming him.*

"How about joining us?" Kari looked from one to the other. "Have you eaten yet?" She turned to Slade. "I guess I should have asked if you're okay with this."

"Listen," Beau began, "we don't want to horn in—"

Slade held up a hand. "We'd love to have you join us. Please. Sit down."

They shuffled the chairs around and everyone settled in their seats. The waiter took their order for more margaritas and brought more baskets of tortilla chips and bowls of salsa.

Kari thought how nice it was just sitting there, making small talk, enjoying herself for the first time since forever. She enjoyed hearing about Megan's job and some of the funny things that had happened. As a sports reporter she had entry to a world filled with colorful bigger-than-life characters. She told them about locker room interviews, arriving at the home of one athlete to be greeted by the man himself at the door, nude. And the time she'd been interviewing an athlete and his wife and they'd been interrupted by a police raid…on the wrong address. She explained she did a variety of pieces, everything from personal feature interviews to investigative stories on what was good and bad with professional sports.

Kari assumed the two had spent the night together. They had that kind of electricity between them that people got when they fell into bed together for the first time and had outstanding sex.

Then she was jolted by the thought that she and Slade might be in the same boat. Was there sexual tension in the air? Slade's deep voice broke into her thoughts.

"You okay? You look a little strange."

Get it together, girl.

"No, no. I'm fine. I think maybe hungry, though." She picked up the menu in front of her. "Let's order before I eat the basket the chips came in."

It amazed her how easy the atmosphere was at the table, any sexual tension aside. She liked both Megan and Beau and hoped that at least while Beau was here the two of them could enjoy each other. Despite the fact that she wanted alone time with Slade, she actually felt a little regret when they finished their meal.

"Okay." Slade pushed his chair back and stood. "I think we're getting out of here. I'm glad we ran into you."

"Yeah," Beau agreed. "Same goes."

Megan pulled a business card from her purse and handed it to Kari. "I'd love it if you'd call me sometime." She winked. "We could get together and rake these guys over the coals."

"Hey!" Beau frowned. "Wait a minute here."

"Just kidding. But really, Kari, I'd love it."

"Me too. I've only been here a short time and haven't taken time to meet too many people." She handed her card over to Megan.

"Beau, you okay for transportation?" Slade asked.

Beau looked at Megan who nodded. "I'm good. Thanks."

"We'll be getting along then. Nice to meet you, Megan. Keep a short leash on this guy."

Megan laughed and slipped her hand into Beau's as they walked away.

"That was nice." Kari smiled. "Your friend is very nice. So is Megan. He's got good taste."

"That's one thing about Beau," Slade agreed. "He's got very good taste in women." He leaned down and put his mouth to her ear. "But not as good as mine."

The server returned with the check and his credit card. Slade signed it and tucked the card back into his wallet. "How about if we blow this place? Maybe stroll along the river a little?"

"Okay. Sounds good to me."

She was quiet as they walked along the busy pathway, thinking about the man who'd stopped at their table and her reaction to him.

Slade studied her intently. "Is there something worrying you, Kari? Are you in danger of some kind? Maybe from someone you've prosecuted?"

I only wish I knew if that was it.

"I'm fine." She curved her lips in a smile. "And having a great time."

He stopped and looked down at her. The heat in his eyes warmed her body. "If anyone is bothering you, if you are in danger of any kind, I want you to tell me." His voice and his face were dead serious.

"Are you going to tell me you know fifty ways to kill someone?" she joked.

"Without a doubt." And he wasn't joking.

"Okay. I'll remember that. Is that what you do for the Army?" she teased.

He hesitated a moment before he answered. "Among other things."

She stared at him, all levity gone. "I'm sorry, Slade. That's nothing to joke about. I've read what's out there about Delta Force. It's hardly fun and games."

He nodded. "We don't usually discuss it. Everything we do is top secret."

Another brick fell into place. "And that's why you don't want a permanent relationship."

He shook his head. "It isn't that I don't want it. It's that I'm not sure I can handle one. I can't afford to split my focus. Plus, I don't want to think of someone back home worrying about me. Or worse, getting a visit from the brass to tell them I bit a bullet." He shook his head. "I don't want to put someone in that situation."

They started walking again. "Don't you think that's a decision for the other person to make? What if they are willing to take the chance?"

"What if I'm not?" he came back with. "What if I can't live with it and it affects how I carry out my missions?"

Okay, she thought. *Enough of this bad stuff here.*

"Maybe we're getting way ahead of ourselves here." She gave him a tiny grin. "Maybe after ten days we won't even be able to stand each other."

The slow, lazy smile he gave her matched the desire in his eyes and made every one of her girl parts quiver with need.

"I don't think that's a problem," he drawled.

One of the river boats filled with people cruised by. During lunch Kari had watched them moving slowly along the water. They were flat-bottomed barges with rows of bench seats and wooden railing painted myriad colors. At one end, facing toward the passengers, a guide stood at a wheel steering the boat, giving what looked to be a narrative of the river and what they were seeing.

"Looks like fun," she said.

"I'll bet you haven't ridden on one of these yet, have you? You aren't considered a resident until you've had at least one boat ride."

"Is that a fact?" Her lips curved in a smile. She had seen pictures of the sightseeing tour on the water but hadn't had the courage yet to get in a boat with a couple dozen other people she didn't know. But Slade was with her and probably the man who'd bumped into their table really did not know who she was. And —

Oh, for God's sake, Kari. It's a boat ride and Slade will be right next to you.

Yes, Slade. The icon of masculine strength. He'd never let any harm come to her. She hated herself for being so paranoid, but that unnerving feeling she'd lived with since the first episodes in Chicago still clung to her like a second skin.

"Okay." She pushed herself out of her chair. "Let's do it. I'm up for some fun."

And she did relax, to a point. The ride was fun and she loved hearing about all the interesting places on either side of the river, which she noted was more like a stream. They passed the riverside of the colorful pubs and restaurants, saw the tiny Honeymoon Island just big enough for two people and an officiant, the many historic buildings that had been there since the late 1800s — Kari loved every minute of it. Despite that, as if he knew she needed the added reassurance, Slade kept hold of her hand the entire time, at one point casually draping his arm around her shoulders and pulling her closer to him.

She had to admit no one on the boat looked threatening, or showed any unusual interest in her. She had to get past this somehow. Not every place was a trap waiting for her. She hoped.

When they returned to the landing spot, Slade helped her out of the boat then took her hand again.

"How about an ice cream?"

"Wow! That sounds really good."

"We'll have to climb the stairs to street level, but there's a great place right by the Alamo."

"Sounds good to me." She wondered if her life was changing enough that she could at last put the stalker out of her mind. If she'd even be able to.

And just as the thought turned around in her brain, a sudden chill skittered over her skin. She looked around, slowly, trying to spot whatever might be causing it. But nothing seemed out of the ordinary. People were strolling along the sidewalks, crossing the bridges over the river, hurrying up and down the stairs from the lower level. No one seemed to be paying them—*her*—any undue attention.

I'm losing my mind.

It stunned her to realize her hands were shaking. How had she let some unknown person take this kind of control of her life? She needed to get her act together here.

She jumped when Slade's hand closed over hers and he curled his fingers around it.

"Are you going to tell me what this is about?" His voice was low, even, warm. Soothing.

But no, she wasn't about to dump this on him when they'd spent barely twenty-flour hours together. If they never had more than this interlude, she didn't want him to carry with him the memory of someone who was a nervous idiot. Worse yet, who attracted someone like her stalker.

She swallowed, smiled up at him and did her best to make her voice reassuring and light. "It's really nothing. Honestly. Let's just forget it." She paused. "Please?"

He turned her so she faced him completely and studied her as if memorizing every inch of her face. Finally he nodded, his body relaxing.

"Okay." He lifted her hand and kissed it. "For now."

Chapter Eight

The man filled his mug from the single-serving coffee maker and carried it back to his den. He'd come to realize he was getting into the Scotch too much doing his fruitless Internet searches so he'd switched to coffee. He had a professional demeanor to maintain and showing up anyplace hung over wouldn't do his reputation any good. But sometimes it was the only thing that could take the edge off the frustration.

He wouldn't have believed it was possible for one person to disappear so completely off the face of the earth. He knew criminals who would like to be able to do that. That damn Delahunt had helped her. He would swear to it. Otherwise, how else could she have accomplished it? She didn't have those kinds of contacts, no matter how good a prosecutor she was.

If she would only listen to what he had to say. He'd admired her for so long. He wanted to cherish her, to do everything for her. To make her his prize. How could she not see that? He'd try to be very specific with the gifts.

Okay, yes, again he had to agree that the break-ins had been a foolish move on his part, but he was getting desperate. He wanted her with such a burning need. From the first moment he'd laid eyes on her, she'd become everything to him. He thought she was the best prosecutor on the Chicago State's Attorneys staff. If only he could have approached her out in the open, but people would have misconstrued. One night with him, he was sure, was all it would take. Then she would be his precious little flower.

If only he could find her.

Fucking damn!

He knew Delahunt had been quietly asking questions and doing some investigating as to who her mysterious suitor was. Suitor, not stalker, as the idiots kept saying. Well, maybe he could do something to give that a shove in the right direction, and use that to get a lead where she'd disappeared to. But he'd have to be very careful how he handled it. Hardly anyone could be trusted these days.

Chapter Nine

The creamy confection was, as promised, outstanding. Smooth ice cream, hers in a salted caramel flavor, sat in a waffle cone, perched for easy consumption. The rich taste burst on her tongue as she slowly licked it, tasting each drop. She'd had ice cream, but this was *ice cream!* Sitting on a low stone wall in Alamo Plaza's parklike area, consuming the treat one lick at a time and enjoying the late-afternoon warmth, Kari felt truly normal for the first time in months.

"Have you been to the Alamo yet?" Slade asked.

She shook her head. "I'm ashamed to admit I have not. Actually, I haven't done much except work, to tell the honest truth."

"Not even taking time to make friends?"

Kari concentrated on her cone. "I will. Eventually."

"You made one today. I hope you follow through on it. Megan Welles seems like a nice person to know."

"Yes, she does." She sighed. "I guess I'm sadly lacking in the girlfriend department."

Slade's inner antennae were still working overtime. He could understand if she'd only connected with a couple of people so far, but not to hook up with *anyone*? There was definitely something else going on here with her and one way or another he was going to find out. He knew the smart thing was to let it go, not get all up in her business. Another few days and he'd be gone again. He was so used to not leaving entanglements behind he wasn't sure if he could be comfortable doing it.

He was fighting an internal battle with what he wanted

and what he was afraid to do. His insides were in turmoil, his muscles tense and his mind sending him silent messages he didn't want to receive.

Don't pry. Don't ask questions she probably doesn't want to answer.

No, ask her. Maybe she has a problem you can help her with.

Yeah? Like what?

Don't ruin this, cowboy. Not when you've finally got the woman you've been dreaming about for five long years.

Slade didn't know which bothered him more, her evasiveness or that sexy twist of her tongue. Remembering the feel of it on his body, his cock popped to life and tried to push its way out of his slacks.

He knew whatever had hold of Kari wasn't just nothing. He'd been in too many situations like this not to know and his Spidey senses were on full alert. He wanted to tell her she could drop anything on him, but he realized despite the super spectacular sex that had knocked his socks off, they hadn't really spent much time together. Or gotten to know each other. He hoped that was what today was about.

He knew come Monday she had to go back to work and he needed to spend time with his men. The shooting competition was next weekend and he was hoping Kari would come along to watch. He wanted to get her down to the ranch too. See how she liked it. If maybe next time he was on leave, they could spend some time there.

He was playing a dangerous game here. He still had so many reservations about permanent relationships, regardless of the many successful examples he'd seen. He knew he was being selfish, spending as much time with her as possible if he didn't let this go anywhere. She wasn't the kind of woman you used and discarded. But damn it all, anyway. He wanted her, more than any other woman who had ever walked into his life. If only he could get his own shit straight so he could figure that out. But all that aside, there was something going on with her that gave him an uneasy feeling. Solving problems was his strength, but this time he wasn't sure how to go about it. For once in his life he was at a complete loss.

One thing he did know was if he had to watch her pink tongue in action another minute, he'd have a hard-on it would take a bucket of ice to tame.

"You about finished with that cone?" he asked.

"Oh. Yes. Wait. One more lick here." She swiped her tongue around the bottom of the cone, all that was left, then popped the little bite into her mouth.

Damn. He could have an orgasm just watching her.

"Here. Give me the trash." He dumped their debris in the nearby garbage can then took her hand and urged her to her feet. "Come on. The Alamo is right here. No time like the present to start appreciating Texas history."

He was always awestruck whenever he visited the mission where the battle for Texas freedom had begun. He hoped it would relax Kari and ease some of the tension vibrating around her. Since the stranger had bumped into their table she'd been nervy. The boat ride hadn't seemed to help nor had the ice cream cone. All normal fun things that shouldn't have been a big deal.

But he'd been in Delta Force long enough to pick up on someone's fear. She was on edge—no, make that on guard—every single minute, always looking around, checking for—what? He wanted to ask her what the hell she was afraid of? Was it someone she'd convicted? Some criminal who held a grudge? In her line of work it was probably more common than he wanted to know. But this wasn't the time or the place to get into it. Maybe when they were back at her place, when they were relaxed, after some more really good sex. But he'd have to be careful. If he went about it wrongly, she'd draw in walls around her and maybe even tell him she didn't want to see him again. But his life was assessing threats and demolishing them. He wanted to put that skill to use here.

"That was awesome," she told him when they exited the building. "I've been looking forward to this since I moved here."

"Too busy to come before now?" He asked the question casually, wondering if it had something to do with this tension she wore as a permanent cloak. Everywhere except in bed.

She shrugged. "Just, you know, getting settled in and stuff. Besides, by the end of the week, I'm usually so bushed I just want to veg out."

"Maybe we can do a few more things while I'm in town." He was holding her hand so he felt the involuntary twitch of her fingers.

"I-I think I'd like that."

"Only think?" he teased.

"I mean yes. Yes, that would be fun." She stopped and turned to face him. "Have you got your guys all squared away for tonight? Do you need to call them or hook up with them or anything?"

"Here. Let's sit for a minute on this low wall here while I check on everyone." He pulled out his cell. "Beau is certainly all set. And then some. But let me double-check with him anyway."

"Miss me already?" Beau joked.

"Like a case of the plague," Slade told him. "Just checking on your transportation situation. I'm assuming you're good until tomorrow?"

"Hell to the yeah. Megan's not on assignment this weekend so we're taking advantage of her free time. She said she'd give me a ride back to the ranch tomorrow. That okay?"

"Sure. It's not like it's some secret hideaway."

"Good, because I told her about it and she wants to see the horses."

"Bring it on. See you tomorrow."

Trey was next on his list. "I'm good to go, boss man."

"You behaving yourself?"

"Hell, no." Trey laughed. "What fun would that be? Hey, Kenzi," Slade heard him call out. "Am I on my best behavior?"

Slade heard the faint sound of a musical laugh. "You'd better be."

Trey came back on the line. "It's all good, Slade. I'm not doing anything to embarrass us. Just having a good time. Oh, and Kenzi said she'd deliver me back to you tomorrow."

"Everything okay?" Kari looked at him, her eyes full of concern.

"Let's say it's seventy-five percent okay. Let me call Teo so I can satisfy myself Marc at least won't be alone. Yeah, hey, amigo," he said when Teo answered. "You in a place where you can talk?"

"About the basket case you brought me?" Teo grunted. "Yeah. I'm out in the barn. What's up?"

"That's what I'd like to know. What's he doing?"

"Sitting on the patio. He's been there so long I told him he's going to grow roots."

"Damn." Slade thought for a minute. "Has he been drinking?"

"Coffee, only. He may be a depressed dumbass, but at least he's not stupid. What do you want me to do with him?"

"Has he taken one of the horses out today? Maybe get him to ride with you, or take him out on the four-wheeler. Pretend you're checking fences."

Teo's sigh was loudly audible. "Only for you. And I get extra for babysitting."

"Only as long as you tuck him safely into bed. I'll check with you later. And, Teo?"

"Yeah?"

"Thanks a lot."

He disconnected the call, but instead of getting up he continued to sit on the wall, lost in thought about Marc.

"Problem?" Kari's soft voice broke into his thoughts.

"You didn't meet Marc at the party, but I told you about him. Remember? He was hiding out in some corner waiting until he could make an exit." He rubbed his jaw. "You know

I'm worried about the guy."

"I know you said he's in a dark place, but that you can't find a way to help him. But, Slade, listen to me." Kari rested her soft hand on his arm. "There's only so much you can do besides just being there for him. You know you guys need to give him some room to come to terms with all this."

"Yes, but it's damn hard. He keeps telling us if it wasn't for the team, he doesn't know what he'd do. But still, most of the time he shuts us out. I'm just happy he didn't decide to crawl into a hole and never come out."

"I know this is something that's very hard for him to come to terms with." Kari paused. "I don't know Marc, I've never met him, but I'm going to make an assumption here. If he's Delta, he has to be smart, disciplined, trained to examine things from all sides and sniff out problems. He's beating himself up because he believes he was stupid enough to let his dick do his thinking for him there." She laughed. A soft sound. "Pardon the crude language."

Slade took her hand, laced his fingers with hers and lifted them so he could brush his lips over her knuckles.

"You can say dick any time at all, darlin'."

She laughed again. "I'll keep that in mind."

"Which was why, when all of us left the party with someone last night, he left to return to the ranch as soon as it was politely possible. He just doesn't have the stomach for social situations anymore."

"I can understand that. One hundred percent. But give him time. Be there for him. He'll come out of it. And who knows? When he's least expecting it he might meet a woman who'll pull him out of it and be just what he needs."

"God, I hope so. Anyway, that's enough discussing that for now." He stood and pulled her with him. "Now, what was on your mind when you asked about my team?"

Her eyes sparkled with mischief. "Oh, how about a thick steak, baked potato and some exercise to work it off?"

Slade decided to pack all the garbage in the back of his mind for now and just enjoy tonight.

"Sounds perfect to me. Let's go."

* * * *

The dinner was as promised and they returned to the apartment pleasantly full and a little buzzed on the excellent wine. But instead of falling into bed, Slade coaxed her into that incredible shower with him. He looked at the woman standing there and wondered how the hell he'd gotten so lucky. She had occupied his thoughts for the past five years, a mixture of desire and regret. Regret that he'd probably never find her again.

Then, boom! There she had been, an unexpected surprise at the party. He was torn between wanting to store up every minute with her because he'd probably end up walking away and wanting to find a way to make this last. He knew how to do everything else. Why didn't he know how to build a permanent relationship?

Despite whatever it was that was plaguing her, beneath it all he sensed a strong, determined woman who'd created a place for herself as a corporate attorney. She was confident, funny, smart and sharp. And a wildcat in bed. God! The images that had popped into his head of the things they'd done together. He was pretty sure when his ten days were up this time he wouldn't be able to just walk away from her. And how did he handle that?

Sex with her was beyond incredible and he'd had enough in his life to know. As they stood in the shower, water sluicing over them, he wondered idly if that was her way of letting the real Kari out, the one who hid inside the shark-like prosecuting attorney. Tiny droplets of water clung to her very thick lashes and highlighted the deep emerald green of her eyes. More drops coursed their way down her body, running in gentle rivulets over her nicely rounded breasts and dripping from her tightly beaded nipples. Over the curve of her stomach and down to her neatly waxed mound. That alone gave him the mother of all hard-ons.

He ran his hands gently down her shoulders and arms, loving the silken feel of her skin. Indulging himself, he licked the line of her jaw, moved down into the valley between her breasts and caught the droplet on the rosy flesh of one nipple. Closing his lips around it, he sucked deeply, pulling it into his mouth. When he was satisfied with the taste and feel of it, he turned his attention to the other breast and the other nipple, licking and sucking until she clutched his biceps and moaned softly, tilting her head back.

His cock, already semi-hard, responded at once. It seemed just touching her made his body ready for her. No one would ever accuse Slade of being shy with either women or sex. He'd enjoyed more than his fair share, but there was something different about Kari Malone. He wondered if there was something in the drinks he'd had that made him so obsessed with her, so hungry for her.

There was a convenient little bench in her shower and he lowered her to it, splaying her legs wide and running his fingers through the soft thatch of curls on her sex. She hummed her pleasure, leaning her head back, eyes closed. Kneeling on the tile floor, water cascading over them both, he parted her sex, sucking in a breath when he saw the tempting pink flesh. He blew softly on her inner lips, reveling in the tiny shiver that raced over her.

The water made her skin even silkier, and he ran his tongue over the inside of her thighs, her belly, the crease where hip and thigh met before flicking his tongue over her tempting pink clit. God, she tasted so delicious, sweet and salty, her liquid better than any drink he'd ever had. To give himself better access, he lifted her legs and draped them over his shoulders then took a minute to just stare at her gorgeous, gorgeous pussy.

When he clamped his lips over that swollen nub she cried out and dug her fingernails into his arms. He pulled it into his mouth, pressing it between his lips while he stroked his fingers over the crease on either side of her slit. He was so tempted to let one finger stray a little farther, down, down, and back to where that hot, tempting rear opening begged him. The thought of his cock inside that scorching channel made him so hard he nearly cried out.

Instead he eased two fingers inside her while he continued to suck on her clit.

"Oh, oh, oh." The little cries floated from her, almost as arousing as the feel and taste of her.

He added a third finger, stretching her and curling his fingers to scrape that oh so sweet spot and drive her wild. He felt the quiver in her inner walls that signaled the onset of her orgasm. Her muscles clamped down on him, her breathing sped and tiny moans drifted from her mouth. He worked his fingers faster, driving her up and over. Lowering her legs, he opened the shower door to grab the condom he'd stashed there as a just-in-case. He rolled it on with hands shaking with need, lifted her up and lowered her directly onto his cock. Pressing her against the shower wall, he began the slow in-and-out glide, the friction so delicious it nearly drove him out of his mind.

"Oh, my God, Slade," she gasped. "You're going to kill me."

"Not yet, sweet thing. And not for a long time. This is just too good. Come on now, put your arms around my neck."

She hung on for dear life while he drove in and out of her, winding her legs around his waist to hold herself in place. He felt the clenching of the walls of her sweet, slick pussy and increased his pace. They came together in wrenching spasms, bodies shaking so hard he worried they'd slip and kill themselves. At last the shudders, the tremors, all subsided, leaving them both drained.

Slade eased himself gently from her body, settling her on the bench while he disposed of the condom. Then he took the bottle of shower gel, worked up a good lather and proceeded to soap her entire body. He might have finished sooner if he hadn't stopped so frequently to treat himself to the taste of her lips, the feel of her mouth and her tongue.

He ran his hands over every inch of her, every crevice, every bit of skin, then forced himself to rinse her off lest he find the need to have her again. God. At this rate he'd kill himself before the weekend was over.

"I think I worked off that dinner," she told him with a grin as he dried her off. "What about you?"

He chuckled. "Oh yeah."

She took his hand and led him back into the bedroom. When she'd pulled back the covers, she slid in and moved over to make room for him. He stretched out beside her, inhaling her scent, so sweet now from the floral shower gel. Her breath fanned his cheeks like a wisp of a breeze. She settled her head on his shoulder, the line of her body fitting itself perfectly to his.

Slade closed his eyes, the glow of satisfaction from the orgasm still surrounding him. And one thought kept running through his brain.

I can't let her go.

Chapter Ten

Kari watched the jury file into the courtroom, their faces solemn, and take their seats in the jury box. She tried to read their expressions, but they gave away nothing. The trial had been long and arduous, one that had required hours and hours of preparation. A woman and her lover had systematically looted her husband's corporation, siphoning money to offshore accounts until some person with a passion for numbers had caught the situation. In a panic, they'd killed both her and the woman's husband. They had appeared remorseful and sad and pleaded their innocence with desperation, but Kari thought that was mostly because they'd been caught. She'd given her closing argument that morning. Then it was sit and wait. The afternoon had felt two weeks long. Then, just before closing time, she was finishing up a brief in her office when she got the call from the judge's clerk. The verdict was in.

The banging of the judge's gavel brought her back to awareness and she straightened in her seat. Next to her she could feel Jerry Broder, her second chair, vibrating with controlled anticipation. They'd worked hard on this and had presented a solid case. But you couldn't control the human factor and sometimes it did you in.

"Ladies and gentlemen of the jury." Judge Swimmer's heavy voice boomed at her. "Have you reached a verdict?"

The foreman, a thin, gray-haired man who'd shown no reaction to either testimony or evidence during the weeks of the trial, rose from his seat.

"We have, Your Honor." He unfolded the sheet of paper in his hands. "In the manner of The People versus Harold

Webster, we The People find the defendant"—he paused for maximum effect—"guilty of first-degree murder."

Kari forced herself to breathe as the courtroom erupted. Jerry pounded her on the back, the murder victim's family was crying in the row behind her, reporters were clamoring for sound bites. Judge Swimmer pounded his gavel again.

"Silence. All of you. I will have order in here or the bailiff will clear the courtroom. Officers, please remove the prisoner at once."

Then, finally, nearly everyone had filed out and the place was blessedly quiet.

Beside her, Jerry stuffed folders into his briefcase. "You rocked it, Kari."

"With your help." She could afford to be gracious. He really had been a huge help, with his research and witness interviews. She shook hands with him. "Good job. Go take your wife out for a fancy dinner."

"I just might do that." He waved as he walked up the center aisle.

Kari was glad to have this finally over with. The trial had dragged on for a week longer than she'd expected, but in the end she'd gotten the verdict she wanted, that she knew was the right one.

Rod Ciruli wasn't an easy defense attorney to beat. Although still in his mid-thirties, he had already built a strong reputation for himself as a shark for his clients and she respected him. He didn't cut corners and, if his client was blatantly guilty, he did his best to work out the most advantageous deal for him.

She'd heard the other prosecutors in her office talk about him, people who'd lost to him and griped about him all the time. Kari usually just smiled to herself, loath to point out to them that they needed to prepare their cases better. Kip Reyes had warned her about him when he'd handed her that case.

"I don't like facing him myself," he'd said, only halfway joking. "This office doesn't have a real great track record against him. Your old boss gave you high marks against people like him, and I think we need a fresh face."

But she'd done her research, not just on the case but the attorney himself, and went into court confident of a win.

"Nice job, Kari. Even if I did lose."

She looked up to see him standing beside the prosecution table.

"Thanks." She laughed. "But your client made it easy for me. Too many things pointed to him." She zipped her briefcase shut. "But I'll take the compliment."

He grinned. "Got time for a drink? Maybe you can give me some pointers."

"Thanks, but I really just want to get home, take a hot shower and pour myself a shot of fine Tennessee whiskey."

"Most women I know usually crack open a bottle of wine. But I guess a tough prosecutor has some strong tastes in alcohol." He walked with her to the doors leading from the courtroom out into the corridor.

"We all have our own tastes, Rod," she joked. "Have a good night." She turned and nearly bumped into her boss. She hadn't even been aware of him approaching.

"Good job, Kari." Kip held out his hand. "Excellent job."

"You were here? I didn't see you?"

He chuckled. "I don't think you saw anything, you were so focused on what you were doing. I saw the closing arguments this morning. When we got word the jury had already reached a verdict, I wanted to be here to give you some well-deserved praise."

"But what if I didn't get the verdict we wanted?"

He cocked an eyebrow. "After this morning there wasn't a doubt in my mind. So. Big celebration tonight?"

She shook her head. "No, just some time to unwind."

When she'd driven Slade home Sunday afternoon, he'd hugged her, given her a hot kiss and wished her luck. He hadn't said when he'd see her again and she'd wondered if he was pulling back, not interested in getting too intensely involved. She'd bitten down on her disappointment. If she heard from him, she heard from him. She was getting very good at shutting herself away.

By the time she got to the lobby, she was sure a hundred people had shaken her hand or pounded her on the back. Invited her out for drinks. Dinner. Whatever. She waited at the elevator, anxious to get to her office, unload everything and head for home. When the door opened, Sasha was swept out with the crowd and she threw her arms around Kari.

"Congrats, girlfriend! The word is all over the office that you hit a home run."

"Thanks." Kari managed to loosen herself from the bear hug. "I'm feeling really good about it."

Sasha stepped back and studied her friend carefully. "You look beat. Wrung out. I prescribe a session at Frankie's to pep you up."

Kari shook her head. "Thanks, but not tonight. I'm going home and crawl into a hot bathtub with a shot of bourbon on the rocks." And wait for a phone call.

"Jeez, Kari. You're no fun." The woman pretended to pout then grinned. "I'll have an extra drink for you. But maybe this weekend we can do something to celebrate."

"I think she might have plans for tonight." The deep voice came from behind her.

Kari turned, pulse fluttering and heat coursing through her body from her breasts to that oh so sensitive place between her thighs. The place still recovering from the most erotic weekend she'd ever spent.

Sasha stared up at Slade, eyes wide. "Oh, hey. I'd take him over Frankie's any day, girlfriend. Are there any more like him at home?"

Slade laughed, a warm sound that accelerated the throbbing in her body.

"I think they might all be taken, but I'll be sure to check." He looked back at Kari, effectively shutting out Sasha and everyone else. "That hot bath with a shot of bourbon sounds real good. Is there room in the tub for two?"

Kari looked around her to see if anyone besides Sasha might be listening to the conversation. Fortunately they all seemed more focused on getting the hell out of there. Which, at the moment, was exactly what she wanted to do.

"Let's get out of the mob scene." Slade closed his fingers over her upper arm and guided her away from the elevator and out of the stream of traffic, moving them off to the side. "What do you have left to do?"

"Actually, I'm good. I just need to get my purse and I can leave. Where did you park?"

"I had Trey drop me off earlier. He's hanging out with the woman he met at the Huttons'." He grinned. "And spent the weekend with. By the way, she's an attorney, too. You think we're having an epidemic in our team?"

"I don't know about that, but at least you'll have good legal support if you get into trouble. Let's get out of here. I need a shower and a drink and not necessarily in that order. And food. I was too nervous to eat today."

"I think I can handle all that for you."

"So how did you know I'd won my case?" She was curious as to where he'd got his information.

"I didn't. But I figured if you lost—slim chance—I could console you and if you won, we could have a hell of a celebration. Your office told me you'd gone to court for the verdict. I was there when it was read, but I ducked out and waited for you upstairs."

"That's— I'm floored. You even remembered about the case."

"Of course I remembered." He stopped, turned her to face him and touched his lips to hers in a gentle kiss. "There's more where that came from, but I need to get you alone first." He winked then nudged her toward the car.

They had just walked up to her car in the underground parking garage when her cell phone rang. She glanced at the screen and every muscle in her body clenched.

"Bad news?" Slade asked. "You look like someone just punched you."

"It's my old boss in Chicago. Probably just checking up on me. He still does that every now and then."

But she had to work hard to keep her hands from shaking. There could be only one reason why Ross was calling her. She walked a few steps away from Slade to take the call, aware that he was watching her.

"Ross!" She forced a smile. "I hope you're just calling to see how I am."

"Well, that too." His tone of voice gave nothing away. "I hear you knocked one out of the park today."

She relaxed a fraction. Kip Reyes had apparently called to tell him about her win.

"Kip give you a call?"

"He did. Said thanks for sending you his way and he has no intention of ever giving you back."

She actually managed a smile. "You know I miss you, but thanks for arranging this opportunity for me."

"Gave away one of my best prosecutors." Silence hummed across the connection. "Listen, Kari, this may be nothing, but I feel compelled to pass it along."

The tension returned, sharper than before. "Something's happened."

"Maybe, maybe not, but I don't want to take any chances."

"So spit it out. What's the situation?" *Yes. Ross, what the hell happened?*

"Our office has had three or four calls in the last couple of weeks asking for you. When my admin told them you were no longer with us, whoever it was tried to get her to tell them where you went."

"Did—? Did whoever it was leave a name? Or say why he wanted to get in touch with me? I'm assuming it was a he."

"Yes. It was." He cleared his throat. "Janine told him she didn't have that information, but if they'd leave a name she'd try to get in touch with you."

"So whoever it is hasn't given up, have they." Nausea bubbled up in her throat.

"That's not all." Another pause. "Remember how we

decided that you should close all your accounts everywhere at your address here and open new ones in San Antonio with a post office box? And the forwarding address we gave the post office was here? So Janine could send it along every couple of weeks?"

"Yes, yes, yes. And every couple of weeks Janine puts it in a big envelope and mails it to me." She nibbled her lip. "I haven't changed all the addresses I need to yet. Is that a problem?"

"Not in the way you mean. We had a few that had dribbled in over the past couple of weeks. Janine had them on her desk getting ready to address a big envelope to you, and it disappeared."

"Disappeared?" Her hand tightened on her phone. "How could it just disappear? Did it get thrown out or something?"

"No." She could hear his sigh across the connection. "This is my fault as much as anyone's. Todd Barber won his first case as first chair and we were doing a bit of celebrating. A bunch of people came by to congratulate him and it got a little crazy in here for a while.

"A little crazy," she repeated. Now she really did want to throw up. "So tell me how it disappeared?"

"Well, Kari, that's the thing." There was a second of silence. "When Janine went back to her desk, it was gone."

"*Gone?*" Oh, God. "What do you mean *gone*?"

"Just that." She could hear the note of apology edged with anger in his voice. "Someone had swiped it. All of it. Listen, I chewed her ass out good for that, but it doesn't help the situation."

"They'd have had to go into her office to get it. Did anyone see who wandered in there?"

"I wish I could say yes, or that I'd kept a better eye on things, but no." Ross sounded more upset than she'd ever heard him. He hated screw-ups like this. "And the truth is, Kari, embarrassed as I am to say this, I was so caught up in the success celebration I totally forgot the mail was even there."

"But it all has my old address on it, right?" She had to be sure of that. "That's the one?"

"Right. It does. And the chances that they can use that to follow a trail to you are practically nonexistent. Not with the way you set things up."

"Practically," she repeated.

"However," he added, "they could take the return addresses on each envelope and, if it's someone who's smart and has connections, check with those places to see if they have new information on you."

"Nobody's going to give that out just like that," she reminded him.

"If this guy is sharp—and I have a feeling he is—he can figure out a way around that. Unfortunately shit like that happens all the time. If he's desperate. He's going to tug on this thread like it's a lifeline."

"Kari, I am just fucking pissed that this happened." She could hear the edge of anger in his voice. "We worked so hard to wipe away any trail to you. But I do believe it won't be a problem. I think you'd need the FBI to track you from the mail that was left."

"I hope you're right, Ross. Uh, who all was at the celebration?"

"A real mixture. Attorneys, some judges, of course everyone in our office." He cleared his throat again. "I've asked everyone to try to reconstruct a list from memory, just in case. Told 'em we need it for future events."

"So now what?" She felt suddenly weak.

"Now you spend tonight celebrating your big win and tomorrow morning you go back to work." She could hear his sigh across the connection. "There were no real strangers here. I'd sure hate to think one of those people is your stalker."

"Me too." She swallowed, hard, and willed her hand not to shake. "I don't want to have to leave here, Ross. Start over somewhere else. I'm just getting to where I don't jump at every shadow here. I can't do this again."

"I don't expect you'll have to." She wished his voice sounded more reassuring. "I'm putting out a full court press to check again on everyone who was here. Someone had to see something. Believe me, I'm keeping my eye out now on all these people. I'll see if any of them does something hinky."

"Keep me up to date, please."

"Count on it."

Kari disconnected the call but couldn't move. What she'd heard had frozen her in place.

"Kari?"

Slade's voice tapped her consciousness, kicking her brain into gear. She had almost forgotten he was standing there.

Oh, God! It was bad enough that she'd gotten this news from Ross. But to get the call while she was with Slade? He'd know something was wrong and he'd want to know what it was. One of the last things she wanted was for him to get dragged into her problems. Would she never be free of this person, whoever it was?

"You look like you're about to faint." Slade was suddenly right next to her, his strong arm around her, guiding her toward her car. "Give me your keys. I'll drive."

She wanted to tell him she was okay, but that was so far from the truth. She had to agree she probably shouldn't get behind the wheel, so she handed over the keys, glad to see her hands only had a slight tremor. Slade unlocked the passenger side and helped her into the car, putting her purse in her lap and her briefcase in the back seat. She sat there, still trying to absorb what Ross had said, while Slade buckled her seat belt. Then he crouched down next to her, tilted her chin and gave her a warm kiss.

"We'll talk about this."

But what could she say? She certainly didn't want to dump the whole mess in his lap. He'd run as fast and as far as he could and she couldn't blame him. Who wanted a woman who dragged this kind of problem around with her? He dealt with things far worse than this on his missions. He didn't need her trouble spoiling his downtime.

God! Would she never get away from this nightmare? And who the hell could this be? Who was so obsessed with her? She shuddered as a chill raced over her skin.

Slade knew the way to her apartment complex so she leaned back, closed her eyes and wished by the time she opened them this had all gone away. He reached across the console and took one of her hands in his, giving it a gentle squeeze. He continued holding it all the way to her apartment, the warmth of his touch infusing itself into her body. When they got to her complex, he helped her out of the car and up to her apartment, where he dumped her purse and briefcase on the floor and nudged her to sit on the couch.

She waited, still too numb to move, while he prowled around the apartment. She heard the sound of water running, then glasses clinking in the kitchen. Then he took her hand and led her into her bedroom.

"Okay." He stroked one cheek with his fingertips. "Here's how it goes. The bath is running. Strip and get into it. I'm fixing your drink and will bring it in to you."

"But—"

He touched the tip of one finger to her lips. "No buts. Tonight I give the orders."

"Orders? Are we trying something new?"

Slade cupped her chin in his palm. "Maybe a little, when you're ready. Not tonight, though. Right now I want you to just get into the tub."

A weak laugh bubbled up from her throat. "Yes, sir."

"Okay. Get cracking."

She left her clothes in a pile on her bedroom floor, something she rarely did, while Slade finished getting her bath ready. Pulling her hair to the top of her head, she then twisted it into a messy bun and pinned it in place. The bathroom was filled with a wonderfully fragrant mist. Slade had obviously dumped a generous portion of her bubble bath into it plus some of her scented bath salts.

118

He had also pushed the button for the Jacuzzi jets and the water was whipping into a froth. She slid down until she was immersed and leaned her head back, closing her eyes, enjoying the soothing feel of the jets pulsing the water. Wouldn't it be nice, she thought, if the bath could wash away this nightmare the way it washed away the grime of the day?

She heard the clink of ice and the twist of the taps as the water was shut off. When she opened her eyes, Slade was standing there holding a rocks glass with ice cubes and a generous portion of bourbon.

"A woman after my own heart." He grinned. "I didn't look during the weekend. I was afraid you didn't have anything except wine and I have a feeling whatever this is calls for something stronger."

She took the glass and swallowed some of the smooth aged whiskey. The burn as it slid down her throat was a pleasant feeling and almost at once began to soothe her jangled nerves. Was she overreacting to this? After all, it was just some mail. Wherever it came from, the sender couldn't just give out her new address, right? And the thought that this might be someone she knew, someone she worked with, maybe even someone she thought of as a friend— She couldn't help the tiny shudder that raced over her.

Slade sat on the edge of the big tub, facing her, watching her sip the rich bourbon. Kari wanted to close her eyes, take a deep breath, and when she opened them, everything would have gone away. But no, it was still there. All the fear, all the terror, everything she thought she'd at least tucked away with the move had come rolling back like a thick black fog. She drank as slowly as she could, but Slade was not moving and nor apparently was he going to let her move until she told him what was bothering her.

"Slade," she began.

He held up a hand. "Don't even think it. We may have only been together for a couple of days, but this thing between us started five years ago. We have strong feelings for each other, Kari. There is something here that's way beyond casual. I'm not sure I know where it's going and I'll bet you don't, either, but it won't go anywhere if we keep secrets from each other."

There was such concern in his eyes she had to look away.

"You don't need my problems." She wanted to sink beneath the bubbles and pretend this wasn't happening. How could she bring her troubles into his life? "You have a job that requires all your concentration. I don't want this to spill over onto you."

"Sugar, you were nervous as a cat when you got that call. Right now you look like you'd spring if I touched you. There's something wrong and I want to know what it is." He grinned. "If I have to feed you the entire bottle of booze to get it out of you, I will."

Kari studied his face, set in stubborn lines. No, he wasn't going to let her keep quiet about it. Nor was he going to get up and walk away. Maybe telling him would ease some of the fear she still lived with, the fear that had exploded after Ross's call.

"Slade, I—"

He shook his head. "Whatever you're going to say, forget it."

"You're going to be sorry you asked," she warned.

"You let me be the judge of that, but I don't think that's a worry here."

He wasn't going to give up. She could see it in the line of his body and the set of his jaw. If she told him, he might decide she was too much trouble and get up and walk away. But if she didn't tell him, she knew for sure he'd be gone in the next five minutes. She might just as well give up and give in.

"Okay." She took another fortifying sip of her drink and set the glass down.

Slade took her hand and wove his fingers through hers. "Take your time, darlin'. Don't rush it. Just…however you want to tell it."

She hadn't thought the retelling would be so painful, or dredge up even more fear. Somehow, putting it into words brought it all back. But Slade's hand locked with hers gave her strength and comfort. She leaned her head back, closed her eyes and gave it all to him, chapter and verse. The flowers with their special meanings. The notes. The hang-up phone calls. She held it together pretty well until she got to the part where she'd woken up and someone had been in her bedroom.

Slade's fingers tightened with hers, but when he spoke his voice was low and even, unhurried, calm.

"He didn't touch you, did he?"

"No. I think I frightened him away, although it was a toss-up which of us was the most scared." She rubbed her forehead. "I've had the nightmare so often that I'm not even sure what's real and what's my imagination anymore."

"You don't strike me as someone who'd just imagine something like this, especially with all the things leading up to it," he reminded her.

"I can still feel that brief touch on me, still hear that whisper of a voice. God, Slade. I can't seem to stop dreaming about it and…" She let her words trail off.

He brought her hand to his mouth and brushed a kiss over her knuckles. "Nightmares can really fuck with our minds, but they are most often rooted in reality. And with everything else that happened, including this latest episode? I'd say you didn't imagine it."

"I came here to get away from it, you know." She unwound her fingers from his and reached for the bourbon. "I left Chicago like a thief in the night. No forwarding address. No goodbye party. No anything. Ross helped me a lot. He even helped me get this job. I'm very grateful to him."

He looked at her through narrowed eyes. "So, were you and he…you know…?"

"What?" Kari's eyes flew open. "You're kidding, right? Ross and me? He's a good boss and a good friend who is very happily married." She found herself smiling for the first time since Ross' phone call. "Why Slade Donovan, are you jealous?"

"Damn straight and don't you forget it." He leaned forward and brushed his mouth against hers, lips firm and warm and still tasting faintly of the ice cream.

"You know," she told him, "you've got enough to deal with doing what you do. You don't need my baggage to deal with on top of it."

His smile almost wiped away her reservations about his involvement. Almost, but not quite.

"You have the sexiest baggage of anyone I know." His voice was low and soft. "And I've had a lot of practice as a baggage handler. Let me help you with this."

"B-But we hardly know each other. We've just—"

"Picked up where we left off five years ago only now it's bigger and better." He reached out to cup her chin. "We have a week left before I have to report back to the base. Let me see what I can find out during that time. You'd be surprised at the connections my team and I have accumulated."

"I don't want this to get in the way of whatever missions you have once you get back to base," she protested.

"I'm very good at compartmentalizing. Believe me." He gave her a look that she was sure could see clear through her. "We're going to get to the bottom of this. I am not going to let anything happen to you. Count on it." He picked up the sponge. "Now let's finish this bath. I have other activities in mind. Then we need to talk about this again. Any and every little detail can be a help. You never know what triggers something."

Now she saw heat and hunger in his eyes. Surprised, considering the shock of Ross's call, she felt an answering fire in her body.

"Lean your head back and close your eyes." His deep voice was low and seductive. "Let me relax you. You're wound up tight as a drum. That's it," he said, when she took in a breath and let it out slowly. "Good girl. Keep your eyes closed and just feel."

Kari took another sip of the rich drink, the pleasant burn beginning to settle her nerves, and did as he asked. She felt the bath sponge coasting over her skin, skimming her neck and shoulders and arms. The soft material danced over her breasts, circling the mounds before stroking across her nipples. Little by little, as Slade moved the fluffy sponge over her body, her muscles relaxed and the tension that gripped her slowly eased.

The phone call from Ross, the worry about who her stalker might be and if he'd found her, all faded until she was wrapped in a cocoon of sensation. Slade swept the sponge from side to side over her stomach, gliding back and forth before sliding it down her legs and nudging her thighs apart. The touch of the sponge moving over her mound and down her slit was so erotic the walls of her pussy pulsed with need.

Then she felt it press between the lips of her sex and rub lightly on her now ultra-sensitive clit and her hips lifted off the bottom of the tub, rising toward Slade's touch. She wanted his hands on every part of her body, inside her body, touching every inch of her. She tried to signal him to press harder, move faster, but he seemed determined to go at his own very slow pace. Kari couldn't believe how easily and quickly he aroused her.

"Mmmmm." The sound drifted from her lips as her body clenched with need.

Slade pressed the sponge harder, rubbing the inside of her labia. Electricity jolted through her system and she lifted her hips slightly to meet the pressure. The glass with the whiskey in it wobbled in her grip until he took it from her grasp. Good. She didn't need the alcohol. Slade's touch was more than enough. She pinched her nipples, squeezing them until pleasure spiked in a painful surge.

"That's it." Slade's deep voice was low in her ear, his breath a warm breeze on her skin. "I like to watch you play with your nipples. Squeeze them like that. They're so pretty, such a nice dark rose. They get even darker when they tighten and swell. Did you know that?"

Kari had no idea what she knew. Her entire focus was on the pleasurable pain in her swollen nipples and the throbbing in her clit. She clenched her internal muscles as they flexed and pulsed. The little ruffles on the sponge brushed back and forth on her swollen nub in just the right way to drive her even crazier.

When the orgasm came, it roared up from inside her, seizing her body and sending the inner walls of her sex into a frenzy of throbbing. She tightened her grip on her nipples, moaning loudly. Then, at the very peak, Slade dropped the sponge and thrust two fingers deep inside her. She pushed down on them, gripping them with her internal muscles as she spasmed over and over.

"That's it, darlin'." He worked his fingers in and out. "Let it come. Give over to it. That's all you need to focus on, the pleasure, the sensations. Yeah, like that."

The water sloshed as she hitched her hips and bore down on his fingers again and again, until the last of the tremors subsided. She lay there, head back, eyes still closed as at last her body relaxed. She unbent her legs, letting them slide down in the water. Slade kept his hand in place until she was at last so limp she could barely move. Then he removed it, let it drift up her body to caress her nipples before cupping her chin. Next, his mouth was there on hers, his lips firm, his tongue probing oh so lightly.

At last she opened her eyes and looked into Slade's hazel ones, flecks of gold and brown gleaming like polished metal. What she saw there rocked her. There was so much feeling, so much caring, so much desire. How had they gotten here so fast?

Or maybe it wasn't fast at all. He kept reminding her this had all started five years ago. She was ready to believe it had been simmering and building since then, waiting for them to find each other again and reconnect.

"I think I'm ready to get out of the tub." Her voice was a little shaky.

"No problem," he assured her. "Leave it to me."

He lifted her out and stood her on the large mat while he dried her off with a fluffy towel. Then he wrapped her in it and carried her back to the bedroom. He left her sitting there hugging the towel to her body while he dug through her drawers and found a sleep shirt.

"That's not very glamorous." Kari gave a little hysterical giggle.

"We have plenty of time for glamor. Tonight it's just plain Slade and Kari."

In what seemed like seconds, he had the towel whisked away, the sleep shirt over her head and her body tucked into bed, the bedclothes pulled up to her chin.

"Don't move," he ordered.

"Okay."

She huddled into the warmth of the covers while Slade jogged into the bathroom. She heard him drain the water from the tub, then the sound of the shower came on. She closed her eyes and tried to recapture the peace she'd found when he'd made her feel so good in the tub. Then she wondered if she'd ever find that serenity again. If whoever this was would ever get tired of the game and leave her alone.

Before she knew it he was back, showered and dried, and climbing into bed with her, his naked body curled around hers. His muscular arm wrapped around her waist and he slid her close to him.

"Later we'll worry about dinner," he told her. "I want to get some food into you and another drink. Then I want to go over all this again so I have a good starting point."

She frowned. "Starting point for what?"

"For finding out who this is. And for how I'm going to keep you safe while I'm on my next mission."

Her stomach knotted. *His next mission.* Of course. He'd be gone and she'd be here wondering if whoever this was had managed to get her new address. Maybe he was right about a permanent relationship between them being impossible.

He kissed her cheek. "Close your eyes, babe. I'm going to take care of it."

Kari was sure she would spend the night lying there wide awake, but within seconds she felt herself falling into a deep and thankfully dreamless sleep, spooned against Slade.

Chapter Eleven

The bath had been the best medicine Slade could have given her. Shower, bath, he seemed to know exactly what she needed. Despite the disturbing phone call Kari had received and the details of her hair-raising situation she'd shared with him, he'd relaxed her enough so they'd managed to have a great evening celebrating her win in court. If there was an underlying note of strain, well, he couldn't blame her. But he felt uneasy about leaving her to go back to work.

"I'm fine when I'm at work," she assured him. "I'm surrounded by people and I'll even eat lunch in the break room, if that will satisfy you."

"It would," he agreed. "Have someone pick it up for you."

"Slade, I'm pretty sure whoever this is doesn't know I'm now in San Antonio." But her words didn't have the ring of positive assurance he'd have liked.

"Pretty sure isn't good enough," he pointed out.

"Okay, very sure."

She smiled, but he could hear the strain in her voice.

When Slade got his hands on whoever this was, there'd be very few pieces of that man left. And he *would* get his hands on him. He would go after this like he did a regular mission. It was unfortunate, however, that his day job would soon interfere with that. He and his team were due back on base Sunday and he had no idea how long it would be until he got some downtime again. He'd have to make some kind of arrangements to ensure Kari's safety. At the moment he just didn't know what those would be, but he planned to do some digging while he was at the ranch.

Beau had spent the night with his lady so he picked Slade up Tuesday morning to take him home. But Tuesday and Wednesday Slade left the SUV for the guys and used the pickup to drive into the city so he could spend those nights with Kari. Thursday morning she told him she'd be working very late that night.

"I've got depositions all day," she explained, "and then hours reviewing case law for a new trial I'm just starting to prep for. By the time I'm finished with everything, all I'll be good for is to fall into bed and collapse."

"You could fall into bed with me," he teased.

"It's very tempting." She shook her head. "But even when I'm asleep my mind will be a million miles away. I'd rather save it all up for a great weekend."

"You don't get much of a rest between trials, do you?" he commented.

"It's okay," she assured him. "The busier I am the better."

He wasn't comfortable not being with her, especially with this new development in her situation. He was trying to walk a fine line between protection and obsession. He did get her to agree to text him regularly and had to be satisfied with that until he could get something better in place.

According to Trey, the woman he'd hooked up with was also an attorney, but not criminal, like Kari. She worked for a silk-stocking corporate law firm in San Antonio that represented high-ticket clients. At first Slade had wondered what the two of them could possibly have in common. Then he gave himself a mental kick for selling his team member short. Trey had graduated from the University of Michigan with a history degree and a concentration in military science. He could hold his own with anyone. But Kenzi was off to Miami for two days to meet with a client, which left Trey at loose ends for the moment.

Beau was also spending time with a woman he'd met at the Huttons'. Slade had started to wonder if the JAG attorney and his wife were running a dating service. In any event, the woman currently front and center in Beau's life was a reporter for a sports magazine based in San Antonio. To Slade's way of thinking, that made her an excellent match for Beau who was a fanatic about almost any kind of athletics. But she was currently in San Francisco to interview a hot new baseball pitcher.

And Marc? Slade had done his best to draw Marc out of the darkness, but he was making very little headway. Teo reported that he'd had the man out riding horses every day, that he seemed to enjoy it but rarely said a word. Although Marc had asked to borrow the beat-up pickup they used to haul hay.

"Told me he didn't need anything fancy," Teo repeated to Slade.

"And no idea where he's going?"

Teo shook his head.

"As long as he doesn't get drunk and kill himself, let's let him be."

Sometimes Slade just wanted to smack Marc so hard that all that poison and resentment he was holding so tight inside himself would come spewing out and he could begin to heal.

He spent all Thursday and part of Friday with his team. On Thursday they took the four-wheeler to the far end of the ranch, to a pasture where he never ran cattle. There he had a shooting range set up, with targets tacked to bales of hay to catch the bullets. The men unloaded the folding metal tables they'd brought and lined them up in a row. Each of them mounted his own shooting station with their various guns and ammo. They practiced for the match until they used up all their ammunition.

"We done good, boss," Beau joked. "We should shoot the numbers off the competition."

"Like we did before," Trey agreed.

Slade nodded. "I'd definitely say we're good to go. Let's load up and head back to the house."

After stowing their firearms and gear, they congregated at the shaded patio table. Teo had already brought beer in a cooler and had set it up for them.

"Let's talk about this weekend," Slade said after a long swallow of the ice-cold liquid. "We'll have guests here," he reminded them. "Ladies, who need to be treated right."

Beau laughed. "Speak for yourself. I think I'm doing just fine."

"I mean about when everyone's getting here, what we want to serve them to eat, and mostly about explaining the rules of the competition to them. Mostly about the rules and where they can stand to watch."

"I'm good with whatever," Marc said in his usually uninflected voice.

"Speaking for myself," Beau put in, "I'm pretty excited to have a cheering section." He winked. "Show off my skills to my lady."

"Then let's work out all the logistics. This will be our last chance to spend time with them before reporting back to base. I know it's probably not the most romantic of weekends, but it's part of who we are and they should know this. And at least we'll have the time with them."

Slade didn't know the exact situation with Beau and Trey, but he knew what he and Kari had gone way beyond casual.

"When I asked Megan," Beau said, "she told me 'Hell, yeah!' She wants to see the horses again too. Unfortunately she's still in San Francisco getting an interview. Her plane won't get in until late Friday night."

"That's a shame." Slade eyed the other man. "You okay with that?"

Beau shrugged. "She's okay with me going off for who knows how long to who knows where. I guess I have to be, right?"

"Seems as if."

"She offered to get her car and drive herself out Friday night, but I put a stop to that." He shook his head. "Call me crazy. She goes everywhere, all over hell and gone, by herself. I just don't want her on the road by herself that late, even though she probably does it all the time, anyway."

Kenzi and Kari would drive down in their own vehicles after work Friday afternoon.

Slade knew he probably drove Kari nuts as many times as he'd texted her Thursday night and Friday, just to reassure himself that she was okay. He spent a good part of Friday trying to figure out a way to be sure she was safe until he could get back in town again. The others got the message that he was preoccupied and steered clear of him. Trey found him at the kitchen table Friday morning with his cell phone and a notepad.

"We thought we'd haul Marc's ass out of the house and do some four-wheeling again," he said. "I can see you've got stuff to do." He paused. "Whatever's got your knickers in a twist, Shadow, it might go easier if you let us give you a hand."

Slade shook his head. "If I need to I will, but I don't think that would work."

Trey lifted an eyebrow. "I thought there was nothing we couldn't do, for ourselves and for others."

Slade leaned back in his chair and raked his fingers through his hair. He knew these men would lay down their lives for him, as he would for them. But this wasn't something he could bring them in on. At least not yet. They'd be half a world away with him and he was the one with the local contacts here.

"You're right. And I may yet toss it out there. Right now I'm not there yet. Teo said Marc took the old pickup into town one night."

"Yeah." Beau replied. "He say where and for what?"

"I'm hoping he met someone at the party and just hasn't mentioned it. You know how closemouthed he is, especially since the divorce."

Beau nodded. "That's for damn sure. I asked him, real casual, about it when he got home but you'd think his mouth was sewed shut. Still, he wasn't drunk when he came back and he didn't appear any the worse, so I could see that as some kind of progress."

"No kidding, man." Trey fixed himself a cup of coffee. "Slade, we need to take the four-wheeler, stick him in it and ride him around until we maybe shake his brains loose."

"Yeah, do that." Slade shook his head. "That woman really fucked him up good. Time we managed to get him past it. Maybe he already took that first step?"

"I'll see what I can find out. Okay, we'll be off, then. Beau said if you didn't come along to tell you'd we'll back in plenty of time to pretty ourselves up for dinner."

Slade chuckled. "Appreciate it."

He had made some contacts by the time the end of the day rolled around. Put out some feelers. Had some people to call back on Saturday when they got back from the meet, but at least he'd started the ball rolling. He'd even made a couple of calls that he was sure Kari would kick his ass for, but hell. His goal was to keep her safe and he'd do anything to accomplish that.

He wanted to make this weekend as special for her as he could, even if part of it would be spent watching men shoot. Saturday the women would go with them to the competition. He took their eagerness to watch a good sign. Then a relaxed dinner at the ranch and a long night together. He wasn't necessarily looking for off-the-charts sex that night, which surprised him, since that was usually at the top of his list. But with Kari he felt a difference. They had a connection that had meaning, however they did it.

And Sunday it would all come to a crashing halt when they headed back to base. Slade had no idea what would happen in Beau's and Trey's situations, but for himself he had to figure out the best way to handle things. Kari was definitely what he'd want long term. Scratch that. *Who* he'd want long term. But he'd buried his relationship skills and he was still determined not to get into a situation where, if he got killed—which was way more than likely—he'd be leaving someone behind to deal with pain and sadness. Nope. He'd seen it too many times. Only, how was he going to walk away from everything this could be?

I am so fucked up.

By the time Friday evening got there, he had worn out his brain thinking about it. He wanted Kari with an unexpected fierceness, but that same desire wanted to keep her safe from pain. Crap. He tried to mellow out while waiting for her, hanging out on the porch with the rest of the guys. He was sitting on the porch with the others—even Marc, who was a dark, silent presence—when he spotted Kari's car turning onto the drive from the roadway. He set his beer down and headed off the porch.

"Here comes my lady, guys." He spared a quick glance for the others. "Try to act civilized if possible."

"Megan will be here soon," Beau reminded them. "Try not to scare her off."

It was obvious Kari had changed before she'd headed down here. When she climbed out of the car, she was wearing skinny jeans that made her legs seem a mile long and cupped her ass like loving hands. The T-shirt she wore was the exact color of her eyes. Her rich auburn hair was pulled up in a high ponytail, exposing her graceful neck and accenting her sculpted cheekbones and chin. Her lips looked so tempting with a light gloss slicked over them that he couldn't help himself. He hauled her into his arms, bent his head and took her mouth in a hungry kiss.

Kari laughed against his lips, breaking the mood, and he lifted his head, frowning. "What—?"

She nodded toward the porch and he realized the others were treating them to a chorus of catcalls.

"Will you guys please grow up?" he growled. He peered down at Kari. "I apologize for them. They lost their manners someplace."

"No problem." She smiled again. "Really."

"Let's get your stuff inside. Then I can show you around."

The men rose to their feet as she and Slade climbed the few steps to the porch.

"You'll have to excuse us," Trey said. "We don't get to spend a lot of time with civilized people. But we're very

133

happy you'll be watching us at the meet tomorrow."

"Thank you." She looked at them with a straight face. "I should tell you I'm a county prosecutor so if you irritate me, I can have you thrown in jail."

They stared at her as if they hadn't heard right.

Slade burst out laughing. "That ought to keep them on their toes."

He was glad the master suite in the house was on the first floor, almost a separate wing, while the other rooms were upstairs. They'd have at least the semblance of privacy tonight. And he knew that his men, regardless of how rowdy they liked to act, would be very respectful of the women at all times. But it was important to him that Kari saw all aspects of his life and learned that outside Delta, the ranch was at the core.

Her reaction to the ranch was all he could have asked for.

"Oh, Slade. It's beautiful. Absolutely gorgeous." She stood in the yard and turned in a circle, taking everything in with wide eyes. "It totally takes my breath away. That house musty be a hundred years old and look how you've kept it in such good shape." She turned back to him. "Now I want to see the horses."

"Think I might make a cowgirl out of you?" He winked.

"You never know. These horses are gorgeous. The colors, the—what is it? conformation?—are incredible."

She insisted on going from stall to stall with him and petting each one, giving each of them a sliver of the apple Slade had provided her with, holding it out flat on her open palm the way he'd shown her so she didn't get her fingers nipped off. "I might have to hang with you just to get to come out here."

He was thrilled to death with her reaction and wondered if this was some kind of a sign. Then he shut down that line of thinking. He knew what worked and long term wasn't it. By the time they walked back out onto the porch, Kenzi had arrived.

Slade didn't know what he'd expected, but not the petite

woman with the cascade of black hair and the dimple in her chin. Her petite form showed off the skinny jeans and pink sleeveless top she wore. This was Trey's corporate attorney? The shark he'd told them about?

Kenzi shook everyone's hand, smiled at the group, winked at Trey and asked if she could help.

Slade had to swallow a chuckle as he watched Trey roll up his tongue. He tried to speak then just gave it up and pulled Kenzi in for a tight hug. She molded herself to Trey's side, leaning into him although she barely came to his shoulder. He didn't think it mattered though, as besotted as Trey seemed. Another winner, he thought. Smart, sassy, sexy. And looking at Trey as if he was the answer to all her prayers.

How had this happened so fast? Was he the only one questioning everything? Afraid to take a chance? He thought about Marc and his heart pinched at the thought of ending up that bitter and depressed. It was definitely time for an attitude adjustment, and quick, before he lost the best thing to walk into his life.

Teo had the steaks grilling and everyone else pitched in to get dinner and drinks set out on the patio table. The meal seemed to mellow them all out. By the time they'd finished, Slade was shocked to realize how relaxed everyone was. And in most cases, coupled up. He finally reached over, lifted Kari and deposited her on his lap, loving the feel of her firm ass on his thighs. Kenzi sat in Trey's lap while everyone chatted, leaning into him as his hand idly caressed her back. They discovered she had a wicked sense of humor and Slade couldn't remember the last time he'd laughed this much.

If there was one fly in the ointment, it was the sadness and bitterness that continued to surround Marc like a cloak. Although, Slade noticed that tonight the clouds weren't as dark as usual, and Marc actually joined in the conversation. Beau looked at Slade and cocked an eyebrow, but Slade just shrugged. He had no details to give them.

They sat outside long after dinner was over, in comfortable conversation. Somehow, with the wide variety of personalities and new people thrown into the mix, they still managed to fall into a relaxed, easy situation. Then Beau left to pick up Megan and the rest of them cleaned up the debris from the meal.

"I don't think Beau and Megan need us to wait up for them," Slade murmured to Kari as she loaded the last of the dishes in the dishwasher. "Trey and Kenzi slipped out a few minutes ago."

Kari turned and looped her arms around his neck. "I think you're right. What did you have in mind?"

He was hard at once and slid his hands down to cup her ass, pressing her against him.

"Does that give you a clue?"

Her lips curved in the smile that heated his blood. "It seems you have a problem that needs taking care of."

He squeezed the cheeks of her buttocks. "Are you offering to take care of it?"

She nodded and stood on tiptoe so her mouth was closer to his ear. "Just so you know, I've never been like this...in bed...with anyone else. Ever."

Oh, Jesus! Was it possible to get any harder?

"Do you know how great that makes me feel?"

"I mean..." She blew out a soft breath, tickling the skin of his neck. "I know we had the incredible night in Chicago. I'd never been that wild and uninhibited in my life. Ever. And now here we are again. You seem to bring that out in me."

He licked her lower lip, one soft and gentle swipe of his tongue. "And that's the way I want it to stay. That work for you?"

"You mean...?"

"I mean, exclusive." He really hadn't wanted to have this discussion right now, but he also didn't want to leave this kind of thread dangling. "We need at some point, some time, to have a serious talk about the kind of life I lead, darlin'. Strong women have given up on men like me."

She tilted her head back and looked up at him. A tiny frown creased her forehead. "Are you saying yes, exclusive, but no, because of your job? I'm confused here."

A rough chuckle rumbled in his throat. "No more than I am. Yes, exclusive. I want this with you, Kari, whatever this turns out to be. I just want to make sure you know what you're getting into. I still can't make myself believe I can saddle someone with the fallout from what I do, or that I have the ability for a full, emotional relationship."

She took so long to answer he was afraid she was going to shut the whole thing down.

"Two things. One, you're right. This isn't the time or place for this discussion, not when you're going off to God knows where to do God knows what and you need your head clear. No distractions. Two, I can deal with anything as long as the man is faithful. The rest of it? Just let me worry about it. For now."

"That's one thing you'd never have to worry about." He tried to put every bit of feeling into his words. "I promise you."

"Then let's table the rest of this for the moment. Right now let's just be together. And let's get to sleep so you can be on your game for the competition tomorrow."

Slade laughed. "Maybe not sleep but at least to bed."

He lifted her and carried her down the short hallway to his room. He was used to getting by on very little sleep and tonight he wasn't going to waste time when he had something more important in mind.

Chapter Twelve

Kari enjoyed the day way more than she'd expected. Watching the men compete with different firearms, shooting at a range of targets from different distances, had been eye-opening. Four men at a time had lined up behind bales to shoot in each stage. Their targets had been retrieved and scores awarded according to the target areas they'd hit. The four guys swept all the competitions, with top honors going to their sniper, Beau.

"You guys ever gonna give the rest of us a chance to win, Slade?" one of the men joked. "Maybe you guys could shoot with blindfolds, or one-handed."

Slade grinned, knowing the men expected to lose to them but felt honored to compete against them. "We'll think about it."

Back at the ranch, they gathered at the patio table where Teo had provided a variety of drinks.

"I think we need a toast to the champs." Megan lifted her wine glass and the other women followed suit.

She had taken several pictures for an article on competitive shooting she wanted to pitch to her editor. At their request she'd made sure that all the shots of the four men were from behind so no one saw their faces.

"We smoked them." Beau lifted his beer bottle. "Sent them down in flames." He took a long drink of the cool liquid.

"All in all," Slade observed, "a good day."

Trey lit one of the cigars Slade handed out and blew a perfect smoke ring in the air. "No less than I expected of us. If they'd creamed us, we'd never get over the embarrassment."

Everyone was silent for a moment, just enjoying the quiet of the evening and the companionship, the remains of a celebratory barbecue Teo had prepared scattered on the tables. Kari had wondered how they'd all mesh, but she found the other women delightful. They'd formed a cohesive cheering section and during any lull in activity discovered they had a lot of things in common.

This was the first chance she'd had to observe Slade's team and to see how he interacted with his men. She knew about Special Forces. Those men were alert at all times, ready for anything, focused on their mission. But here they were so relaxed and easygoing.

While Beau might look like a candidate for the cover of *Surfer Magazine*, Slade had told her he was the team's sniper and beneath that let's–have–fun attitude she could easily see a man on the alert, never quite relaxed, always aware of what was around him. Always reading other people's signals. Trey was Beau's spotter. While not quite as laid-back on the surface as Beau, he still carried the same comfortable attitude, unruffled by anything. She could also tell they were very much into the women they'd hooked up with, but still with an invisible wall around them. She was sure that letting down their guard was something they'd all been trained not to do. It was definitely the rock in the road as far as Slade was concerned. She was convinced he'd meant it when he'd said he wanted something permanent, but up until now he'd believed the life he led got in the way of that.

The only one she couldn't get a good read on was Marc. She was surprised he'd joined them for dinner, based on what Slade had told her. When he'd lingered over drinks with them after the meal, she'd wondered if maybe this woman he'd spent a little time with at the party had pushed the right button. She wasn't surprised at him suddenly standing up, and his next words made her think she was right about the woman.

"How about if we clean up this mess? I, uh, need to make a phone call."

Everyone stared at him.

Slade found his voice first. "Phone call?"

"Yeah." Marc almost growled the word. He stacked dishes, scraping the leavings into an empty bowl, and carried the pile into the house. "My mama always told me, don't walk in empty-handed."

The others just stared at him, slack-jawed.

Trey cleared his throat. "Well, all right then."

At that the rest of them gathered up the remaining debris and took it inside. With all of them pitching in, they made short work of it. They were just finishing up when Marc came back into the kitchen, holding his cell phone, and pulled a cold beer from the fridge. He nodded to everyone before heading back outside.

The men looked at one another.

Trey cleared his throat. "I'm going to take that as a positive sign."

"Me too," Slade added.

"I hate to say anything and jinx it," Beau said.

They finished the last of the cleanup and quietly wandered off to their own rooms.

"I don't know about you," Slade said, stripping off his clothes, "but I need a shower."

"I can get on board with that." Kari drank in the sight of his naked body. He could have been created by a sculptor, his muscles were so well defined and his body so well shaped. She was so mesmerized watching him she forgot to take off her own clothes.

Slade chuckled. "I'm glad you're enjoying the show, but one of us is very overdressed."

"Oh! Um, yes." She gave herself a mental shake. "Coming right up."

The look he slanted at her was positively wicked. "It sure is."

Get with the program, Kari.

She tried not to think of the fact this was the last night they'd be together for who knew how long.

As much as she'd enjoyed herself today, she'd been gripped by a fine tension she couldn't shake. Tomorrow morning the four men would pack up, Teo would ferry them to the airport and they'd be gone for an indefinite amount of time. Where would they go? What would they do? Whatever it was, she knew it would be one hundred percent dangerous. She did her best to push the thought out of her mind, determined to enjoy every minute together they had left. She stepped beneath the warm spray of the showerhead, hoping the water would wash away the anxiety.

Slade worked the soap into a thick lather in his hands and with slow strokes began to spread it on her body. But the moment his fingers touched her skin, he paused.

"A little uptight tonight, are we? Jesus, Kari, you're tight as a drum." He nipped her earlobe. "Let me help you relax. Tomorrow will be here soon enough." He licked the spot where he'd placed his teeth. "Let's pretend I'm just going off on a business trip."

She chuffed a laugh. "Which you are, only it's a very dangerous business. I know you haven't said much about it and I know you can't. But, Slade, I watch television and read news online. I don't want anything to happen to you again when we've just reconnected."

"I don't want that either. And I'm going to do my fucking best to make sure nothing happens. Now let me help you relax. Close your eyes. Take a deep breath and let it out slowly."

She did, letting his touch soothe her.

He coasted his hands over her, feeling the swell of each breast beneath his palms. He gave each nipple a light pinch, smiling at her little gasp, palming her breasts and lightly pinching her nipples. He stood so close she could feel the hot, hard length of his erection pressing against her. She reached down to wrap her fingers around it, but he gripped her wrist and tugged it away.

"Not yet." The words were so low they had a guttural sound. "I'm too close to the edge. Damn, Kari. I wanted to take it slow and easy tonight, make it last. But it seems all I have to do is look at you and I'm ready to blow."

The realization that she had that effect on the very powerful, very sexy man made her even hotter than she was. He continued to stroke her with a light caress of his hands, following her curves, tracing every dip and swell, slipping between the swollen lips of her pussy. The tip of a finger brushed the sensitive tip of her clit, creating spasms in her inner walls and sending heat shooting to every part of her body.

"Turn around." He breathed the words in her ear even as he guided her body to face the tiled wall. "Brace yourself with your hands."

The pulsing in all her hot spots intensified, vibrating everywhere. The soapy caress of his hands was arousing enough in itself, but when he slid his fingers lightly between the cheeks of her ass, tracing the hot crevice, she thought she might lose it.

"Feel good, darlin'?" he murmured.

"Yes," she whispered. "So good."

"I'm going to do this again, you know. Just like that night in Chicago. But this time I want to build up to it. Pick the right moment."

A shiver raced through her. She'd never forget the hot, hard length of him sliding into that warm, dark tunnel, stretching her tissues and igniting nerves she didn't even know she had. Her sex throbbed and her inner muscles clenched with the memory of the feel of him inside her there and the unbelievable orgasm it had ignited.

By the time he'd lathered every inch of her body, the tension had eased and she was relaxed and aroused at the same time. She turned around and reached for the soap.

"My turn."

Running her soapy hands over that hard-muscled body

was an incredible, erotic experience. She found his hard nipples beneath the swirls of dark hair and scraped her nails over them, drawing a hissing breath from Slade. She had to kneel to lather his legs, drawing her fingers up the inside of his thighs. When she wrapped her fingers around his cock and squeezed, he again moved her hand.

"Darlin', there's nothing I'd like better than to feel those fingers everywhere, especially stroking my dick, but my self-control is about at its limit. Time to get out of the shower."

He dried them off in record time, scooped her up and carried her to the bed. It took mere seconds for him to sheath himself.

"Real quiet," he whispered as he positioned himself over her and spread her thighs. "So quiet we can hear each other breathe. That's it, just like that."

Placing the head of his cock at her opening, he then drove into her in one hard, swift motion.

"Oh." The word drifted from her lips like a soft breeze.

"Ssh. Quiet, remember?" He pressed his mouth to hers, the kiss hot and hungry. He kept his lips there as he plunged in and out of her, thrusting hard, filling every inch of her.

Kari wound her legs around him, pressing her body upward to his and rocking with him in an erotic rhythm that sent heat to every pore of her skin.

They exploded quickly, satisfying a need that consumed them, the joining of their bodies a silent symbol of what this had become. Afterward they lay there, still locked together, hearts thundering, drawing air into starving lungs, straining together to catch the last of the aftershocks. At last Slade eased from the clasp of her body, disposed of the condom and curled himself around her.

"I'd planned for this to last a little longer," he murmured. "I've figured out that I need a minimum of two orgasms with you, one to take the edge off and one to take it slow." He nipped her shoulder. "You just do it for me, Kari."

"Mmm." She snuggled back against him. "Same goes

here."

"Sleep now, darlin'. When I'm in some hot, dirty place and haven't had a bath in a week, I want to remember this."

"'Kay." She drifted off with his body imprinted on hers.

She woke with a start, aware something was wrong. Different. The room was dark, the clock on her nightstand reading four-thirty. She didn't know what had woken her but something told her not to get out of bed. She pulled the covers tight around her and lay there, rigid, waiting.

There. She heard it again, a sibilant sound like the whisper of fabric against fabric. Another sound, like someone breathing. She waited, hardly daring to breathe herself.

Where was her phone? Where had she left the damn phone?

Fingers touched her leg and circled her ankle with a very light touch. The scream bubbling up inside her started to burst free and —

"No!" Kari sat up in bed, hands pushing against air as if to ward someone off.

Slade was awake beside her in an instant, smoothing his hand over her back in a reassuring gesture.

"Ssh, ssh, ssh. It's okay. You're okay."

"He's here." She thought she was screaming the words, but they came out as no more than a whisper. "He touched me."

With great care he wrapped his arm around her and pulled her against him, stroking her arm with a light caress of his fingers.

"It's okay," he repeated. "Easy now. I've got you."

She blinked, hard, realizing where she was, the nightmare disappearing like smoke. But the desperate feeling of fear remained. She leaned into Slade's embrace, taking comfort from his warm, hard body. He continued to murmur soothing sounds to her and caress her with reassuring strokes until she finally began to relax.

"I-I'm sorry." She couldn't look at him. "I'm so sorry."

"Nothing to be sorry for." He dusted her forehead with soft kisses then brushed one lightly over her lips.

At last her heart stopped beating in such an erratic rhythm and her pulse stopped pounding like a trip hammer.

"C-Could I have some water?" She whispered the words.

"Right away." He eased from the bed, making sure the covers were in place, then hurried back with a drink from the bathroom. "Here, darlin'. Have a drink."

She gulped the first few swallows then sipped a little before handing the glass back to him. He set it on the nightstand and slid into bed beside her again.

"You want to tell me about it?" He cradled her against him, his eyes warm as he studied her face.

What was he thinking? she wondered. *That he's sorry he got involved with me? That he'd like to get out of this as fast as possible? That I'm one hundred percent nuts?*

"Just so you know, I'm not crazy." She hiccuped a laugh.

"Kari, we all have bad dreams. My team, the work we do? It's the stuff of nightmares we battle all the time."

That made her feel a little better.

"Remember I told you about the time I was sure someone was in my bedroom?"

"I do."

"Well, I dreamed it." She wet her lips. "Again."

She waited for him to tell her she was nuts, but instead he brushed a kiss over her forehead.

"If I recall, that wasn't your imagination. And it would certainly give anyone nightmares."

"You must think I'm crazy." She couldn't bring herself to look at him.

He cupped her chin and tilted up her face. "No. Not even one bit. I think someone is going out of their way to scare the shit out of you."

"I've been so sure he didn't follow me here. Or find me."

"And you may be right. But I've been doing a lot of thinking about it since you told me all this."

"And? I just need to get my act together, right?"

"Not at all." He reached over and turned on the light. "Kari, you have a real problem here. Imagination doesn't leave flowers or make hang-up calls. I hate that I have to head out of here tomorrow with this dangling in the wind. I don't know how long I'll be gone either, so I did a couple of things. Try to understand that I'm used to planning missions and covering all bases. I hope you won't be pissed off at me."

"So, I'm what...a mission?" Kari accepted the fact that being in charge was part of who he was, but she hoped he hadn't done something stupid in his effort to protect her.

He lifted one of her hands and kissed the knuckles. "I called your boss yesterday. I—"

"You did *what?*" She yanked her hand away. "What the hell, Slade?" What would Kip think of him sticking his nose in her personal business? "I thought we weren't doing the heavy personal stuff."

"That doesn't mean I can't do whatever it takes to keep you safe while I'm away. And see? That's another thing? I should be here with you, protecting you, finding out who this asshole it, not wallowing in jungle mud or fighting bad guys a continent away."

"You don't need this on your mind when you're on an op."

He grabbed her hand again. "Hang in here with me, Kari. You have a stalker who frightened you so much you moved hundreds of miles away. Right?"

"Yes. Okay." A tiny shiver of fear skated over her skin as memories of the situation came back to her.

"And he may have found a way to trace you. Am I correct again?"

The sense of panic became more intense as she remembered the call from Ross.

"Yes." She whispered the word, as if saying it so softly might make the reality disappear.

"I can't be here for however long I'm gone and I can't just leave you out there alone."

Kari frowned. "What do you mean, alone? Is someone moving in with me?"

Slade barked a laugh. "Over my dead body. But there are other things I can do."

"Like what?"

"Kip is going to make sure you're with people at all times. Even when you walk to the courthouse, he'll take care that you don't walk alone."

"Damn, Slade." She jerked her hand away. "He can't turn his office upside down just for me!"

Slade shrugged and grabbed her hand again, giving it a gentle squeeze.

"He says it won't be a problem. And he agrees with me that you shouldn't be alone where someone could make a grab for you."

"Oh, my God!" Her stomach knotted at the thought. "You think he would?"

"If he's that obsessed with you, we can't eliminate any possibilities. Please don't fight me on this, okay? I can't handle a mission if I'm worried about you."

That more than anything made her give in to what he wanted. If the man who didn't do relationships, who focused completely on his team and his missions, might be distracted by what was happening, it was the best indication that what they had between them was more than a passing fad. And the last thing she wanted was to affect his ability to focus.

"Okay." She blew out a breath. "I have to agree that it makes me feel more secure."

"Good. I also want you to wear a new watch I got you. I was planning to give it to you in the morning before we leave."

Kari raised her eyebrows. "A watch? I have a watch."

"Not like this." He reached into the nightstand drawer and took out a small box, which he handed her. "I picked it up Thursday before heading back to the ranch. Go on. Open it up."

To Kari, there didn't appear to be anything unusual about the watch. It had a wide face, the silver case encrusted with

147

tiny jewels that she hoped were decorative glass or paste and not diamonds. The wide strap was a soft-looking white leather. She lifted it free and turned it over and over in her hands, frowning.

"It's a beautiful watch, Slade, but I already have one. And this better not be diamonds on the case. I don't want you spending that kind of money on me."

He gave a soft chuckle. "Kari, I could buy you ten diamond watches, but I figured you'd give me a hard time. No, they're fakes. But the watch has some important features."

Kari wrinkled her forehead as she studied the piece of jewelry. "Like what?"

"Like the fact it has a GPS locator installed, so at any moment in time I can tell exactly where you are." He held up a hand. "And don't give me any shit about it. It will make me feel a lot better to know where you are, just in case."

She didn't want to think what his 'just in case' might mean. "What else? I'm pretty sure that's not all."

He took the watch from her and showed her a tiny button in the opposite side of the winding stem. "This button? It's as good as calling nine-one-one." He went on to explain how it sent an emergency signal both to the police and to a couple of people he knew in the city. "You get in trouble, any trouble at all, just press this. I tested it to make sure it works."

"You have strangers involved in this?"

He closed her fingers around the watch. "Not strangers, but people I trust. They run a security service, mostly monitoring alarm systems from businesses and corporations. I had them set it up with a special code for you so if it pings on their system, they know who it is. Someone is always monitoring it. They know if this alarm goes off to contact me at once."

"What if you're half a world away?" she asked.

"They have provisions for that too," he assured her. "Darlin', if I weren't leaving on a mission, I'd be checking on you myself every day. I really wanted to get someone who could bodyguard you, drive you everyplace, make sure you always got home okay. But—"

She held up her free hand. "Stop. Slade, I appreciate all this. I'll wear this because, well, it would be stupid of me not to. I'll make sure Kip knows where I am at all times and I won't go anywhere alone, even to the courthouse. But no bodyguard, okay? Please? I'm hoping this is just going to fade away on its own."

"We'll see." But his voice was heavy with skepticism. He took the watch from her and placed it on the nightstand. "As long as you're up, maybe we can think of a way to pass the time." He winked. "I've got a sure-fire way to keep those nightmares at bay."

Kari was overcome with his concern for her and the lengths he'd gone to to protect her. Everything he did, including his insistence on exclusivity, gave her hope that this relationship would last. He'd certainly found a place in her heart. Smiling at him, she pressed her fingers against his chest and pushed him back on the pillows.

"I've got a better way. I think you need to let me show you my appreciation."

His half-smile was wicked. "Oh, yeah? What did you have in mind?"

"Why don't you lie there and find out?"

Kari kneeled beside him, her knees pressed against the hard muscle of his thigh, and wrapped her fingers around his cock, shocked to find it already swollen and thick and standing erect. Bending over, she took him in her mouth and tightened her lips around him. The skin of his shaft was so silken over the hard steel beneath it. The moment she licked her tongue around the rim of the head, he sucked in his breath.

"Sweet Jesus, Kari." He hissed the words.

She hummed her satisfaction at his reaction and moved her lips up and down, sliding her hand at the same time, creating delicious friction. Slade thrust his fingers into her hair and tightened them around the strands, cupping her head.

"Yeah," he groaned. "Like that. Just like that."

He filled nearly every inch of her mouth, but she managed to wrap her tongue around the head before licking the velvet surface. She caught a thick drop of fluid and swallowed it, reveling in the slightly salty taste. She slipped her free hand between his thighs, cupping his balls and tightening her grasp. Slade nearly levitated off the bed.

"Holy fucking shit!"

She quickened her strokes, up and down. Suck. Lick. Squeeze.

Slade tightened his grip on her hair. "You better stop or there won't be anything left for you."

She lifted her head long enough to say, "This is what I want for me." Then she went back to work on him.

The heavy pulse of blood in the vein wrapped around his shaft and the thrust of his hips let her know he was reaching the danger point, so she rubbed and licked and squeezed harder. In seconds he exploded, filling her mouth with his semen. She swallowed it, letting it slide down the back of her throat, until she had milked him of every last drop. Only then did she sit back and slip her hands away from his body.

"Come here." His voice was rough with passion as he pulled her to him, pressing her head on his shoulder. "Damn, Kari. I'll be thinking of that every second I'm gone."

"That was the idea." She pressed her lips to his skin. "Except when you're out doing dangerous stuff. Then think only about that."

"Kari." He cleared his throat. "I want you to know—"

She touched the tips of her fingers to his mouth. "Whatever it is will keep until you get back."

She didn't want him making declarations of any kind until he'd had a chance to live with what was happening between them. And she wanted the time to think it over herself. They'd both been chasing the dream for five years.

She wanted to make sure it wasn't just the excitement of fulfillment, but something real. Hard as it might be, she could wait.

"Close your eyes, then." He stroked her arm. "Time to sleep. Morning will be here way too soon."

Chapter Thirteen

Kari dropped the stack of file folders and her tablet on her desk, sat down and blew out a breath. To say today had been the day from hell was an understatement. Among other things, a grueling round of depositions had almost wiped her out. She and Sasha had both been assigned to work a new high-profile assault case that could have heavy repercussions in the city's political and judicial circles.

The asshole Hal Grayson was first chair. She didn't know which was worse, the unbelievable amount of material to wade through or Grayson's condescending attitude. Even Kip got irritated with him, but the truth was, Grayson was a shark in court. Always well-prepared no matter what the defense threw at him, and skewering the defendant. When her phone rang, she was tempted not to pick it up. Sighing, she lifted the receiver, hoping this call didn't take more than five minutes. She was anxious to get the hell out of there.

"You ready to celebrate, kid?" Ross Delahunt's voice sounded across the phone connection.

She was always glad to hear from Ross, but she had no idea what he was talking about. She frowned.

"Celebrate what? Did I miss something?"

"No, but you will be. I've got great news. You'll be missing your stalker."

"*What?*" She nearly shrieked the word. "You found out who it was? Are you kidding me?"

Ross laughed. "Would I kid about a thing like that? But listen." His voice sobered. "You'll never believe who it was."

"Oh, my God. Who? Is it someone I know? It has to be."

She could hardly believe it. The black cloud would be gone?

"Did you ever meet John Schreiber? Judge Glasgow's law clerk?"

Kari tried to conjure up an image in her mind. She had appeared numerous times before the man in Chicago but she didn't remember his clerk. She had a vague image of a nondescript man with brown hair. She did remember he'd always sat at a table to the left of the bench with a laptop and a stack of files. That was about it.

"Maybe a time or two, but I hardly remember him. I don't think I even had that much contact with him. He obviously didn't leave much of an impression."

"Maybe that's his problem in life." Ross sighed. "But yeah, he apparently had a fixation with you. Has ever since the Christmas party at the courthouse two years ago."

"But that's absurd! I hardly remember even talking to him."

"It seems he has some…peculiarities that he'd kept well hidden. Glasgow was shocked."

"God, Ross. I can hardly believe it." She felt as if a thousand-pound weight had suddenly been lifted from her shoulders. "You actually found him."

"Glasgow assured us he'd had no idea and apologized several times. He has a lot of admiration for you, Kari. Said you're one of the most professional lawyers to appear before him in court."

"Wow. That's quite a compliment coming from him." Judge Glasgow had one of the toughest reputations in the judicial system.

"Assured me over and over he had no idea this was going on," Ross continued.

"I'm still trying to process it. I mean, John Schreiber is someone I hardly know. I've only had minimal contact with him, although when I still lived in Chicago, I appeared before Glasgow probably more than I have any other judge since I've been here."

"I had trouble with it myself, kid." He sighed. "We got

lucky, if that's what you want to call it. Janine kept asking people, in conversation, just casually. Someone finally remembered seeing him go into her office the day of the impromptu party. We hauled his ass into my office and after five minutes with me he broke."

"I don't know whether to laugh or cry," she told him. "Someone like him hardly seems dangerous at all. Yet he made my life a living hell."

"Don't kid yourself. Guys like him are sometimes the most dangerous of all. They have no real life to speak of so they become obsessed with someone who's unobtainable. They fixate on them. When we talked to the judge, he said it stunned him. He did admit, however, the kid had been acting weird for a long time. That it got worse about the time you disappeared from Chicago." He paused. "Must have been driving him crazy that he didn't know where you were. He couldn't exactly go around asking."

"So what happens now?" A tendril of fear curled through her as an idea slammed into her. "Do I have to go back to Chicago? Testify? Oh, God, Kip.

"Hold on, hold on." He gave her a reassuring smile. "Luck is with you. They have the evidence so they negotiated a plea deal in exchange for his confession. He gets a lesser term. But at least he's locked down and even when he gets out, he has no idea where you are."

"Thank God. At least I can breathe again. Oh, my God. Thank you, thank you."

"I just wish it hadn't taken so long, kid, but better late than never."

"So it's really over. For good?"

"You have my word," he assured her.

Free. God, it felt so good. But strange. She hadn't felt free for a long time.

Kari leaned back in her chair. "I should let my boss know. He's been so great about keeping an eye on me."

"I'll give Kip a call myself about this. I don't suppose we could talk you into coming back to Chicago now, could we?"

She laughed. "I'm actually getting to like it here." She lowered her voice. "And I've sort of met someone."

"Well, damn!" He chuckled. "I guess that means I'm out of the running."

"Your wife definitely says you are," she teased. "Listen, Ross, thanks for everything on this. You don't know what a relief this is. You'll let me know what happens from here on in?"

"Of course. I'm hoping we don't have to go through the mess of a trial. We're counting on the judge to talk some sense into him. Maybe we can even get him some counseling."

"I don't care as long as he stays away from me."

"Oh, I can bet. Listen, keep in touch, okay? And I'll keep you in the loop on all this."

Kari hung up the phone and took the first deep breath she'd taken in what seemed like forever. She was hardly able to accept what she had just heard. Some lowly law clerk had been making her life hell. She wanted to kick off her shoes and dance, maybe sing off-key, which was the only way she sang. She picked up her cell phone, worrying her bottom lip as she tried to decide about texting Slade. He said his phone was always off and sometimes on an op he didn't even have it with him. But if she texted, he'd pick it up sooner or later.

Before she could change her mind she typed her message.

Stalker outed. Under arrest. Celebration when you get home.

She debated adding the word *love* but decided not to push her luck. She hit Send and stuck the phone in her purse.

Giddy with excitement, she thought this might be a good time to take Sasha up on her invitation to go out for drinks tonight. She hoped the invite was still good. Kari had been avoiding it, politely turning down all Sasha's invitations as well as those of any of her other co-workers. She was sure by now they were convinced she was standoffish. She just hadn't been able to make herself go out for an evening of jokes and drinking, not when she jumped at every shadow. Not when she'd worried about Slade, about where he and his team were. Even Kip, who she knew had Slade's warning playing in his ears, had encouraged her to take a break.

"Your co-workers keep asking me why you're antisocial and if you have a problem with them."

"You know what my problem is," she'd reminded him.

"But you can't keep hiding away. Besides the fact that it generates office gossip, it affects your mental health. You need contact with people outside the office and courtroom."

Now she didn't need to hide away anymore. She could go out without being afraid unseen eyes were watching her, or starting at every noise. She hurried to Sasha's office, catching the woman just as she was shutting down her computer.

"Really?" Sasha's jaw dropped as Kari shyly asked if she could still take Sasha up on her offer to join her and her friends. "This isn't a joke?"

Kari shook her head. "Not a joke. I'm finally ready to let my hair down for an evening."

"Well, hallelujah. You'll love this place we all go to. And you sure picked a good time for this. Get your purse, girl, and let's hit the road."

"On it." She had to admit a night out with a crowd of people from work appealed to her.

If there was one thing people knew about San Antonio, it was its abundance of Tex-Mex restaurants—that particular blend of Texas-Mexican food, cuisine unique to the state. The types of restaurants ran the gamut from tiny neighborhood *taquerias*, through noisy restaurants with busy bars and filled dining rooms, to the most upscale.

Olivia's, located in a shopping center on the north side of the city, was where Sasha and the others gathered tonight. They managed to commandeer one of the larger round tables in the middle of the room.

"We're so glad you decided to come out with us tonight." Across the table one of the paralegals smiled at her.

"Thanks for including me." Kari looked around.

"Didn't I tell you?" Sasha, sitting next to her, nudged her with her elbow. "Olivia's is almost like a second home to us. The frozen margaritas and special salsa with chips are just the recipe after a shit day like today."

Kari, taking another sip of the icy liquid and savoring its sharp taste, had to agree with her. Olivia's seemed to have it all—a warm, friendly atmosphere, a smiling staff and, if the first sip of hers was any indication, killer drinks. Colorful serapes and sombreros hung on the walls, along with posters depicting scenes of Mexico. The waitresses were dressed in colorful skirts that swirled around their legs and white peasant blouses. The bartenders wore matador vests and big grins.

Yes, she had to agree this was a treasure of a place.

Sasha leaned closer, and lowered her voice, although at the noise level in the place it was hard enough to hear anyway.

"Did you hear Hal Grayson's going to be first chair on this case?"

"I know." Kari was doing her best to stuff her resentment in the closet. The case involved a very high-profile accused who'd assembled a very high-priced team of attorneys. "You'd think after I won the Harold Webster murder case, they'd let me take this one."

Sasha gave a ladylike snort. "Are you kidding? I'm not even sure I'd want it. The son of a sitting judge who's been re-elected four times? And has the backing of every politico in the city? Both parties? You'd either be the person who put his son away—and God knows how he'd take it out on you—or else the person who let his attorney get him a not guilty verdict and people would wonder if you'd been bought off."

"You're so cheerful," Kari said with a wry smile. Dipping

a warm chip into the spicy salsa, she then popped the whole thing in her mouth and sighed as the flavors burst on her tongue. "Man, this place makes the best dip I've ever tasted. Anyway, what makes you think as second and third chair we won't get tainted the same way?"

"Because it's always the lead attorney they remember — the one whose ass is on the line with the big boss."

"Truthfully, Kari?" Sasha went on. "I'd just as soon let Hal Grayson take the heat for this one. There'll be others just as tough that won't get us burned. Or on Kip's shit list."

That was the truth. Kip Reyes was in his third term and more than lived up to his reputation as a tough prosecutor. He expected the same of the assistant district attorneys on his staff. Sasha had accumulated an enviable record through sheer grit and guts. Kari was batting a thousand since she'd moved to the city and joined the staff. Still, they knew, like everyone else, that with Kip you were only as good as your last performance.

In some remote ways Kip reminded her of Slade — tall, lean, dark, totally masculine. Always in command. The face he presented to the world was expressionless and hard, but he'd been nothing but kind to her. If not for him and his wife, she'd never have gone to the party at the Huttons' and reconnected with Slade. Nor would she be out tonight having drinks and snacks with people from work. She'd be hiding in her apartment as usual, locked into her pattern of behaving.

Slade Donovan. Just thinking of his name conjured up an image of him in her mind. Since he'd been gone, she'd relived every minute of that incredible week over and over. Despite his very macho image, the ultimate warrior, there was a humanity to him, buried under all those layers of machismo, that she was just beginning to uncover. She'd felt it five years ago at their first encounter, a connection that had gone much deeper than sex. Nothing had happened since to diminish it.

He'd been gone for five weeks now. He'd managed to call

three times and text a few. The rest of the time she knew he probably wasn't near any communications system. Still, she couldn't stop thinking about him. She missed his touch, the feel of him inside her, the caress of his fingers. Tonight she couldn't stop herself from checking her cell phone regularly, just in case he had a break and managed to read her text messages. Even now, she slid a glance at it lying on the table next to her.

"Will you quit looking at that thing?" Sasha's annoyed voice broke into her reverie. "I have a good mind to put it in my purse until we leave here. We're supposed to be having fun, remember? It took me long enough to get you out for a couple of hours. I'm not competing with your cell phone for your attention. Who are you expecting to call, anyway?"

"Just... No one. No one at all." As if to emphasize her words she picked up the phone and dropped it into her tote. "There. All gone."

Sasha picked up her drink and took a sip. "Uh-huh. Why do I think that's all a big act? You've been really weird for, well, forever."

Kari looked at her friend with what she hoped was a confused expression. "Weird? I don't understand. What's that supposed to mean?"

"Well, for one thing, we've been begging you for months to come out with us. Since you got here from Chicago you've been a real social hermit."

"I went to the Huttons' party." Kari did her best not to be defensive.

"And tonight? If we hadn't had the day from hell, I'm not sure you'd have come tonight," Sasha added.

"I've just... I'm only..." There was no way she could explain the fear she had lived with. "You know how I really like to go home and hole up by myself."

Sasha shook her head. "There's by yourself and there's by yourself. You're a regular hermit, Kari. You never ever socialize."

Kari shrugged. "Maybe I just prefer my own company.

No offense intended here."

"None taken. But everyone has to date once in a while, or all those hormones just go to waste."

"Hormones?" Kari burst out laughing. "I didn't think they dried up."

"I've tried three times to set you up with this friend of my brother's and you just blew me off. And look"—she glanced at the bar where a small group of men were laughing together and drinking—"there's that guy I've seen here a bunch who's definitely after you. He sent a drink over to you twice tonight and you sent them both back."

"Puhleeze. I'm just not interested. Truly."

"You don't have to go home with him," Sasha pointed out. "But he sure is easy on the eyes, with his gorgeous body, blond hair and a smile to die for."

Kari peered in the direction of the bar. The man in question turned at that exact moment, caught her eye, grinned and raised his glass to her. She quickly looked away, determined not to give him any encouragement.

"If you think he's so hot," she told Sasha, "maybe you should go after him yourself."

Sasha let out a sigh. "If only I was the one he had his eye on."

Kari shrugged. "I don't think he's my type."

Lydia Farmer, a tall brunette who had been on Kip's staff for five years, licked her lips. "Tell him he can send the drinks to me. I'll be grateful enough to take him home with me."

Everyone at the table laughed.

"What will you tell Dale?" Anna Kenyon, a redhead with a temper to match, waved her straw in the air. "Move over, honey?"

"Maybe he'd like some spice in our lives." Lydia grinned.

Kari chuckled at the byplay. It was fun to talk, and she had a feeling this was common chatter whenever they went out. But none of them ever went home with someone they met here. They'd all talked about it at lunch one day. As prosecuting attorneys, they knew the dangers of situations like that, but it was fun to flirt and pretend.

A sudden shiver rippled down her spine and she slid her gaze around the room. Was there someone watching her too intently? Waiting for her to get up to leave?

Stop it, Kari. The stalker's been caught. You don't have anything to worry about now.

She needed to keep that in mind. Wasn't the stalker's arrest the very reason she was here celebrating? Anyway, if anything else happened she had options. She ran her fingers over the watch Slade had given her, a reassuring contact. If she got in any trouble at all, she only had to push the tiny button and help would be on its way. And not just the police. She didn't know the people Slade had on the hook for this, but she was sure they were lethal. Not anyone to get on the wrong side of.

Sasha heaved a sigh, the sound of it drawing her attention back to the present.

"I'd lick him all over if he'd let me and you won't even give him the time of day."

"Give it a rest." Kari flicked a finger in the air. "He's okay but he's not my type."

"Not your type?" Sasha practically squeaked. "Well, damn, girl. What *is* your type? At this rate, you'll end up being an old maid."

If you only knew. "Besides. You know I don't like blind dates. I'm too old and too particular. And I don't hook up with guys I meet in bars."

"Picky, picky, picky." Sasha took a sip of her drink. "Well, you need to hook up with someone pretty soon or your poor little pussy's going to just dry right up."

"Sasha!" Kari nearly knocked her drink over. She looked around carefully to see if anyone had heard.

"Oh, don't worry. It's so noisy in here people can hardly hear themselves, never mind us. But it's the damn truth." She studied Kari. "Wait a minute… Wait just a minute here."

"For what? What's in that crazy brain of yours now?"

"You *have* met someone, haven't you? Ohmigod, you've met a man and you've got something going. I should have spotted that look in your eyes long before now."

"What look is that?" Kari lifted her glass and took a long drink of the sharp-tasting frosty liquid.

"That 'I've been laid and it's better than Christmas' look."

"You're delusional." Kari let her gaze wander around the room, trying to settle it anyplace but on her friend. "And I'd be lying if I tried to make you think that at my age I'd never been laid before. Besides, you know better."

"Yeah, but this is different." Sasha tapped a brightly polished nail on the varnished tabletop. "This is way different. I can tell. Come on, girlfriend. Dish."

Kari finally looked at her hands. "There's nothing to tell. And if you're going to push this topic, I'm going home."

She was afraid to damage the fragile state of the new level of her relationship with Slade by discussing it with anyone. Besides, then she'd have to tell Sasha where and how they'd met, and that was totally not up for discussion.

"Fine. But I'm keeping my eye on you. You'd better believe it." Sasha signaled the waiter for more drinks.

Kari managed to be sociable for one more round of drinks but passed on a third.

"We have another long day tomorrow," she told Sasha. "We need to have our brains in working order."

"True that," Sasha agreed. "Okay. Time to hit the road, guys. Tomorrow's a working day."

"Aw, you spoil all the fun," Stella Mendez teased and threw a balled-up napkin at her.

"She's our designated keeper." Lydia laughed. "She makes sure we don't get too drunk or go home with strange men. Right, Sasha?"

"Yeah, yeah, yeah." Sasha rolled her eyes at Kari. "Maybe we can do this again Friday?"

"Maybe. We'll see." She wasn't yet ready to hurl herself back into the social swim up to her armpits. Not when she was still looking over her shoulder and jumping at shadows, even though she was sure her stalker was hundreds of miles away.

Chapter Fourteen

Slade cursed the bitter cold of the Hindu Kush mountains and the assignment that had once again sent him and his team to these godforsaken rocks. This was the fourth one since his return from San Antonio. He was beginning to wonder if he'd ever get home again. And see Kari.

Kari.

Just thinking her name made his body heat and his cock harden. He'd never missed a woman like this before. He wanted to think it was just sex, although it was spectacular sex. Emotional connection scared the shit out of him. He tried convincing himself what he felt for her was a result of the sexual chemistry. Even getting the watch for her was something he'd do for anyone in her situation.

You are a stupid fucktard if you believe that.

He could feel himself sucked into this deeper and deeper even while trying to keep his emotional distance.

Yeah, and how is that working for you?

On the very boring flight from Fort Hood to their insertion point for the mission, he'd spent his time staring at the photo of her on his cell phone. He'd had to do some heavy convincing to get her to agree to have her picture taken, but it was an anchor he needed. One minute he was afraid he'd imagined how intense the whole thing was. Another he worried someone would come along before he could get home and pick up where they'd left off. He knew it would be a while, just like he'd told her, before he could get back stateside again.

He tried to analyze how the others were doing. Like him, Beau and Trey had taken advantage of every opportunity to make a cell phone call or send a text. Even Marc, to his shock and pleasant surprise, had huddled a couple of times with his phone. As far away from the team as he could get.

But now their focus had changed. This time they were in hostage rescue mode, a delicate situation that required stealth, sharp eyes and guts. An Army colonel out with one of his men to meet with a local tribal leader had been ambushed, the driver shot and the colonel taken captive. Already the man who had captured him, Faisal Usman, had broadcasted from his camp and shown the colonel bound hand and foot and blindfolded, on his knees in front of him. The message was clear. *Remove your troops from my area or I will execute this man.*

So Slade and his Delta Force team had been tasked with the rescue. He tucked all thoughts of Kari and the future in a corner of his mind and returned to full mission protocol. Another assignment was waiting for them and there was no opportunity for daydreaming. Satellites had pinpointed the location of Usman's camp and given them the layout. The thermal imaging had shown them exactly how many people were there—twelve—and how many buildings—four. They were definitely going to be outmanned but the decision had been made to go with just their team. Any more and their lieutenant was afraid they'd provoke an all-out fire-fight and the first person they killed would be the colonel.

The only additional manpower, besides the helo pilot, would be two shooters ready in the open doorway of the Little Bird if trouble showed up, and a medic who would check out the colonel.

So it was on their heads and they knew they damn sure better not make a mistake.

The helicopter dropped them as soon as it was full dark, the pilot confirming the exfiltration time with Slade—just before the first fingers of dawn would begin to light up the sky. They had to do all this under cover of night. Even then they'd be in danger, but the inky blackness would give them great cover. And no moon tonight... A lucky break. As soon as his boots hit the ground he signaled his team to move forward.

The night was completely still. Not even the birds seemed to be making themselves heard, as if they had silenced their singing so the men of the Delta Force team could hear any other sounds. There wasn't even the distant tinkle of a sheep herder's bell as he urged a flock of yaks from place to place. Not that Slade expected them to be moving at night but weirder things had happened. Almost an entire SEAL team had been wiped out because a young sheep herder had been leading his charges and had stumbled upon them. They'd chosen not to kill him...and he'd chosen to rat them out to the very man they'd been assigned to kill.

Slade concentrated on his movements as he and his team crawled quietly to the ridge overlooking the camp and pulled out their night binoculars to study the layout.

Marc, who had taken point as usual, shimmied back until he was next to Slade.

"Satellite indicates they've got the colonel in the shed off to the side," he whispered and held up his thermal imaging scope. "I agree. It's isolated from the other buildings. They'd want to keep the 'infidel' separate. Plus, it doesn't look like they've even got a guard on him."

"Probably not necessary. They're a cocky bunch of assholes and they're convinced no one will find them. Besides, from what I saw on the video clip, those bastards gave him a pretty harsh beating, so he may not be in any condition to give them trouble."

"Which could also make getting him out of there that much harder," Marc pointed out.

"We'll just have to deal with it," Slade whispered back. "Okay, we need a distraction. Something to draw them to the opposite side of the camp."

"Two people to create chaos and two to retrieve the colonel," Marc agreed.

"We'll let Beau and Trey handle the diversion while we

spring the colonel."

Slade spoke very softly, just enough to be heard through the comm link. As still as the air was in the mountains tonight, almost a total absence of sound, it would be very easy for voices to carry. Not that any of them thought the men below them were paying much attention. The two around the fire appeared engrossed in an animated conversation and everyone else was inside.

He kept the instructions to a bare minimum. It wasn't their first time at this particular kind of ball game. They'd executed the game plan countless times before, in a variety of situations, so everyone was well aware of what had to be done.

Slade and Marc worked their way down slowly until they reached the edge of the camp. It was a cluster of some twenty crudely built huts. Off to the left Slade spotted four transport trucks and two SUV-type vehicles. And, of course, at the opposite end, the requisite camels. Everyone seemed to be inside except for the two campfire-huddling men, rifles slung over their shoulders as they warmed their hands at the flames.

When Slade and Marc were in position, he clicked his mic three times—the 'go' signal. From his position behind a giant outcropping of rock, Beau fired fifty-millimeter rounds directly into the fire. They immediately exploded and sparks flew in every direction.

The doors to the huts flew open and men raced into the area around the fire then jumped back as Beau and Trey unleashed another volley of shots. Slade could visualize them moving stealthily in a semicircle, continuing to shoot to distract the men and pin them down. Over the steady sound of shooting, he heard the men shouting, almost screaming, running to get their own rifles and shooting indiscriminately in the direction of the outcropping.

Crouched low, Slade and Marc made their way slowly around to the front of the shed serving as the colonel's prison. They constantly scanned the area and listened for any sound that would indicate movement. All they heard was the cry of night birds and the snuffling sound of the camels. Step by step, guns at the ready, they inched their way forward until they reached the door. Luckily there wasn't a lock to deal with, just a wooden bar across the door that rested on a claw hook. Of course, where could their prisoner go?

They eased the bar up and out, careful not to make a sound as they lowered it to the ground, opening the door just enough so he and Marc could inch their way inside. His gut churned when he saw the colonel, hands still tied behind his back, lying on his side. His clothes were torn, his body dirt-encrusted and his face a mass of bruises. Rage surged through him, but he forced it back as quickly as it had come. No time for that now. The man's eyes widened as Slade pulled down the black fabric covering the Delta Force patch and pointed a finger at Marc and himself. Slade held a finger to his lips and the guy nodded. The guy was no dummy. He knew silence was key.

Marc pulled out his Ka-Bar knife and cut away the colonel's ropes. They had a little trouble getting the hostage to his feet and he stumbled as they tried to move him forward but mouthed "I'm okay" and pulled in a lungful of air. Slade knew the man had to be in a lot of pain but he also knew he'd suck it up and do what he needed to help them get him out of there.

Trey and Beau were still firing into the camp, moving from place to place on the ridge and staying out of reach of any stray bullets. The men in camp had no idea where the next volley would come from. Each time they tried to send someone in that direction, Slade's team pinned them down.

It was very slow going. They had to be careful not to make a sound, not to kick any loose pebbles or rustle any of the underbrush. The last thing they wanted was to alert anyone. Additionally, the colonel wasn't in much shape to move on his own. He had wounds that appeared painful so Slade grabbed his bandana from around his neck and gave it to the man to bite down on, wrapped an arm around his charge and pulled him against his body, grateful the guy could at least walk without shuffling. Skilled in this, they moved like silent ghosts until at last they reached a point far enough away from the camp to stop for a moment. Slade clicked his mic three times again, knowing the sound would be audible in the earbuds of the shooters even over the gunfire. The next tricky part would come when Beau and Trey stopped firing and had to haul ass to meet up with them without giving away their positions or letting the men in the camp spread out to hunt them once there were no more bullets spraying at them.

But this was a well-trained team, men who knew their jobs. Still in stealth mode, they moved as fast as they dared toward the rendezvous point, he and Marc supporting the colonel between them. By now even with the bandana stuffed in his mouth, the colonel groaned involuntarily if they jarred him too much. Trey and Beau, finished with their covering fire, caught up to them and they all took turns helping the wounded man move along.

Finally they reached the rendezvous spot, just as the helo came in over them, two gunners in the open doorway, rifles at the ready. The pilot set down long enough for them to heave the colonel into the helo cabin then boost themselves in, guns still slung across their chests.

Then they were away.

The medic immediately took charge of the colonel, stretching him out on a piece of canvas on the floor of the cabin, checking the wounds on his face and his chest. When the colonel groaned again the medic rolled him to his side, eased up his shirt and exposed cuts on the man's back. While the team unhooked their packs and their rifles, he cleaned the wounds with materials from the kit he carried with him, and gave him an injection of painkiller. As soon as they landed, Slade would make sure the man was transferred to the nearest military hospital.

Looking down, Slade could see some of the men from

the camp making their way along the path the team had just taken. He didn't let out a full breath until they were safely over the next mountaintop. He was one hundred percent ready for their next leave time and a break from the unforgiving terrain of the Hindu Kush mountains.

There was one downer they discovered when they returned to base camp.

"Good work, Slade," his commanding officer, Captain John Washburn, said. "Glad to see you all back in one piece." The man rubbed his hand over his face. "Too bad they don't all end this way."

Slade stared at the man. "Are you saying someone didn't?"

Washburn nodded, regret stamped on his face.

"Charlie Team was out on a similar mission. They weren't as lucky as you."

"What happened?" A muscle twitched in Slade's jaw. He hated news like this.

Washburn sighed. "They rescued the hostage, but one of the men on the team was killed."

"Son of a bitch."

Washburn nodded. "Exactly."

This always brought home to all of them how very dangerous their work was and how ephemeral life could be. It made him think of Kari, and how deep he was getting into this thing with her. What if it was him in the body bag being ferried home? Any plans they made would be up in just so much smoke, leaving only pain behind. He'd have to find a way to handle this.

"Well, in any event," Washburn went on, "congrats to you and your team for an excellent job. Orders came down to give you and your men another ten-day leave."

"Thank you, sir. I'll let the men know."

Yes!

He wanted to pump his fist. Ten days with Kari. Maybe this time he could find a way to bring up this whole situation with him and Delta Force to her again. Or was he just cutting off his nose to spite his face? Was he being a coward about it because he didn't want to take a chance on losing something?

But when he retrieved his cell, the first thing he saw was her text.

Stalker outed. Under arrest. Celebration when you get home.

Any thoughts about discussing Delta with her and his commitment to it disappeared. He had to get back to her ASAP. He didn't know if she was in a meeting or in court or what, but he texted her anyway. She'd see it when she could use her phone.

On my way to celebrate. Then he added, *Hooah* for good measure.

There was no question about their R and R destination this time. The guys were antsy to get to the women they'd met and even Marc hid in the corner with his cell, making a call. Slade rounded them up and hustled them off to their transportation in record time. All he could think about was Kari and getting to see her again.

God. He couldn't wait.

He didn't stop to think about his feelings. Just told himself he was anxious to enjoy her finally being free of her stalker.

* * * *

Teo waited for them again in San Antonio with the now familiar helicopter.

"Teo!" Beau called. "*Mi amigo.* Good to see you."

"Crank that thing up," Trey told him. "We need hot showers and cold beer."

Slade rolled his eyes at their remarks, but he was glad they felt at home enough to be this relaxed with Teo. He ducked aside and waited until the other three had wrestled their duffels onto the bird before hoisting in his own gear and taking the co-pilot's seat.

"Tough one?" Teo asked.

The headphones were set so Slade and Teo could talk to each other.

"Tough enough. We rescued our target just in time." He swallowed back the bile that threatened to rise in his throat. "Another team wasn't so lucky. They lost one of their guys."

"Damn. That bites the big one."

"No kidding. I'm damn glad this leave came up for us."

The moment the bird touched down at the ranch, his men jumped out and ran into the house, headed for showers. Slade checked his watch and noted Kari's workday should be over. He took only enough time to freshen up before grabbing his phone and calling her.

"Kari Malone." He loved the crisp way she answered the phone.

"Slade Donovan. I may have committed a crime. Want to prosecute me?"

Her laugh was music to his ears. "I'd rather put you in handcuffs."

At the images that evoked, his cock swelled and hardened to steel. "I can get with that program."

"Where are you? The connection is really good."

"Let me look around. Does a ranch just south of the city mean anything to you?"

"You're home?" she squealed. "Oh, my God. Are you really home?"

He laughed. "Yes. And I take that to mean you'll be glad to see me."

"I will. Damned glad. Oh, Slade." Her voice filled with excitement. "You liked my text?"

"Sure did. I want to hear all about it when I get there. Every detail." He checked his watch again. "You got a couple more hours to go, right?"

"Yes. And it's stuff I can't put off."

"No sweat. I'll meet you at your office. Teo will drop me off."

"I'll be waiting." She'd lowered her voice to a sultry tone. "I'll be ready for you. And Slade? I'm glad it's Friday. We have the whole weekend."

His dick swelled so hard he worried it would poke right through his BDUs.

"On my way."

He shaved so fast he was surprised he didn't slice himself open. Five more minutes and he was dressed and yelling up the stairs to everyone.

"Yo! Heads up!"

Trey came into the hall from the kitchen and Beau and Marc hustled down the stairs.

"What's up, Shadow?" Beau frowned at him. "You like to woke the dead."

"Sorry. I have to rush out of here. I'll get Teo to ferry me into the city in the truck and leave the SUV for you guys." He frowned at them. "Can you make do with one vehicle or do any of you need a ride too?"

Surprisingly it was Marc who answered.

"If you can wait five minutes for me to get my shit together, I'll bum a ride and you can drop me off downtown."

"Downtown?" Slade asked.

In stunned silence the others looked at each other.

"What?" Marc gave them a belligerent glare. "I can't go into town? You guys have driven me nuts telling me to get over myself. You change your minds?"

Slade recovered first. "Not at all, my man. Get your shit and we'll split." He looked at the other two. "What about you guys?"

"Beau and I will share the SUV," Trey told him, "if that's okay. Once we get into the city we can work out the rest of the arrangements."

"Um, Shadow?" This from Beau.

"Yeah?"

"We're, uh, taking our ladies out to dinner. Sorry we didn't ask if you and Kari want to join us, but the invite is definitely there."

"Thanks, but not tonight. Maybe another night while we're still here. Okay?"

Beau shrugged. "Whatever works. Say hi for us."

"I'll do that." He looked up the stairway. "Marc? Shake your ass."

Marc came down the stairs three at a time. He carried a small duffel with him. Slade didn't say anything, just raised an eyebrow.

Marc didn't acknowledge anything, just said, "Let's boogie."

Slade did the driving into the city, not sure Teo would be willing to break speed limits the way he was. They dropped Marc at a corner downtown where he could take the stairway to the Riverwalk, then fought the traffic to the criminal district attorney's office. Slade shoved the truck into gear and was out before it had barely stopped moving.

"Don't kill yourself," Teo said. "Not before you get to see your lady."

"I'm good. I'll let you know if I need a pickup."

He remembered from his last visit where Kari's office was. He took the stairs, too antsy to wait for the elevator, and hit the corridor on her floor just as the end-of-day mass exodus was beginning. He gritted his teeth as he made his way through the wave of humanity heading out. She was sitting at her desk when he reached her office, but jumped up as soon as he walked in.

The first thing he did was haul her into his arms in a crushing hug, pressing her tight to his body so he could feel every one of her delectable curves. The kiss could easily have started a small fire in the office. At last he stepped back and feasted his eyes on her, from her slightly mussed hair to her kiss-swollen lips to the silk blouse caressing her breasts that he itched to palm, to the sedate business skirt that flared just slightly over her hips.

"I'd run my hands over every inch of your body," he told her in a low tone, "but someone might come in and I'd get arrested either for sexual harassment or indecent behavior."

Then he pulled her in for yet another hug.

A breathy giggle bubbled up from her throat. "I take it you're glad to see me."

"Hell, yeah. Damn fucking glad." He took her hands and gave them a gentle squeeze. "Now tell me. It's all over, right? The stalker business?"

Her smile was so wide it made the corners of her eyes crinkle. "Over for sure. God, Slade, it feels as if a ton of concrete has been lifted from my shoulders."

"Let's go back to your place and you can tell me all about it. And does pizza sound okay for dinner? I don't think I want to share you with anyone tonight."

"Suits me just fine. Let me get my purse."

It was obvious to Slade that Kari's smile was more genuine, her face less tense, her body language more relaxed. It pissed the hell out of him that she'd been going through that for more than two years. At least now he could be there for her.

Can I? Be there for her? Can I really deal with that kind of relationship?

God, I'm such a fucked-up mess.

But he parked that whole internal conversation in a dark corner of his mind. Nothing would ruin tonight. He kept repeating that as he held Kari's hand on the elevator ride and the walk through the parking garage to her car. He could not believe how much he was looking forward to the evening. Or how glad he was they could celebrate without the shadow of the stalker hanging over her head.

Chapter Fifteen

The man had to hold himself back from rubbing his hands with glee. Things were working out so much better than he could have hoped. He had to pat himself on the back for being such a fucking strategist. More than two years of waiting were finally coming to a conclusion. Soon, very soon, he would have her and she would be all his.

He dropped two ices cubes into a rocks glass and poured some very fine bourbon over it. Then he lifted he glass to his lips and sipped very slowly, enjoying the fire and warmth of it.

Fire and warm. That could just as well describe Kari Malone.

He dropped into his chair and set the glass on a coaster on his desk. Unlocked a drawer, pulled an envelope from it and removed the bit of her lingerie he kept there. Lifting it to his nose, he inhaled a deep breath. He believed her essence still clung to the soft fabric. He closed his eyes, leaned back in his chair and licked the garment. Even though it had been in her lingerie drawer, her taste and scent still clung to it.

The plan had worked to perfection. So what if it had cost him a bundle? It had been worth it to have a tool to find out where she'd gone. At last he would have her as his own.

He needed the right location, a place that afforded the privacy he would need. He had time to find one, using the computer to narrow his search for him. Only a few days from now and it would be accomplished. This time he was not walking away. This time he would make her understand they were meant to be together. And tell her he would never let her go.

Chapter Sixteen

Kari was sure she'd never had so much sex in her life, yet still she wanted more. Her desire and need for Slade just kept growing. She ignored the fact that this could come to a crashing halt at any moment and made up her mind just to enjoy it while she could. They had this incredible connection. Finding each other again after five years had to be some kind of sign, she was sure.

They barely made it inside her apartment before they began tearing each other's clothes off like two sex-starved teenagers. No matter what they did, the raging desire never seemed to abate.

"Tell me what happened with your stalker," he urged when they were lying in bed, temporarily sated.

"There really isn't all that much to know." She gave him every detail she had, answering whatever questions she could. "The thing is, I hardly even remember him. I'm sure I saw him several times. I appeared in Judge Glasgow's courtroom a number of times, but I just never paid attention to him."

He was quiet for a moment. "And they're sure they got the right person?"

"Oh, yes." She heaved a sigh of relief. "Ross did the questioning himself. He said Jerry confessed to everything."

"Then we definitely need to do a lot of celebrating." He tugged her until she was lying on top of him. "Whatever will we do?"

They took a break to devour the pizza later that evening, and slept in intermittent snatches. In the morning Slade went out for fresh muffins while she made coffee. He was like a man starved for sex. But then, she had to admit, so was she. She reveled in it, feeling totally hedonistic. She had never enjoyed sex the way she did with Slade. Finally, late in the afternoon, he demanded they get up and dress.

"I want to take you out someplace special."

"I'm happy just to stay in," she assured him. "I don't need special. Being here with you is all I need." She didn't know long she'd have him for this time and she didn't want to waste a minute. She'd decided that where Slade Donovan was concerned she was addicted to sex.

"I know, but this calls for a celebration." He rolled over until he was on top of her, his very hard erection pressing into her.

She laughed. "Are you sure you don't want to just celebrate here?"

"No, but we're going out anyway. This will keep until later." He brushed his lips over hers. "But then I expect you to give it your full attention."

"That's a promise."

So here they were at Morelli's, one of San Antonio's top-notch restaurants with a reputation for the best in Italian cuisine. In her self-imposed isolation she hadn't had a chance to check out any of these places. She certainly hadn't accepted any offers of dates. Slade was the first man she'd been able to let down her guard with.

Kari looked around. "This place is everything I've heard about it and more."

The restaurant was broken up into small intimate dining rooms. Barely audible music drifted on the air from concealed speakers just enough to set the mood without interrupting conversation. People spoke in hushed, muted tones, punctuated by the tinkle of fine crystal as glasses were filled and people lifted them to drink. Exquisitely framed prints adorned the walls along with dimly lit wall sconces. And the fragrant scents of gourmet food enfolded it all like a sensual cloak.

The maître d' pulled out Kari's chair and waited for her to

sit then took the fan-shaped napkin, opened it with a flick of his wrist and placed it in her lap. He nodded to Slade, who folded his lean body into the opposite chair.

"Your waiter will be with you shortly."

Slade thanked him and reached across the table to take Kari's hand, wrapping his fingers around it.

She smiled at him. "Thank you for bringing me here."

"I wanted to make this special," he told her. "We have something big to celebrate, right?"

"Yes." She smiled, something she'd been doing a lot of for the past few days. "We most definitely do."

A waiter materialized from someplace, setting menus in front of them, and Slade ordered a bottle of champagne. He waited while the waiter filled the crystal flutes.

"We're in no rush," he told the man now. "Just keep an eye on us, okay?" He looked back at Kari. "That all right with you?"

"Yes. More than."

"To the end of the stalker," he said in his deep voice.

"I'll definitely drink to that." She took a sip, enjoying the taste of the bubbles on her tongue. "God, Slade. You have no idea what it's like to have that off my back. I've been afraid to check my mail or answer my phone since this started. And that's more than two years ago."

When he picked up his glass and took a deep drink from it, she was fascinated by the workings of his throat muscles, the way his head tilted slightly as he drank. The long, lean fingers holding the glass—fingers that had stroked every part of her body. She remembered the feel of them, their touch. The pulse between her legs throbbed to life and her nipples tingled, wanting those fingers to pinch and tease them.

Oh, my God. All that incredible sex and yet it took so little to arouse her.

He caught her hand in his again and gave it a gentle squeeze, the press of his warm fingers sending little flames of heat rushing through her. Oh, she'd missed him a lot when he'd been gone, but she'd been able to compartmentalize. But now it seemed as if, with the end of the stalker situation, her body was on high alert for his every touch, every caress. She was afraid that with very little urging she might rip off her clothes and straddle him right there at the table.

At the thought, a tiny giggle escaped her mouth.

Slade quirked an eyebrow. "Something I said? Or did?"

"No." She shook her head. "Maybe a little hysterical laugh at not having to be afraid anymore."

"And now you can put it behind you."

"And we can talk about other things," she added.

It occurred to her with a sudden jab that in all the time they'd spent together, they hadn't really discussed the things most couples dug into. Common interests. Shared interests. They hadn't really looked beyond the upper layers of who each of them were. Kari was sure it had been because Slade was so afraid to create something that had the appearance of a relationship. She hated to tell him but they were well on their way to one, whether or not he wanted to accept it. She was getting damn sick and tired of the same old song. She often wondered if he was protecting himself, more than another person. Whether he was more worried about the death of a relationship than getting killed himself and leaving mourners.

I'm strong, she wanted to tell him. *I can survive. I survived the stalker, didn't I? Trust me to not be afraid of this.*

But not tonight. Tonight was about celebrating and talking about the other things that made up their lives. Movies, books, even sports. Slade had a sharp mind and a depth of interest that she hadn't found in a lot of men. Or maybe before she'd left Chicago she'd just been hanging around with the wrong men.

Slade Donovan was a man of many faces. He was a warrior first. She'd started watching movies like *Lone Survivor* and *Zero Dark Thirty* to try to get a better understanding of what he did. He was a rancher. She could visualize his lean, muscular figure sitting easy in the saddle, well-worn jeans outlining his long legs and fantastic butt. And he was a man with an incredible mind and a thirst for knowledge. Conversation flowed so smoothly dinner was over before she realized it.

"How about a carriage ride?" he asked when he'd settled the bill.

Outside in Alamo Plaza were fancy horse-drawn carriages available for romantic rides.

"Oh! That would be nice. I've never done one before." They were both silent for a moment as they realized why that was.

"Then tonight is the right time for it. Come on."

He held her hand as they walked the two blocks to Alamo Plaza. Slade negotiated with one of the drivers and before she knew it she was sitting in the seat, nestled against Slade with his arm cradling her. It was a typical old-fashioned buggy, with large wheels, two steps up to the body of the carriage and bench seats lined with plush velvet. A variety of colorful flowers decorated both the carriage and the horse, and bells attached to the horse's bridle jingled as the animal slowly trotted around downtown San Antonio. All around them people enjoyed the warm night, strolling, stopping to chat, sitting on the low wall where she and Slade had enjoyed their ice cream cones. They rode in silence, neither of them requiring conversation. *It was nice*, Kari thought, *to just* be.

That same feeling of latitude still wrapped itself around them on the ride back to her apartment and after they were inside. Kari did her security check then, by unspoken agreement, they undressed slowly, gazes locked together. When they were naked, Slade simply stood and looked at her for a moment. She loved the hunger and heat flaring in his eyes. She loved even more the way he ran his hand so slowly over her curves, following the line of her hips and her buttocks. Coasting up her arms and over to cup her breasts. Hefting them in his palms, he brushed his thumbs lightly back and forth against the nipples, now tightly beaded. Kari sucked in a breath at his touch. Her taut buds were so sensitive to his touch that the lightest caress had them tightening even more and flashes of heat racing through her system right to her core.

He took his time, stroking and caressing. It amazed her again that no matter how much sex they'd had last night and today, he wanted her just as much. Maybe even more. And certainly as much as she wanted him. When he lowered his head to string kisses along one shoulder, she tilted her head back, giving him access to that delicate spot at the hollow of her throat where she could feel the heavy pounding of her pulse. He traced the indentation with the tip of his tongue, shivers racing over the surface of her skin. And in her pussy her inner walls flexed as her body demanded his cock.

By the time he slipped his hands over the curve of her hips again, she was shaking so badly with need she had to sit on the edge of the bed. Slade nudged her to lean back, urged her thighs apart and kneeled between her legs. His thumbs were hot when he used them to gently open her labia, but that was nothing compared to the heat that shot through her with the first swipe of his tongue over her clit.

Oh, God!

How was it possible that sex with him just got better and better?

The soft swipes of his tongue lit every nerve in her sensitive tissues. Her muscles quaked each time his tongue took a pass over her sensitive bud. He licked the smooth skin of her inner lips and drew lines with his tongue the length of her slit. She tried to urge him with her hips to go faster, do more, but he went at his own pace, determined to torment her. She was so ready for him, hanging off the edge of that erotic cliff.

Now! Please, now!

In the next instant, he had her legs resting on his shoulders, his thumbs holding her apart and his tongue probing her with strong, hard thrusts. She quivered and shook at the assault on her senses, locking her ankles behind his back to keep him in place. He moved his tongue faster now, in and out, easing one thumb to her center to torment her aching clit. God! She wanted to come so much she was willing to beg for it.

"Please, Slade. Please, please, please."

"Please what?" His deep voice was muffled against her flesh.

"Please let me come."

He looked up at her for a brief moment. "Slow and easy wins the race, darlin'."

She had to stifle a cry of impatience, knowing there'd be no rushing him now. And there wasn't. He held her just at that place, so close to the edge, for what seemed like forever. Until her limbs were like jelly, her pulse stuttered and her body begged for release. When her orgasm rocked over her, it came so slowly she didn't realize it at first. It wriggled its way up from deep inside her, uncoiling with maddening slowness until her entire body shook with the force of it. The spasms went on and on and on, as if they'd never stop, the release hitting her everywhere, her inner muscles clenching and clenching. Slade's tongue still did its sensuous dance, lapping up every bit of her juice.

By the time the last of the tiny aftershocks had subsided, she was little better than a wet tissue. She didn't even have the strength to lift herself from the bed. Fortunately Slade took care of that for her, stripping back the covers and arranging her just the way he wanted her. He grabbed one of the condoms he kept in the nightstand, rolled it on while his gaze still locked with hers, then he was *there*. Right *there*. His thick shaft easing into her pussy made slick by the juices of her orgasm.

Again he took her on a slow ride, thrusting in and out in slow motion, until she was ready to beg him to just do it. *Do it!* When he did, with her legs over his shoulders again and his hands beneath the cheeks of her ass, their shared release exploded through her, seeming endless, on and on.

Slade collapsed onto her, catching his weight on his

forearms. "I could stay like this forever."

A little bubble of hysterical laughter burst from her. "We might have trouble going to work."

One corner of his mouth kicked up in a half-grin. "Maybe they'd let us work from home."

Kari had no idea how much time passed as they lay there in that position. At last Slade eased himself from her body, went to dispose of the condom and slid into bed next to her, spoon fashion.

"Thank you," she said at last.

He chuckled against her ear, his warm breath tickling her skin. "My pleasure."

She dozed off curled into him, wishing things could stay just like this forever and wondering if there was a way to make it happen.

Chapter Seventeen

The night had been perfect—the elegant dinner, the romantic carriage ride and the slow, delicious sex. Now they lay in bed together, sated for the moment, her head on his shoulder, his hand stroking her arm. She felt freer than she had in a long time, now that her stalker had been caught and was safely tucked away in jail.

She woke about three o'clock and went to get a drink of water. When she came back into the bedroom, Slade was also awake and sitting up in bed.

"I'm glad you're here this weekend to celebrate with me." She set her glass on the nightstand and crawled back into bed. "I can't begin to tell you what it feels like not to be running from shadows all the time."

"But you haven't been running from them here, right?" Slade asked. "Nothing's happened since you left Chicago? He has no idea where you've disappeared to and it doesn't matter now as he's been caught?"

"Right. Not a sniff or a sign of him, thank the Lord. But that doesn't mean he's given up—he won't be in jail for ever." She rubbed her upper arms as if trying to warm herself. "That stolen mail still spooks me. I don't know how he would have used it to trace me. In any event, I'm relieved to have it over for now."

Slade scratched his cheek, frowning.

A familiar sense of foreboding tied her stomach in tiny knots. "What is it? God, Slade. I've barely had time to enjoy being free of all this. What's bothering you?"

"Don't be upset with me, okay? I'm just having a hard time thinking of someone like this person you describe, almost a nonentity, being as inventive and clever as your stalker has been."

"You'd be surprised what kind of people turn out to have obsessive personalities."

"But that's just part of it, right? You have to be clever and devious to pull it off."

"Stalkers come in all sizes and shapes," she pointed out. "They can be aggressive, insanely jealous and possessive, insecure and obsessing from afar. There's no set personality type."

Slade rubbed the back of his neck. "I hear what you're saying, but—"

"So you see?" she interrupted. "He fits one of the two stalker profiles." When he didn't comment, she nudged him. "Slade?"

He stroked her arm again, a lazy sensuous gesture, his fingers raising little goosebumps on the skin, but still made no comment.

"Okay." Kari pushed herself up to a sitting position, uncaring that the sheet fell to her waist, leaving her breasts exposed. What the hell. He'd already spent time worshiping every inch of her body. "Tell me why this has got your brain in a twist? I can smell it burning and I'm not sure I like it."

Slade sat up beside her, shoving pillows behind his back. He took one of her hands in his, rubbing her knuckles the way he had a habit of doing, but Kari jerked away. That little thread of panic she'd had as a constant companion since the first 'gift' from her stalker was wiggling inside her again.

"I'm trying to look at this as if I were analyzing one of our missions. Sometimes when we have to identify a target, it's not as easy as it sounds. Terrorists stay alive by being clever. There are times we have to question ourselves three or four times to make sure we've identified the right target."

"I thought your commanding officer got that information and handed it off to you to plan the mission. At least that's what I've been given to understand."

He nodded. "Except it isn't always as clear as we'd like it to be. Every so often we get what we call a false positive. Someone who appears to be the target, but is in fact covering for someone else and taking their place."

She stared at him. "But that's absurd. Why would anyone do that?"

"Terrorists are a unique breed. They'll gladly accept death for what they consider a martyr's cause."

"Please don't tell me you think they've arrested the wrong man here?"

When he didn't answer her at once, a chill slithered the length of her spine. She wanted to bury herself against Slade, take the heat from his body. Pretend he hadn't said what he had. Instead, she slid out of bed, grabbed a robe from her closet and belted it in place. She began to pace, something she did often when she was trying to work out kinks in a case.

"Kari, listen to me."

"Listen to what?" She had a feeling that for a smart woman, she was becoming unreasonable, but she couldn't seem to help herself. Just when she thought she could breathe again, Slade and his damned reasoning knocked her sideways.

He was silent for a moment. Then he rose from the bed and walked over to her in all his naked glory, resting his hands on her shoulders. "I'd be a lot happier if I didn't get this uncomfortable, itchy feeling that what happened is just that—they might have the wrong man."

Kari raked her fingers through her hair. "I don't understand. He knew everything about it all, down to the last tiny detail. How is that possible if it wasn't him?"

"I don't know, darlin'." He planted a soft kiss on her forehead, a gesture obviously meant to soothe her. "Could be I'm seeing trouble where there isn't any. But like I said, I just have this crazy little itch I get when things feel off kilter. I want to make sure they've got the right person and you really are free of this whole thing. That's all. And something about this has been bothering me all weekend."

She dropped into the slipper chair and leaned her head back, rubbing her temples.

"Slade. I have lived with this over my head for nearly two and a half years. It got so bad I had to leave Chicago and move to Texas, and do it under the radar. I couldn't contact any of my old friends, for fear whoever this was would be watching them to see if they knew where I was."

"I understand," he began, but she held up a hand.

"Kip Reyes had someone else listed as the lead attorney on all my cases. No one cares about the second chair, even in a big case. And it wasn't as if anything I tried was even that newsworthy. Besides, the only time the media haunt the courthouse is when there's something very high profile or extremely salacious. So my name never made it into the media."

She stopped and drew in a breath.

"Kari," he began again.

She shook her head. "I'm not done. I was afraid to start a social life here for fear somehow, someway word would get out." She stood and began to pace the floor. "That night at the Huttons' was the first time I'd been anywhere except work and home for three months. I feel like I've been let out of prison, finally, and you want to make me question that?"

"Not one bit. I'm trying to make sure you're really safe."

"I trust the people who uncovered the stalker and questioned him," she insisted.

"Okay, tell me again how they identified him." He crossed his arms and glared at her. Even naked he was formidable.

"I told you. Someone saw him stealing mail meant for me from Kip's admin's desk. Ross just kept asking questions in a low-key way until someone finally remembered."

He stopped her pacing. "Just ask yourself this. Could someone so meticulous about sending you specific flowers and other things, and breaking into your home without getting caught, be so disorganized as to allow himself to be found out that way?"

"First of all, could you please put some clothes on?" Staring at his cock wasn't helping her state of mind any.

He chuckled. "Sorry about that." He grabbed his boxer briefs from the foot of the bed and dragged them on. "Better?"

"One hundred percent."

He crouched down, taking her hands in his. "All I'm saying is, sometimes the wrong person gets arrested. Maybe it's a misidentification. Maybe it's circumstances. Hell, it could be almost anything. You're a prosecutor. I'll bet anything you've had a case go south at one time or another for one of those reasons."

"But Schreiber admitted it," she protested. "He pleaded guilty in return for a reduced sentence." She brushed her hair back from her face. "I'll bet mistakes don't happen in your world."

"You're right, but the parameters and environment are a little different." He lifted her hands and squeezed them, as if infusing her with his strength.

"You understand the people who caught him aren't amateurs, right? They know what they're doing. It's not their first rodeo."

"Are you saying you don't want to call your boss and ask him to double-check? Kari, I don't understand why you're fighting me on this."

Because! she wanted to shout.

But that was no answer. Shouldn't she want to make sure they got the right person? Except she wanted to believe there was no doubt about it. If she questioned it, that meant someone could still be out there searching for her. Stalking her.

She pulled her hands from Slade's grip. "I know I'm not making any sense to you," she told him. "But I want to believe—no, I *have* to believe—that people I trust got this right. Why would they arrest this man and tell me everything was wrapped up if it wasn't? Ross wouldn't do that to me."

"Listen to yourself, Kari. You're a smart, savvy woman. A sharp prosecutor. Tell me that you don't have questions about this. That you don't have a gut feeling something is off here. Tell me that and I'll back off."

The problem was, now that he'd opened that door, she couldn't tell him that and it was killing her. The objective Kari knew she should pay attention to him, but the emotional Kari hated the fact that he had planted doubts in her mind. That the fear was creeping back again, gripping her in that invisible vise.

"Okay." She blew out a breath. "Tomorrow morning first thing I'll call Ross and be sure he and the police double- and triple-check this John Schreiber."

"Thank you. I don't mean to rain on your parade, Kari, but something about this just doesn't feel right. Okay? I'm used to reviewing mission details a dozen times, until every piece of it adds up. Something here just doesn't make sense to me. I'm glad I'm here, not off in some hellish hot spot, so I can look at this thing from all angles. When I leave, I'll feel a lot better if I know this thing is really over."

Why was she fighting him so hard on this? She wasn't stupid. She was well aware that people got things wrong. A lot, as a matter of fact.

Because I'm scared to admit to myself that might be the case here. I want this to be over. I want my life back.

"Come on. There's nothing we can do right now. Let's put this aside until you can make your calls." He stood and pulled her body against his and stroked his hand up and down her back. "I bet I can think of something to keep us occupied until tomorrow morning."

Kari hated to tell him, but the mood had changed. She didn't want to admit that Slade might be right. Hadn't Ross told her this took someone very smart, very clever, to pull all this off without detection? John Schreiber had graduated at the top of his class from Yale Law, but did that make him knowledgeable and sophisticated enough to do all this and escape detection? If so, then how could he have been stupid enough to get caught stealing mail? The fear she'd lived with for so long and thought she'd now been able to bury came roaring back, throwing everything else out of sync. She wanted to crawl back into bed and pull the covers over her head, wishing the whole thing would disappear.

Slade tightened his arms around Kari. He could have kicked himself. What he should have done was call her boss himself. He'd already spoken to the man once and he seemed like a smart, savvy guy. He was sure if he explained his misgivings that Kip Reyes would know who to call and what to do about following through on things. He wanted this settled one way or another before he had to report back to base.

But what if this was still not resolved by the time he left? Who knew when he'd be back again to provide help and support? This was why he never got emotionally involved with anyone. Never tried to become part of their lives. He'd known that from the beginning, yet he'd broken his own rules. *Fuck!*

The whole thing had bothered him all weekend. The story was just too neat. Too pat. A stalker who had managed to send her flowers and gifts and not be detected wouldn't be caught stealing mail from the district attorney's office. In fact, he wouldn't steal the mail to begin with. Or would he? Was whoever this was so desperate to find her, so over-the-top obsessed with her that he was making little mistakes? Of all the things he'd learned as a member of Delta Force, questioning things was at the top of the list. His first commanding officer had drilled it into him. When something looked too good to be true, too easy, it usually was.

Kari pushed away from him. "I'm going to make some coffee. I have a sudden chill."

One he knew he'd caused, because with the heat they'd just generated, there was no way she could be cold.

"All right. I'll have some too."

But not even the hot liquid could take the edge off the icy-cold feeling that had dropped over them with such suddenness. Why couldn't Kari see he was just interested in her safety?

But when they sat at the breakfast bar, each with a steaming mug, the silence surrounding them was uncomfortable. Slade kept running through his mind everything Kari had told him about the situation. The one thing that baffled him was the stalker's confession. If he hadn't done it, why say he had? Was this one of those situations where someone was so anxious for the fame that came with the notoriety that they'd confess to anything? Jesus, he sure hoped not.

Chapter Eighteen

The other side of the bed was empty when Kari awoke in the morning. Last night, for the first time since they'd found each other again, they had not made love. Had sex, she reminded herself. No one had said anything about love so she wasn't going to put lipstick on it and fool herself.

She grabbed the robe she'd discarded the night before and made her way into the kitchen, where she found Slade drinking coffee.

The atmosphere between them was stilted and she blamed herself as much as him. Why hadn't she been grateful for him looking at her situation from all sides and questioning things that bothered him? It was dumb for her to resent his determination to make sure everything had been done properly. But she knew Ross and the people who worked with him. If they were convinced John Schreiber was the one, then so be it. She didn't want to spend her time wondering if whoever this was had traced her to San Antonio and was even now following her around, planning and plotting to get her attention.

"Teo's on his way." Slade took a healthy sip of the hot liquid. "The other guys have plans and I didn't want to interfere. Listen, I'm sorry —"

"Slade, I'm sorry —" She spoke at the same time, then gave a nervous little laugh. "I apologize for last night. You're only looking out for my welfare and I appreciate that."

God, could she have sounded any more stilted?

"I didn't mean to upset you." His words were as stiff as hers. "I'm sorry that I'm the type to question things. I'm especially sorry you thought I was questioning the efficiency of your friends. I know you want to believe this is over and done with. I want that too."

"It's fine." She drank some of the orange juice. "You don't have to leave, you know."

He shrugged. "You're off to work and I have things to do at the ranch."

She nibbled her lower lip. "Will you be back later?"

"I'll call you." His cell phone dinged and he looked at the screen. "Teo's here. He's outside waiting for me."

He rinsed his mug, kissed her forehead then he was gone. Kari wanted to cry. Then she wanted to smack herself. Stupid, stupid, stupid. She'd behaved like an idiot child. Of course he would question things. It was who he was and the nature of what he did. She should have been grateful instead of acting the way she had. No wonder he was pissed off.

Well, nothing for it now. She might as well dress and get to the office early. Maybe she could catch Kip before he got caught up in the business of the day.

All the way to the office and all the way up in the elevator she kept replaying the conversation with Slade in her head. She did her best to blank the tension between them before he'd left, although she knew she'd have to deal with it. She also knew she'd have to be the one to reach out since it was she who'd acted like an idiot. Hopefully when she called him to give him a report, she could convince him to come back up to spend the night.

There were very few people in the office at this early hour. A couple of the assistant prosecutors were hard at work on whatever cases they were handling and a few of the support staff were busy. She fixed her coffee in the break room and carried it back to her office. She didn't know if Kip was in court today or had other things scheduled, but she didn't want to wait until the end of the day to talk to him. He'd been so good to her she wanted to run this past him prior to calling Ross.

At seven-thirty she heard the ding of the elevator and a

minute later saw Kip stride down the hallway. She took her coffee with her and headed for his office. Anita Navarre, his admin, was already there, computer awake, working through a stack of papers on her desk. Kari often wondered if the woman ever slept, or if she just woke up fully clothed and made up.

She looked up at Kari. "You need to see the boss?"

"If I could, please?"

"Let me check real quick." Anita hit a button on her computer to bring up the calendar. "He's free for a few minutes right now. Will that do?"

"I'll take it. Thank you." She rapped on the doorjamb. "Anita says I can steal a few minutes with you if I hurry."

Kip Reyes looked up from the folder on his desk and smiled. "Always. Come on in."

She sat in one of the two chairs in front of the desk, holding her coffee carefully. "This is probably going to sound crazy, so I wanted to run it past you before I called Ross."

"This have something to do with your stalker?"

"It does." She took a sip of her coffee, organizing her words in her brain. "Do you think there's any chance they got the wrong man?"

Kip frowned at her. "What makes you think that's even a possibility?"

"I'm just wondering if Schreiber fits the personality profile of a stalker." She took another sip of her drink, hoping the hot liquid would steady her.

"You should know there really isn't any rigid personality profile. Something's got your knickers in a twist. Out with it."

She took another swallow of coffee, framing her words. Was it just Slade's paranoia or did she really have doubts?

"It's just odd that someone who was so careful and so meticulous with every task while I was in Chicago would be sloppy enough to get caught snitching mail."

The way Kip eyed her, she knew his brain was going a mile a minute behind those dark eyes.

"Have you called Ross about this?"

She shook her head. "I wanted to run this by you first." *And hope you'll tell me I'm nuts.* "If I'm just seeing shadows where there aren't any then I can relax. But if not, that means someone is still out there and still looking for me."

"I'll tell you what." He checked his watch. "I've got a meeting in five minutes that should take about an hour. Can you be available right after that? We'll call Ross together. In situations like this, you can't be too careful. If they've made a mistake, he'll want to get on it right away."

Kari released the breath she'd been holding. At least he hadn't told her she was crazy.

"Thank you, so much. Really."

"No sweat. We'll get this taken care of and then you can get on with your life without any shadows hanging over you."

An hour had never dragged so slowly for Kari. She had trouble concentrating on the brief she was preparing. The situation wasn't helped any by the strained parting with Slade that morning. The chemistry had still been there, but it was affected by the tension between them. Maybe she shouldn't have taken off at him when he'd suggested her stalker might still be at large, but it had been a knee-jerk reaction. She'd just wanted it to be over and done with. And he, the big alpha dope, didn't appear to know how to soften his stance. He couldn't understand why his attitude had upset her.

In a way, neither could she. She'd reacted without thinking then didn't know how to back down. Crappity crap crap.

She booted up her computer and pulled up a document she was working on, but she found it difficult to concentrate. She didn't know what she'd do if it turned out Slade was right.

His voice echoed in her brain, replaying over and over. *'I just want to make sure you're safe.'*

Safe. She hadn't felt that for too long a time. Probably the reason she'd reacted the way she had to Slade's words. She didn't want him to be right. It meant the nightmare was far from over.

She alternated between glancing at her watch and at the clock on her computer, willing the minutes to pick up the pace. When her intercom buzzed at last, she almost jumped out of her skin. She depressed the button and Anita's voice squawked out at her.

"Kip says to come on down to his office now."

"Thanks." She wet suddenly dry lips. "On my way." She wanted to stop and refill her coffee mug, but as nervous as she was, she figured she might just spill it all over herself.

Kip was behind his desk again and waved her into the office.

"Come on in and close the door. I'm going to call Ross on his direct line. If he doesn't pick up, I'll try his cell. I don't want this to go through the switchboard unless it has to."

Kari wrinkled her forehead. "Why? What's the problem?"

"On the off chance you might be right, I don't want this on a line anyone else might be able to tap into."

She hadn't thought of that. In these days of advanced, sophisticated electronics, anything was possible. One more thing to be nervous about. She nodded and sat on the edge of the chair, clasping her hands together to still their trembling. She was nauseous with anxiety, hoping she didn't throw up on Kip's carpeting.

"Take a deep breath," Kip told her. "We'll make this right, one way or another."

She just wished she could believe that.

"Yeah, Ross." Kip leaned forward in his chair. "How's everything in the Windy City? Good, good. No." He laughed. "I didn't call for a weather report. Kari's here with me. Got something to run by you. I'm putting you on speaker so we can do a three-way here."

"Got it. Hey, Kari." The familiar warm voice floated into the room. "You must be feeling pretty damn good now that we've got your stalker locked up."

Kari looked at Kip, waiting for him to speak.

He cleared his throat. "Actually, Ross, that's the reason we called."

He laid out Kari's misgivings for Ross, short and succinct, the way he did everything. Kari sat there with her hands clenched so tightly she was worried she'd break the bones or at the very least cut off the blood supply. When he finished, there was a long moment of silence before Ross spoke.

"Kari? I hate to say this, but that may be a valid point."

Her stomach heaved and she had to swallow hard to keep her coffee from coming back up. "I was praying I was wrong, you know."

God, God, God.

"If it turns out you're right," he went on, "I owe you a huge apology. This means that asshole is still out there."

Kip cleared his throat. "Can you fill us in on the details of the arrest?"

"I'll fax the file over to you," Ross told them. "Then I guess we'd better go back and take this asshole's confession apart word for word."

"What was he like when you arrested him?" Kari asked. "Nervous? Frightened? Remorseful?"

"You know," Ross said, his eyes narrowed as if his thoughts weren't on her question, "it's a funny thing now that I think about it. I think we were all so relieved to have this put to bed and give you back your life that we let things slip through the cracks."

"How was he identified?" Kip asked.

"This is going to sound stupid." Ross' voice had an edge to it. "Especially since I'm no greenhorn prosecutor and I should know better than this." She could hear his sigh over the connection. "We got an anonymous tip from someone who said they'd seen this guy stealing things from Janine's desk during that little party we had."

Kip grunted. "I'm guessing he didn't resist arrest and he had every detail you needed without putting words in his mouth."

"Give that man an award." Ross sounded disgusted with himself. "Damn, Kari. We were celebrating the fact we'd gotten this bogeyman off your back we didn't look at it all as hard as we should have. But shit! He had every single detail."

"You know what that means, right?" Kip asked.

"No shit." She could hear the hard edge in his voice. "It means the real stalker is a close friend of his and he's still out there."

Kari forced herself to take deep, slow breaths in an effort to calm her racing heart.

"I just can't picture someone confessing straight out the way he did. Who would voluntarily go to prison for a crime they didn't commit? Especially someone with a good job and in the judicial system to boot."

"We've all seen a lot of people do twisted things for ungodly reasons," Kip reminded her. "Attention. Notoriety."

"God, Ross." Kari blew out a breath. "I don't know if I can deal with this."

"You will because you're strong," Kip told her. "And because all of us will help you."

"As soon as we hang up, I'll get things in motion," Ross told them. "I'll get the detectives who arrested and questioned him and we'll go through the whole process all over again. Examine what evidence we've got. We still have the tape with the anonymous call so we'll work on that. Kip, you make sure to keep an eye on Kari, okay?"

"You don't even have to ask. You know that."

"I also think I'll have a heart to heart with Judge Glasgow," Ross added. "He was some pissed off that his law clerk would do something this stupid and dangerous. After all, it also reflects back on him."

"Thanks, Ross." Kari hoped she didn't pass out in her boss's office. Now she wished she'd stopped for that cup of coffee. She was such a caffeine junkie she needed it to settle her nerves. "I appreciate you doing this."

"Don't thank me yet, kiddo. If everyone had done their

job to begin with, we wouldn't be in this mess now."

"Remember the motto," Kip put in. "If something's too good to be true, it usually is."

"Oh, and Kari? Speaking of Glasgow, he'll be in San Antonio this week for a judicial conference. When I thought we had this wrapped up, I mentioned to him that's where you'd gone. He asked if I thought it would be okay for him to get in touch with you. I'm guessing he wants to make sure you don't blame him for this."

"Of course I don't. And I'll be happy to see him. I sure appeared in his courtroom a lot."

"He could even be there already." Ross' sigh was audible over the connection. "I hate to spoil his trip by dumping this on him, but he'll want to know."

"Okay, then." They heard Ross clear his throat. "I'll be back in touch with both of you as soon as I have something."

Kari just stared at Kip after he disconnected the call. "I can't believe this."

"I'm so sorry, Kari." His eyes were filled with concern. "This has to be a real blow to you. Just when you thought you were safe, right?"

"What's worse," she told him, "is I had an argument with the very person who brought this up to me and told him he saw ghosts where there weren't any. I have some groveling to do and I don't know if I'll get the chance." She caught her bottom lip between her teeth, biting down on it, using the pain to stop from falling apart.

"I'll be happy to speak to anyone for you, if you like," Kip assured her.

"No!" She swallowed. She hadn't meant to just spit the word out. "I-I'll talk to him." She blew out a breath. "In fact, I'm going to try calling him right now, as soon as I get back to my office. Then I'll get to work and see if I can keep my brain occupied."

She made it back to her desk on shaky legs, closed the door and dropped into her chair. She picked up her cell phone from where she'd left it next to her computer and stared at it. How was she going to do this? Maybe she could get Slade to come over tonight and she could greet him at the door, on her knees. They'd joked a couple of times about the subject of submission after he'd told her he'd experimented at a BDSM club. Well, whatever it took.

With a shaking hand she dialed his number and waited for him to answer. What she got instead was his voicemail. Okay. Maybe he was out somewhere on the ranch and out of cell range. He'd told her he sometimes took a satellite phone or a radio with him if he was going to be too far away from the house. Just in case, she dialed him again, with the same result. This time she left a voicemail message.

"Slade? Seems you were right. And I was wrong to argue with you. They're having to go back and start over but they'll keep me in the loop. Please call me. I'd really like it if—"

The recording chose that moment to cut off so she redialed.

"Me again. I'd really like it if you'd come over tonight. I can apologize for my idiotic behavior in person."

The beep ending the recording sounded again, so she hung up. Hopefully he'd call back soon.

The morning dragged beyond belief. Kari found it difficult to concentrate, rereading the same brief three times. She might have concentrated better if she hadn't stopped to check her cell phone every fifteen minutes. After a couple of fruitless hours she finally decided to call the ranch directly then realized she had no idea what the number was. They'd exchanged cell phone numbers and that was it. Well, she was an assistant district attorney, right? She could get any phone number she wanted. But after thirty minutes when she still had nothing, she wanted to scream.

That was when she realized the phone might not even be in Slade's name at all. She entered Teobaldo Rivera's name in the search engine she used and bingo, there it was.

"I'm sorry, Miss Malone," he told her when she answered the phone. "He saddled his horse right after he got back from town and I haven't seen him since then." There was a pause. "I hope everything is okay with you guys. I haven't seen him this happy and relaxed in a very long time."

And, of course, I had to go and ruin it with my stubborn stupidity.

"No problem," she assured him. "I plan to fix it just as soon as I can get hold of him. Will you please have him call me when he gets back?"

"I'll do that."

She called one last time and left him the same message.

"Please, please call me," she ended. "Please."

She disconnected, wondering if she should have begged a little harder.

Chapter Nineteen

Slade sat astride the big gelding, catching his breath, although he didn't know why he was winded when the horse had done all the work. He'd urged the animal from a fast canter to a full gallop, the wind blasting his face with what felt like hurricane force as if it could blow away his demons. But by the time he pulled up at the stream at the far end of the property, all he had was a good case of windburn.

He dismounted and led the animal to the water, giving him time to drink and rest. He wished a bottle of water and a few idle moments could fix what was wrong with him. Except he didn't know exactly *what* was wrong with him. He hadn't been in this much emotional turmoil since he'd been a horny teenager.

God damn that woman, anyway!

He smacked his palm against the tree, but that didn't accomplish anything except to nearly break his hand.

He'd violated his own rule and this was what he'd gotten. It was no more than he deserved. He'd confused good sex — scratch that, extraordinary sex — with emotion and this was what he'd gotten. He was much happier when he had no emotional connection to anyone or anything except his men and his ranch. But fuck! He couldn't help the way he felt, no matter how much he wished it. For the first time ever, he'd allowed himself to think about a future with someone. He'd opened his heart, even if he hadn't gotten around to telling her yet.

Stubborn woman. Why hadn't she seen that his theory made sense? At least enough to ask the police in Chicago to double-check everything. Okay, he got it that she needed to believe it was all over. That she was finally safe. He just wanted her to make sure. Somehow it had escalated to a point where a big invisible wall had popped up between them. That had really shocked him. Kari wasn't one to run away from the truth, at least as far as he could tell. She worked in a profession where she had to dig out truth every day. Why had she reacted this way?

Maybe he'd read her feelings for him wrongly. Maybe he'd just assumed things that were not true. She was the first woman he had ever felt anything for that was more than occasional lust. There was a rare connection there, a strong one. He'd even begun to think about his next leave and taking things further. Now he wondered if he'd just been too hasty. That's what he got for letting himself get attached to someone and stick his nose in their business.

Well, fuck!

There was one thing, however, he intended to do regardless of how he felt at the moment. His concern for Kari's safety hadn't diminished, despite their argument. He'd contact Jamie Ramone, who was monitoring the panic button on Kari's watch. Any time she pushed it, like a security system, it would ding on Jamie's electronic setup and they could bring up her GPS signal. He wanted more than anything to be wrong about his suspicions and for that watch never to be used except to tell the time.

He glanced at his own watch and saw that it was close to noon. Beau and Trey had both texted him earlier to say that they'd be heading back to the ranch. Kenzi was tied up as part of a team handling a corporate merger and had told Beau she didn't think she'd see daylight, never mind him, for the next couple of days. Megan was leaving town again for two days on assignment so they were at loose ends. He hadn't heard from Marc yet, which he hoped was a good sign, but he and the others could certainly occupy themselves.

Mounting up, he then turned the horse back the way

they'd come and headed toward the ranch. He'd give Kari a couple of days to get her shit together. Maybe that was harsh, but he wasn't about to apologize for wanting to be sure she was safe. Hopefully by that time there'd be a resolution to her problem, one that proved him wrong. He sure hoped so.

* * * *

Kari's cell phone rang just as she was deciding what to do about lunch. She wasn't about to head out by herself but in her present mood she didn't want to give Sasha the opportunity to ask her what was wrong. She thought she'd done a pretty good job all morning of keeping herself on an even keel when people popped in and out of her office for things. Every time the phone on her desk rang, she jumped, hoping it was Kip or Ross with news for her, but no such luck.

They'll call me as soon as they have something concrete to say.

She was just trying to decide whether to send someone down to the coffee shop on the main floor of the building or order something delivered when her cell phone rang. She looked at the screen, hoping it was Slade but instead saw an unfamiliar number.

"Hello?"

"Kari? That you?" The Midwestern twang of Judge Robert Glasgow sounded in her ear.

"Judge Glasgow." She smiled. "Ross said that you might call. Welcome to San Antonio."

"Thank you. I told Ross I was happy this conference brought me here. It would give me a chance to apologize to you for the obscene situation with my law clerk." He paused. "Former law clerk, that is."

"I don't think anyone blames you for that, Your Honor. You can't be responsible for someone else's actions."

"Nevertheless, I want you to know how very sorry I am. I'd love to take you to lunch today. The conference begins tomorrow and I'll be a little tied up, so I hope today works for you. Sorry for the short notice."

"No, no, that's fine." Lunch with him would be good. She had a longstanding professional relationship with Glasgow, as many times as she'd appeared in his courtroom, and he had an impeccable reputation. He had to be upset at what John Schreiber had done. Maybe she could poke and prod and get a better picture of the law clerk, a picture that would convince her one way or the other. "Today works out well for me."

"Excellent, excellent. My club in Chicago has reciprocity with some of the private clubs here in San Antonio. I thought we'd have lunch at one of them. Quieter than your usual restaurants."

"Thank you. That's very nice of you, but—"

But she really wasn't much in the mood for a country club lunch today. Besides, there were plenty of good restaurants right near the criminal courts building.

"No objections," he interrupted. "It's the least I can do. I rented a car at the airport, so how about if I pick you up in front of your building in ten minutes?"

"Ten minutes?" Wow! "Uh, okay. Sure. Just let me tell the office where I'm going."

"You might just say you're having lunch with an old friend," he put in. "Some people are funny about judges and prosecutors lunching together like this."

"But we're not even in the same state anymore," she reminded him. "You no longer hear my cases."

"Just humor an old man, okay?" She could almost hear his smile.

"Sure. Fine. Whatever you think best."

"Ten minutes."

"See you then."

She spent a few minutes in the restroom making sure she looked presentable. Then she grabbed her purse and stuffed her cell phone in it. She thought about telling Kip where she was going, but neither he nor Anita were at their desks. She settled for just letting the receptionist know she was going out to lunch and would be back in an hour or so.

Judge Glasgow was waiting for her at the foot of the long flight of stairs from the entrance to the sidewalk.

"I'm in a No Park zone." He grinned at her. "I figured a judge could get away with it, though. Right over here."

He cupped her elbow to guide her then opened the passenger door and helped her into the black sedan he was driving.

"Thank you." She glanced over at him as he climbed in behind the wheel. He was just as she remembered him, tall with a thick shock of brown hair lightly shot with silver. She was sure the navy suit was made to specifications as were most of his clothes, custom tailored to his tall, broad-shouldered build. It was well-known around the Cook County State's Attorney's office that the Honorable Robert Glasgow was a clotheshorse.

"This is an unexpected pleasure," he told her as he pulled away from the curb. "We've missed you a lot. I myself miss your fiery presence in my courtroom."

Kari laughed. "Fiery presence? I'm not sure I'd describe myself that way."

He chuckled, a deep-throated sound. "Don't sell yourself short. You set the courtroom on fire plenty of times with your passion for justice."

For whatever reason, his words made Kari a bit uncomfortable. She didn't know why. After all, he was complimenting her work as a prosecutor, right?

"Which club will we be having lunch at? I should have told you there are plenty of excellent restaurants downtown."

"I'm sure there are, but I wanted to take you someplace you normally wouldn't go." He reached over and squeezed one of her hands.

Kari tried to snatch it back without making it too obvious, but he was making her very uneasy.

"That's very nice of you, but I do have to get back to the office in a reasonable time. I have two cases I'm very involved in at the moment and Kip likes his prosecutors' noses to the grindstone."

"If it makes you feel better, I'll call him when we get to where we're going. I'm sure it will be fine with him."

The thread of unease was wriggling harder in her body.

"Perhaps we could leave that for the next time you're in town," she suggested, "or maybe the weekend. You know. When I'm not so pressed for time."

"We'll be fine," he insisted. "I said I'd call Kip and I will. I don't often have the pleasure of lunch with a woman as beautiful and sexy as you are."

Okay, now warning bells were going off inside her, clanging loud and hard.

"Uh, Judge Glasgow? I think we'd better head back to town and reschedule. Really." She glanced out of the window and was startled to realize they were a good distance from San Antonio, heading into the Hill Country. "Where did you say we were having lunch? Because I don't think there are any private clubs out this way."

"Yes, there are." He glanced at her, his mouth curved in a smile that reminded her of predator just before he devoured his prey. "Very private. You know, Kari, I've admired you for a long time. A very long time. You're everything a man could want in a woman." He reached over and squeezed her thigh.

The bells were ringing harder and panic surged up in her throat.

"Oh, shoot. It's later than I figured. Kip will be looking for me before long." She glanced at her watch, taking the opportunity to push the tiny panic button. If this was a false alarm she'd apologize later.

"We're going to have plenty of time for you to show me just how incredible. I've waited a long time for this and I want to make every moment as amazing as possible. Don't worry. You'll enjoy it." He reached into his pocket and when he opened his hand, she saw he held a small hypodermic syringe.

The surge of fear was so strong it made her nauseated. She tried to get as far away from him as she could, but the door was there and the car was going too fast for her to even consider jumping out. She tried to grab his wrist and keep his hand away from her, but he was too quick for her. She felt the tiny prick of the needle as he stuck it in her neck.

Oh, God!

"Just enough to help you take a little nap, my dear." The tone of his voice had changed.

Whatever he used was strong enough to be fast-acting. In seconds her body went lax, her eyes closed and she was out like a light.

* * * *

Slade arrived back at the ranch just as Trey and Beau were pulling into the parking area. They walked over to watch him as he unsaddled his horse and turned him out into the corral.

"Your lady in court today?" Trey asked.

"No. She's preparing for a trial." His words were shorter and sharper than he intended. He saw Trey and Beau exchange glances. "No questions. Not one."

They looked at each other again then shrugged. If he didn't want to talk, there was no way they'd push the issue.

"Listen, Marc texted me," Trey said. "I guess he tried to call you, but you were out of range?"

Slade gave an abrupt nod. "What did he say?"

"He's having lunch with the woman he met. Then he'll be back here." He checked his watch. "Should be almost any time now."

"I hope this woman doesn't screw him over," Beau remarked. "Anyone here know anything about her?"

"I can ask Paul Hutton. If she was at that party, he'll be able to tell me."

"It's the first time we've seen any life in him outside the missions." Trey frowned. "If she screws this up, she'll have all of us to answer to."

Slade snorted. "I'm sure she'd be thrilled to hear that. I just—"

Whatever else he might have said was interrupted by the ringing of his phone. When he saw the number, every muscle in his body tightened.

"Yeah, Jamie?"

"You wanted to know if a particular panic alarm ever went off. Well, it just did."

"Shit. Is the GPS pinging?"

"Yes. It's heading out on Interstate 10 out of the city."

"Fuck, fuck, fuck. Okay, I am on my way. Give me two minutes. I have to get some stuff and make a call. Then I'll call you back. You can give us directions." He glanced at the other two men. "Okay, load up. Guns, ammo, Ka-Bar knives, anything we've got here."

He raced toward the house.

"What's up?" Beau asked, hard on his heels.

Slade filled them in on the situation even as he headed to his room to get his gear.

"We'll be ready in one," Trey assured him.

At that moment the back door opened again and Marc walked in.

He looked at Slade jogging out of his bedroom and Beau and Trey taking the stairs down two at a time. "What's going on?"

"Kari's in trouble." Slade bit off the words. "I set her up with an alarm on her watch and she just activated it. Get your gear."

They were so used to reacting in situations like this that in less than another two minutes they were loaded into the SUV and headed away from the ranch. Slade rattled off Kari's cell number to Trey, who was riding shotgun, and asked him to dial it. The phone rang several times before going to voicemail.

"Hey, Slade? Did you know you've got a ton of texts and voicemails here from Kari? Don't you ever answer your phone?"

"I told you I was out of range," he growled. And out of sorts, he might have added. "Play them."

When he listened to them, he turned hot and cold by turns. She'd done what he'd asked and he hadn't even been available for her to tell him about it. He had been off on his horse licking his wounds.

Fucking shit.

"Okay," Slade told him. "Call Kip Reyes, her boss. His card's in the glovebox." Kari had given him the card in case he ever had to get hold of her and she was unavailable. When he told the man's admin it was an emergency regarding Kari, she put him through right away.

"Slade." The man's voice boomed over the connection. "What's going on? Is Kari in trouble? She threw me a curveball this morning when she said we might not have the right guy for her stalker."

"I gave her a watch with a panic button on it and she just activated it. Do you know where the hell she is?"

Kip was silent for a moment. Slade wanted to reach through the phone and shake him.

"She didn't tell anyone where she was going," he said at last. "But Judge Glasgow is in town and her old boss said he'd be calling her for lunch."

"Fuck." Slade spat the word out. "How likely do you think it is that Glasgow's the stalker and not his clerk?"

Again a momentary pause. "Four days ago I'd have said impossible, but now I'm not so sure. Her former boss said as soon as this Schreiber character was booked, the judge hotfooted it to his office to offer his apologies for this going on under his nose. He asked if Ross could tell him now where Kari is so he could apologize to her."

"And no one suspected the fucking judge, right?"

"We'll talk about that later. Right now can you track her, whoever she's with?"

"I can. It would also help if you could use your prosecutorial muscle and find out who he rented a car from at the airport and what kind."

"Done. I'll call you back. Listen, Slade, we're all sorry that—"

Slade cut him off. "Time for that later." He disconnected and punched in Jamie's number. Then he put the phone on speaker and set it in the holder on the dash.

"Okay," he said, "we're on our way. Give us what you've got."

Chapter Twenty

He was there again, in her bedroom. Whatever had awakened her, she realized he had broken through her alarm system. How the hell did he do that? She lay very still, hardly daring to breathe, getting her eyes accustomed to the dark. Maybe this time she could see who he was?

Lying motionless, she listened for movement. There it was again, that whisper of sound. It came from somewhere near the foot of her bed. If she kept pretending to sleep, would he go away and leave her alone?

But then she felt a hand on her ankle, through the covers. It moved in a slow motion up the line of her leg to the curve of her hip and squeezed, oh so gently. She kicked, an automatic reaction, trying to dislodge his hand. Strange, the hand tightened its grip on her, despite her movement.

She forced her eyes open and —

She came awake, her brain fuzzy. Opening her eyes had been a bad idea, because even the soft light of the room stabbed at her pupils. When she realized she was lying down, she tried to sit up. That was when she discovered her arms were outstretched and her hands tied to the posts at the head of the bed. Her head pounded as if a jackhammer was trying to break out, and the hand — *the hand* — was stroking her calf through the fabric of her pantyhose.

"I know your head hurts." The voice was male and familiar. "I am sorry about that, but it will wear off shortly. I just wanted to be sure you slept until we got to our little hideaway."

Kari took a deep breath, let it out and forced her eyes open again, hoping this was all a dream and she was in her bedroom. Alone. The hand moved on her calf again and she tried to kick it away. Except it appeared her legs were tied in a similar fashion to her hands. Wherever she was, she was spread-eagle on a bed and some stranger was touching her body.

"Take it easy. Just relax."

The voice was probably meant to be soothing, but she found it both irritating and frightening. Making another valiant effort, she managed to pry open her eyelids and focus her eyes. They were in a cabin of some kind, very rustic, with just basic furnishings. There were two doors against one wall and she hoped one of them led to a bathroom. A man stood near the foot of her bed. His features were still unclear, but she did see that he was tall, fairly well built and wearing only a pair of boxer briefs.

Panic surged.

Who the hell was this?

Then, as if a hand had slid across her pupils and wiped away the fog, the picture leaped into startling clarity and she nearly passed out again. Watching her expectantly, with a hungry smile on his face, was Judge Robert Glasgow. She tried to speak, but her throat was so dry and her lips wanted to stick together.

"I know you're thirsty." He spoke as if they were having a normal conversation. "I apologize for all the discomfort but as I said before, it was important that you not wake up too soon. But let me get you a little drink."

This is a nightmare. I've had them before. I'll wake up and this will all disappear.

But instead Glasgow moved to stand beside her head, bracing it with his hand while he fed her water from a cup with a straw.

"Little sips. We don't want you to get sick."

Kari didn't know about him, but she certainly wasn't anxious to get sick. He held her head until she'd consumed enough water to lubricate her mouth and her throat, then gently placed her head back on the pillows. She was grateful at least that he'd piled more than one pillow to support her so she wasn't lying completely flat.

"Why are you doing this?" She hoped that as long as she kept him talking, he wouldn't be doing other things, things she didn't even want to think about. And there was Slade. She had to give him time to get here. She'd pressed the button so he had to be on his way. No matter how upset he was with her, he would never just turn his back on her. That wasn't who he was.

And it wasn't who they were either. She had been so idiotic and stupid. If she could she'd smack herself in the face. And maybe she'd have been on her guard about Judge Robert Glasgow. After all, it had been his law clerk who'd confessed to everything.

"Why?" He trailed his fingers over her leg again. She had to grit her teeth to keep from trying to jerk away from his touch. "Since the first day you appeared in my court I've wanted you. I looked at you, all that auburn hair, that gorgeous figure in those lawyer clothes. Saw your fire and passion as you prosecuted your cases. You have no idea how many nights I've dreamed of having you in my bed, naked. Showing you how I feel. Licking every inch of your body. Having you all to myself. Giving you my love."

His love? The thought made her skin crawl. When he stroked himself through the fabric of the boxer briefs, she had to work hard to suppress a gag, as well as the fear still bubbling so close to the surface.

"You never spoke up," she told him.

"It would have been improper. After all, you tried so many cases in my court. There would have been rumors of favoritism. At first I contented myself with sending you little gifts, flowers with special meaning, other things. But pretty soon that wasn't enough."

"You broke into my house." God, how many times had he been there? "How did you do that? I had an alarm installed."

"Easy enough to bypass," he bragged, "if you're as smart

as I am and know what you're doing."

"You touched my things," she cried, unable to stop herself. "Why did you invade my privacy like that?"

"You're sharp, Kari. You know the satisfaction a man can get just from touching the intimate things of a woman he... loves."

Love? This was far from any kind of love.

"You broke in while I was sleeping." She tried to steady herself. "You scared me half to death."

He nodded. "I know and for that I'm very sorry. I couldn't restrain myself any longer. I just wanted to...see you, when you were vulnerable. To see how you'd be when we were together at last. *Intimately.*" His whispered the last word.

At the thought, her stomach heaved. Still, she had to keep him talking. The longer she held him off, the greater the chance Slade would have time to find her. *If* he still cared after she'd acted like such an idiot. *If* he still wanted her after she'd argued with him the way she had.

"But if we couldn't be together forever, what good would it be?"

He smiled, a smile so smarmy she wanted to smack his face. On a different man it might have been warm, or exciting or even sexy. With Glasgow parading around in his boxer briefs that barely restrained a hard-on, it just creeped her out.

"Oh no. If we worked it properly, we could have. Eventually I'd find a way so we could come out in the open, so to speak. By that time our love would be sealed forever and I'd have you to myself all the time."

Holy God! The man wasn't just obsessed with her. He was insane. Real fear threatened to paralyze her and she couldn't have that. She needed to keep her wits about her until Slade could find her. She was pinning a lot of hopes on that watch with the panic button.

"You got John to admit to this, didn't you?" It wasn't even a question. "How did you manage that?"

There was that nauseating smile again. "It seems John

has a bad gambling habit and was in need of a great deal of money. We agreed that I would provide the funding and he would confess to the situation. I refuse to call it a crime. I gave him every detail so he could pass muster in the interrogation."

Kari frowned. "And he would go to jail for you?"

"Oh no, no, no. This was never about anyone going to jail. I had to find out where you'd disappeared to. It was driving me crazy. I'd phone in the tip, John would confess, I'd tell Ross how very sorry and embarrassed I was. Then I'd ask him where you'd taken yourself off to, reminding him he could tell me now that the danger was passed. It was the only way I could think of to find you. I tried everything else. You'd done a very professional job of disappearing."

How devious and clever he'd been. And his plan had worked, damn it.

She wet her lips. "Where are we? I know we aren't in the city."

"That's correct. I arrived here a few days ago to scout the area. There is a group of cabins on a side road up on one of the many hills for which the Hill Country is named. Every cabin has a separate path leading up to it. We're completely alone, Kari. Just the two of us."

No wonder he hadn't wanted her to tell anyone where he was going.

Slade! She had to focus on Slade. He might be upset with her, but he wouldn't ignore the danger signal. He was her secret weapon. He'd find her. He had ways. And she'd spend the rest of her life apologizing to him, if he let her.

She swallowed, aware that her throat was dry again and scratchy. "What about your conference? They're expecting you."

"I can work that out. I'm sure you won't mind being left here when I have to go into town. But I'll return each night and we can have more time together."

He stroked his fingers along her cheek. Kari had to clench her fists to keep herself from shuddering. But when he pressed his open mouth to hers, she couldn't keep herself from gagging.

Glasgow recoiled and before she could try to shift her head, he lifted his hand and slapped her with such force it made her teeth rattle.

"Perhaps," he said in a soft voice, leaning down so his mouth was close to her ear, "I need to teach you some discipline first."

Kari closed her eyes and prayed.

* * * *

Slade pushed the SUV as hard as he could, ignoring Trey's caution that they didn't want to risk getting stopped for speeding. In between steadily cursing, he bugged the shit out of Jamie every two seconds to make sure the GPS was still transmitting.

"Slade," Jamie grumbled. "Fuck! If it changes I'll let you know."

But Jamie knew him and reported to him every few minutes, sometimes every few seconds.

"They turned off Interstate 10, Shadow. They're off on one of the Farm to Market Roads. Hold on. Okay, here's the one." He rattled off the numerical designation of the two-lane country road that broke off from the Interstate. "I've still got the GPS signal. Let me bring up my topographical map." Another pause. "They're heading up into the area of those twin hills. Damn, Slade, there isn't shit up there."

"Just keep following the signal," he told the man through gritted teeth.

"I am. No sweat."

"Have you been up this way, Slade?" Beau asked.

"Yeah. There are a few ranches out this way I've visited, but for the most part it's just raw nature."

Where the fuck is he taking her? Does he know someone up here? How the hell could he have made contact so fast?

Then he realized it had been four days since the fake

stalker had been caught. Four days since Glasgow could have flown down here and made whatever arrangements he needed. Four days to plan.

Fuck! Fuck! Fuck!

At that moment his phone dinged.

"It's that guy Kip," Trey told him.

Slade was grateful he'd had the new radio with Bluetooth and cell phone capabilities installed in the vehicle. He pressed the button to connect the call.

"Go ahead," he barked.

"He rented a black four-door sedan, an Infiniti. And get this. He rented the car three days ago. He's been here all this time."

"He must have hotfooted it down here the minute he found out where she is. Damn." Slade pounded his fist on the steering wheel.

"Right after he went to apologize to her boss and get her location." Kip's voice was tight with strain.

"Where is she now, Jamie?" Slade demanded, disconnecting his call with Kip.

"About five miles from the Interstate. Hold on, I'm pulling up Google Maps on one of the other computers."

Slade thought he'd grind his teeth to dust waiting for Jamie to get back to him. Beside him Trey checked his weapon and made sure the clip was loaded. The clicks in the back seat told him the others were doing the same. He cursed himself a hundred times over for the way he'd handled the situation with Kari. He should have ignored her anger at him and her need to know the stalker was actually in jail. No, he should have brought it up when she'd first told him about it. So maybe they wouldn't have had such an incredible weekend, but if he'd insisted she call her boss right away, at home, maybe this wouldn't have happened. She wouldn't have gotten into a car with a man she trusted.

"Okay." Jamie's voice crackled from the speaker. "You know that road, Slade. There's mostly nothing on there for miles except a few scattered ranches."

"Mostly?"

"Except for a collection of cabins someone built on top of one of the big hills. Got a picture of them. I'm sending it to your phone."

They had exited the Interstate by now and were speeding along a narrow two-lane highway. The terrain was a mixture of rolling land dotted with oak and cypress and mountain cedar and what the locals called small mountains but were really the hills that gave the Hill Country its name. Where the hell could someone build cabins? There weren't even roads going up most of these rises.

His phone beeped with an incoming email. He depressed the button to open it and a photograph filled the scene.

"Got it," he told Jamie. "Trey, describe it to me."

"Near the top of one of these hills, or whatever you call them. Seven cabins, pretty rough looking. There's a level place for parking and then narrow paths leading up to each cabin. They're pretty far apart, Shadow. Kind of like spokes in a wheel."

"Jamie, is there an entrance from the highway? How the fuck do people get up there?"

He took a sharp curve in the road so fast the SUV rocked up onto two wheels. Then they landed with a thud and he goosed it even more. No one said a word about his driving.

"I got it, Slade," Trey told him. He was moving the picture around with his finger to take in all the details. "There's a narrow dirt road. Lots of trees. You could miss it if you didn't know it was there. Who the hell would stay in a place like this?"

"People who don't want to be bothered." Slade grated out the words.

"There it is," Beau called from the back seat. "Right up there. Turn, Slade."

"All the signals still beeping, Jamie?" he asked.

"Yeah, but we got a slight problem."

What the fuck?

"What kind of problem?"

"Her GPS has been stationary for the past few minutes but it indicated the car is stopped in the parking area."

"Not in front of one of the cabins?" Beau asked.

"Nope. That's the closest I can pinpoint."

Slade hung a sharp left onto the dirt road that was barely more than a cart path. The mountain cedar was thick on either side of them.

"We're almost at the parking area," Trey announced after a few seconds.

Slade spotted a small clearing just to the left and he yanked the wheel hard, nosing the SUV into the space.

"Jamie, we're going silent. Thanks for everything."

"Good luck," the man said. "Jamie out."

Trey had the binoculars out, focused on the parking lot, visible through the trees.

"The car's there all right." He read off the license plate number.

"That's it," Slade confirmed.

They planned this like a mission, because no one doubted for one minute that was exactly what this was. They'd done hostage rescue more times than they could count. They might not have all the sophisticated tools this time, but they had enough and they had what they needed.

"You all know the drill," Slade began. "We've done something like this a thousand times before. Ease out of the vehicle, as little sound as possible. We can make our way up there through the trees. I don't want to risk him spotting us pulling in to park and wondering who the hell we are and what we're doing. If he feels trapped he could kill Kari."

"Okay," Trey agreed. "Then let's split up, two of us to the left two on the right."

"That way we can scout the cabins one at a time," Slade agreed. He took the binocs and focused on the area of the cabins himself.

"What do you see?" Beau asked.

"We'll have to be careful as we approach each unit. The

ones I can see all have a window in the front and where I can see the sides I also see a small window. They're high enough we can crouch beneath them. Let's number them left to right."

"We don't have the comm gear we use on our missions," Marc reminded him. "We'll have to improvise."

"Right. Okay, Beau, you're with me," Slade ordered. "Trey, you're with Marc. Everyone set your phones on Vibrate. Whoever finds the right cabin first signal me by speed dialing me with the cabin number. I'll respond. If I'm the one that finds it, I'll signal Marc. We'll respond."

They made one last check of their firepower and their phones. Then they were ready.

Like the Shadow for which he was nicknamed, Slade eased out of the SUV, closed the door so it was barely a click and began his ascent to the cabins. He used the covering of trees as much as possible. He had no idea what view the cabin had and he didn't want Glasgow to see him coming, in case he happened to be looking outside. Stealth was their name, however, and they all used the trees and wild shrubs as cover while they split up and headed to the far cabins on each side.

Since there was nothing to signify which cabins were occupied, they decided to start at the far ends and work their way toward the middle. Beau took the left with Slade, who forced himself to go slow and do nothing to give away his presence, even though his brain screamed at him to hurry.

Please let her be okay.

* * * *

"I, uh, have to go to the bathroom."

Kari had tried to think of a way to get this madman to untie her. The ropes were cutting into her wrists and ankles when she tried to move and she was beginning to lose the feeling in her hands. She did her best to avert her eyes from

Glasgow, who kept walking around the bed, moving from side to side, stroking her, touching her, telling her all the things he wanted to do to her and how he'd make plans for them to always be together. At one point he kissed one of her hands and ran his tongue over her knuckles and she wanted to vomit. It was almost as disgusting as the sight of the man in his boxer briefs that did nothing to disguise the bulge of his cock beneath the fabric. She knew, however, how important it was to maintain control. She clung to the belief that Slade was on his way and she needed to find some way to stall things as long as she could.

Glasgow looked at her through narrowed eyes. "Is this some kind of trick? I'd hate to have to punish you for lying to me."

"No, no, not at all," she hurried to assure him. "I really do have to go. And then maybe instead of tying me back up we could, you know, enjoy each other a little."

He studied her face for a long time.

"Why are you suddenly so agreeable?"

She found a smile from someplace. "I've been thinking about it and watching you. Maybe I'm wrong to fight you. After all, how many women can say a judge is in love with them, right? I should see it as an honor."

His face lit up and he actually licked his lips. "An honor. Yes, yes. Now you get it."

She wiggled as much as her restraints permitted. "So, bathroom? I really need to go."

"All right, but absolutely no tricks."

"No tricks," she agreed.

She forced herself to lie still while he unfastened the ropes and again not to move while he massaged her wrists and ankles. When he reached out a hand to help her from the bed, she even responded when he gave her fingers a squeeze, even though she felt like shuddering at his touch. She sensed his eyes on her as she walked to the bathroom. Inside, she closed the door and leaned against it, drawing in a deep breath and letting it out slowly. She only had a few minutes in there, positive that if she took longer he might even break down the door to get to her.

She was still reeling from the realization that her stalker was a well-respected judge, an important community figure. An icon in the courtroom. How in all that was holy had he gotten his law clerk to confess to a crime like this? Even if, as Glasgow had hinted, there was proof he couldn't have done it, the stigma would follow him wherever he went. Who on earth would even hire him?

She stalled as long as she could, using the facilities and taking a long time washing her hands.

"Kari?" A fist banged on the door. "I think you need to come out of there now."

Another deep cleansing breath and she opened the door, pasting a smile on her face.

"All freshened up," she told him in as bright a voice as she could manage. "Perhaps, like I said before, we could just sit and chat a while."

"Maybe later." His fingers closed over her wrist in an iron grip she was sure would leave marks. "When I am sure to my satisfaction that this isn't all just a ploy on your part."

She thought about fighting him as he tugged her over to the bed again, but then what? He was a large man, not someone she could overpower. Maybe if she could aim a well-placed kick to the crotch she could double him over long enough to get out of the place. Too bad he seemed to guess her intent, because he made sure to hold her in such a way it was impossible as he propelled her toward the bed again.

She was at least glad he hadn't tried to undress her yet. She forced herself to lie as still as she could while he restrained her wrists and ankles again. But this time when he pulled her legs apart he took a moment to run the flat of his hand over her stomach and down between her legs, rubbing her mound through the fabric of her slacks.

"I have such plans for you, Kari. For us. Once you commit to this fully, think what a wonderful couple we'll make."

Not if she had any say in the matter.

Then a sickening thought rolled through her. What if the panic button on the watch hadn't worked? Or what if Slade had discontinued the monitoring? No, no, no. He'd never do that. He might be pissed off at her, but he'd never do anything to put her in danger, or to ignore her need for help. Even assuming everything was working, she had no idea how long it would take him to identify where she was and get here.

Okay, then. She needed to hold herself together as much as possible. If that meant playing his sick little game, so be it. She might have walked around in fear for more than two years because of this maniac, but now she needed to find her inner core of strength. She needed to be the person she was in court.

Think of him as a defendant or a reluctant witness. I know how to play that game.

But when he opened a drawer in the little nightstand and removed a knife, she couldn't help the small surge of fear. She'd worried about rape, about whatever sexual deviations he might enjoy. She hadn't thought about torture and pain. But if he loved her, as he'd said, why would he cause her to suffer torment? Her mind scrambled frantically for some answers, seeing the wicked blade glint in the light.

"Please don't be afraid of the knife." That sickening smile reappeared on his face. "I like to play with it. It has so many uses. For example, it's much more exciting to cut your clothing away than it is to just undress you. Exposing your skin a little at a time."

That fear now rolled into a cold, hard ball in the pit of her stomach and she had to force it back. How was it this madman had existed for so long without anyone being the wiser? He had to have played his sick games with other women, even if he hadn't stalked them first. Had he done more with the knife? Used it on them in other ways? She'd prosecuted a murderer who liked to carve his initials into his victims. Was that what he had in mind for her?

She swallowed back the revulsion surging up and forced herself to lie still and make no movement at all. But in her head, silently, she was praying.

Please, Slade, hurry, hurry, hurry.

Chapter Twenty-One

The first four cabins they checked out yielded nothing. Three of them were empty. Slade heard something coming from the fourth that made his muscles tighten, noises that sounded like screams. However, when he managed to peek in the window he discovered a couple having athletic sex accompanied by appropriate noises. Damn!

While he was cursing silently, his cell phone vibrated in his pocket. He looked at the screen and every nerve went on alert as he read Marc's text.

"Target identified. Cabin three."

Slade moved up to the cabin in a low crouch, Beau right next him. They rendezvoused with Marc and Trey at the side of the small building.

"We have zero intel on what's happening inside," he reminded everyone in a whisper. "We don't know if he has a gun or what, so we have to do this with great care. We can't put Kari in any more danger than she already is."

They all four crouched below a small window. Slade had a desperate need to see what he could, but he didn't dare risk a peek and have Glasgow spot him. Not until they knew more about what was going on.

Constantly checking the area around them to make sure no one was around who could spot them, they finally settled on a game plan they thought would work. While the others waited on either side of the door, Beau banged on it with his fists.

"Clara, honey? Hey, it's me. I forgot my key. Open up, now."

There was no answering sound from inside.

"Sweetheart? Come on, now." He banged on the door again. "I'm sorry for what I said. Open the door and I'll make you glad you did."

"You have the wrong cabin," a man's voice called out. "Go away."

"Hey!" Beau shouted even louder. "You got another man in there with you? Damn you, Clara. Open this damn door before I blow it open." He pounded again, several sharp knocks in rapid succession. The others flanked him with their weapons at the ready.

"I said go away," the voice called again.

"Not until you open this fucking door, whoever the hell you are. I want my woman. You let me in or I'll just wait out here and blow your fucking head off."

Then they heard a sound that made Slade's heart beat faster.

"Slade? Is that you? Help! Help, Slade."

Kari's voice sliced right through him. Without waiting any longer he lifted his booted foot and kicked the door hard, splintering it. At the same time the others put their shoulders to it and knocked it into the room. When he saw Kari spread-eagle on the bed, for a moment he forgot to breathe. A man he assumed was Judge Glasgow was standing beside her. He had one hand on her forehead, pressing back on it. The other hand held a knife, poised over her body. A sharp crack sounded in the room, the explosive sound of a shot being fired, and Glasgow stumbled back, cursing. The knife fell from his hand as he clutched his shoulder.

"It should have been your fucking head," Beau told the judge. "You just better be glad I'm such a damn good shot or it *would* have been."

Trey walked over. "I've got him. You did your part."

He backed the judge over to the chair, pushed him into it and stood with his gun pointed at him. "I'd love it if you'd move right now," he growled. "Nothing would give me more pleasure than blowing a hole in you."

Glasgow huddled in the chair making little sniveling noises. "I'm bleeding," he whined, holding his shoulder.

Trey grabbed a towel and threw it at him. "Truthfully, I'd rather just let you sit here and bleed to death, but I think getting you into court for this would be a lot more satisfying."

Slade was already untying Kari. He sat on the edge of the mattress cradling her in his arms. She was shaking all over and crying silently.

Beau crouched beside her and took one of her hands. "I just want you to know, darlin', that I'm a deadeye shooter. I know where and how to hit so he didn't cut that pretty throat by mistake." He grinned at her. "Besides, Slade would have cut off my balls and I kind of like them where they are."

"Thank you." Her voice was so soft Slade had to strain to hear the words.

"Hey, Slade," Trey called. "We got company."

A man in jeans and a plaid shirt stood in the doorway, observing the ruins of the door and holding a shotgun.

"What the fuck is going on here? I just called the cops so you'd better all back up and sit on the floor until they get here."

"Good thing you did." Trey stepped forward and held out his hand. "Trey McIntyre. United States Army Special Forces. We got ourselves a stalker turned kidnapper here."

"Don't believe them," Glasgow shouted. He cowered in the chair against the wall, the towel pressed to his shoulder, still wearing nothing but his boxer briefs. "I'm a district judge from Illinois here for a conference. I came to this cabin to get some rest first and these assholes broke in and shot me."

"That's not true." Kari looked at him from where she sat in the circle of Slade's arms. Her voice sounded shaky but determined. "He's been stalking me for two years and today he kidnapped me." She pointed to the ropes still attached to the bed and to the burns from them on her wrists and ankles.

"It was just a game," Glasgow shouted. "She likes it rough."

"Not from you, asshole." Slade hurled the words out as if each one was a bullet.

"Everyone just put down their damn guns," the man in the doorway ordered, "until the sheriff gets here and we get this sorted out."

Slade shook his head, the signal to his men not to leave themselves unarmed. The screech of a siren split the air just then.

"Good," the man said. "There's the sheriff now. We'll see what's what here. Nobody move until he gets in here. And for God's sake, watch those trigger fingers."

It took longer than they would have liked to sort it all out. In the end it meant calls to both Kip Reyes and Ross Delahunt, not to mention the team's commanding officer, before the sheriff was satisfied and told them all they could go. He made arrangements to have Glasgow handed off to the Bexar County Sheriff's Department, where they'd get him medical aid and a spot in a cell. Texas and Illinois could fight it out over who got to try him.

Slade watched as the man was marched out in handcuffs with little care for his wounded shoulder.

Kari leaned into Slade. "I can't believe it's over at last."

"And this time for real," Slade assured her.

"If only I'd listened to you," she began.

"Coulda, woulda, shoulda. I'm just glad I gave you the damn watch." He leaned down and kissed the top of her head. "I may never let you out of my sight again."

"Does that mean I get to go on missions with you?" she teased.

She might have been joking, but Slade heard the edge of hysteria still lingering in her voice.

"We'll negotiate." He tightened his arm around her. "Let's get the hell out of here."

The ride back to San Antonio in the SUV was completed

in silence for the most part. Slade asked Trey to drive so he could hold Kari in his lap, seat belt and regulations be damned. He couldn't stop himself from stroking her hair and her arms, from leaning his head against hers so he could feel the smoothness of her cheek. And if his men were right there? Too damned bad. He might have lost her altogether and that would have been unbearable. He couldn't believe it had taken almost losing her to realize how deep his feelings for her went, or the strength of them. The question was, how did she feel about him? They'd danced around the subject in the short time they'd been together but neither had really expressed their feelings or emotions. He and Kari needed to have a long talk, but not right now.

Delayed reaction had set in and he could feel her trembling, hard as she might try to hold herself still. It wasn't just today that had done it for her. This was the culmination at last of months and months of being afraid, of trying to deal with that fear and not knowing who it was out there doing this to her.

When the SUV pulled up in front of her apartment building he pushed the door open and eased himself out, still holding her until he could set her on her feet.

"Don't even think about not letting me come up with you."

She gave him a weak smile. "I don't even think I'd want to."

"Good." He nodded to the guys that they could take off.

"Call us whenever," Trey said. Then he put the vehicle in gear and rolled back into the street.

"Come on, darlin'," Slade said. "I've got just the prescription for you. A hot bath and a stiff drink and I don't mean wine." He tilted her face up. "You held up so well. I don't know what went on but I'm guessing you kept your head pretty good or you would have been in a lot worse shape."

"I can't believe I was scared of that weasel." She looked

down at her feet as they rode up in the elevator.

"Kari, weasels can be very dangerous. They're nothing to ignore."

"I guess you're right."

Her hands were shaking so much it took two attempts for Kari to get her key in the lock to open her front door until a strong hand closed over hers and helped her with it. Slade wrapped an arm around her as they finally made it into her little front hall. When the door was closed again and locked and the alarm set—she was far from ready to let go of that yet—he turned her to face him, grazing her cheek with the knuckles of one hand. Even as knocked off balance as she was, his touch electrified her, heating her blood and setting the pulse in her cunt to throbbing with a heavy beat. His gaze locked with hers in a look so intent she could feel it strumming every one of her nerve endings.

"Bath first before anything," he insisted, leading her to her bedroom.

She started to undress, but the aftereffects of today's episode still had her body off kilter. Her hands still shook, her legs were still weak and she still felt as if she'd collapse at any moment.

Slade picked her up and sat her on the bed. "Hold on one second."

He strode into the bathroom and in a moment she heard the splash of water going into the tub, followed by the clink of glass. Then he was back, kneeling before her and undressing her with such exquisite gentleness she wanted to cry. All she could think about was how concerned he'd been for her and how she'd tried to argue with him about his misgivings. She was just damn lucky he hadn't taken back the watch and left her hanging out there in the wind.

She ran her tongue over lips that were dry. "Slade, I want to tell you—"

He lifted a hand and touched two fingers to her lips. "Ssh. Not now. Now it's all about getting you past this."

As he removed each piece of clothing she tried not to remember Robert Glasgow and his plans to do exactly that but in a more vicious fashion. She made a deliberate effort to try to blank that whole scene from her mind. It helped that as each item fell away, he took the time to place gentle kisses on the exposed skin. There was nothing erotic about any of this. It was more of a calming nature, more reassuring that she was safe and she was okay with him touching her.

When at last she was completely naked, he lifted her and carried her into the bathroom. Fragrant steam rose from the tub, which was now filled to the top, bubbles floating on the surface.

"I dumped some of your good-smelling stuff into it," he told her, smiling, as he turned off the taps. "I thought a few bubbles might be nice too."

Kari swallowed a smile at the thought of this big, masculine soldier, a warrior, preparing this bath for her. He lowered her slowly into the water until she was submerged up to her neck. She leaned her head back against the bath pillow she kept in place and closed her eyes. It was heavenly, the heat, the bubbles, the scented water all working to ease the tension and wash away the fear. To help her relax.

Slade stripped off his T-shirt and kneeled beside the tub, picking up the flower sponge she kept on the ledge.

"You'll have to excuse me if I stink from the ranch," he told her. "I'd just gotten through riding when I got the call that you'd pushed the panic button."

"You can smell like anything you want. It's all good to me." She let out a sigh. "It's really over now, isn't it?"

"It is. In fact—"

"Just let me say this. Let me get this out before we go any further." She closed her eyes, unable to look at him while she spoke. "I am so very sorry, Slade. I acted like a child, refusing to listen to you. My brain knew you were right, but I wanted it to be over with so badly I couldn't entertain the alternative."

"I know, darlin'. It's okay." He began smoothing the

sponge over her arms and shoulders.

"No, it's not. I'm a prosecutor, for God's sake. I know how this stuff works. The best cases sometimes go sideways because of just this sort of thing. I just didn't want it to be that way with me." She blew out a breath. "You have no idea how grateful I am to you. Not just for rescuing me but for not being so angry with me you wrote me off."

"Never." He eased the fluffy sponge over her breasts, first one, then the other, a caress more soothing than sexual.

"I don't know why, but—" She caught her lower lip between her teeth. "Thank you. I promise you that's the last time I'll ever act like an idiot."

Slade rocked back on his heels and laughed. "Even *I* won't promise that, but it's nice to hear." He leaned forward, ignoring the bubbles brushing his chest, and placed a soft kiss on her lips. "I've been kicking myself for waiting all weekend to bring it up to you. Maybe if I'd figured out a way to do it earlier—"

She shook her head. "I'm not sure I would have listened then. But I will from now on."

He stared at her, his eyes dark with some unknown emotion. "Does that mean you want to keep this going? Us? This thing between us?"

"Damn straight. Like you said in the beginning, you lead an uncertain life and you never know what's going to happen. I understand you not wanting to—"

Now it was his turn to shut her up, but he did it by pressing his mouth to hers. "Forget all that. Forget everything else I said about not knowing how to have a relationship or not wanting to have someone at home worrying all the time about me or the rest of that crap. When that panic button set things in motion today I wasn't sure I'd survive if something happened to you. But then I realized, whatever came in life, I'd always be grateful for whatever time we had together." He rubbed his jaw, leaving a trail of soap bubbles.

Kari giggled then reached out to swipe them off. "It's far more likely to happen to you than me, although you know that old saying. Car accidents can happen to anyone and right in front of your eyes."

"My point is, I don't want to waste any more time because of my hang-ups. This is fast, Kari, and maybe we skipped a bunch of steps, but…" He blew out a breath. "Here it is. I love you. I do. And I don't want to take the chance someone else might grab you up while I'm being an indecisive idiot."

"Come here." When his mouth was a breath away from hers, she tugged him closer that last little bit.

Slade's tongue slipped into her mouth, another gentle caress as he lightly licked and stroked. He tasted sweet and salty and sharp, all the flavors of who he was. When he finally lifted his head, she gave him a hard, intent look, as if asking him to see into her soul.

"I love you too."

For the first time since she'd met him, she saw his face completely relax, felt the same release of tension in his body. The smile he gave her reached into every corner of her body.

"How about we finish this bath, take a nap and order in some dinner? For what I have in mind, you'll need to be well rested and well fed."

She laughed. "Keeping up my strength?"

"You know it." Then all traces of humor left his face. "I'm serious about all this, Kari. I almost went nuts today when Jamie, my security guy, called to say you'd pushed that button. I realized then that I didn't want to be the idiot that missed the best thing to ever walk into my life."

"Then let's not. Let's make every minute count."

Chapter Twenty-Two

Kari came awake with a start, not sure for a moment where she was. Blinking the sleep from her eyes, she realized she was in her own place, her own bed, and Slade was right beside her, talking to someone on her cell. The last thing she remembered was listening to the shower running while she'd waited in bed for him. Then he'd slid his warm body in beside her and pulled her into his arms, cocooning himself around her and allowing her to just drift off to sleep.

Who on earth was he talking to?

"Oh, wait," he said. "She's awake now. Let me put this on speaker."

She frowned. "Who is it?"

"Your boss. He has information to share." He pressed the Speaker button and held the phone between them.

"You doing okay, Kari?" Kip asked. "Ross is about to kill himself over letting this happen."

"He didn't *let* anything happen," she corrected him. "He's not responsible for the judge's actions."

"He believes everyone was so happy to wrap the thing up that they didn't look beneath the surface. John Schreiber knew all the details, even appeared to brag about some of the things." His heavy sigh transmitted across the connection. "You know what they say, if something looks too good to be true, it usually is."

"Kip had said the same thing yesterday. We all live and learn."

"I just hate it that my learning put you in a desperate situation."

"It's all good now, though." She leaned closer to Slade, who circled his arm around her. "Was this trip to San Antonio just a coincidence? He only just learned where I was."

"Sort of. He knew about the conference and was wavering about attending. He got John to do his shtick and figured he could use his fake apology to get Ross to spill where you were. No more danger, right?"

"The conference was his cover," Kari guessed.

"It was," Kip agreed. "An unfortunate circumstance of timing for us."

"I think it's disgusting the way he bribed John to take the fall for him."

Kip snorted. "Paid him an obscene amount of money and promised him he'd make sure he got a good position with a top firm when the time came."

"Not if Schreiber was in jail," Kari pointed out.

"Well, that's the thing." Kip paused. "The dates some of these things occurred, like the break-ins at your house? Schreiber had proof he was somewhere else."

"But wouldn't it then be an open case again?" Slade asked.

"It would," Kip agreed. "But that could be months away. Glasgow was crazy enough to believe by that time Kari would be thrilled to be in a secret relationship with him and the whole thing would just die out."

Kari felt a chill skitter down her spine. A secret relationship. He might even have taken it to the extreme of keeping her imprisoned in his house, or some other place.

"So what's happening now?"

"Glasgow's in the hospital until tomorrow," Kip told her. "Chicago's sending two detectives to bring him back to Illinois although San Antonio claims they have dibs since kidnapping trumps stalking." He gave a short laugh. "Either way he'll never see the outside of a prison cell again. And you can finally draw a full breath and live a normal life."

"True, although I'm not even sure what's normal

anymore."

Another pause.

"Kari, Ross asked me to pass along the word that he still has a place on his staff for you. It's safe to return to Chicago if that's what you want."

She looked at Slade who shook his head. "You know what I want," he whispered, "but the choice is yours."

"And what about you, Kip? Would you still want to keep me on?"

"I didn't just make a place for you," he told her. "I had an opening and a real need for a seasoned prosecutor. I'd do a little jig if you decide to stay."

She laughed. "Okay, if you promise to let me watch. Seriously, my life has had some changes to it since I came here. I'll be staying in San Antonio."

"Hot damn! Listen, take the rest of the week off. That's an order. Next Monday when you come back to work, we'll have a little party in the office here."

"Not necessary," she told him.

"It is for me."

"I'll call Ross myself and tell him what I've decided." She looked at Slade again and he nodded.

"Take care." Kip hung up.

Slade put the phone back on the nightstand then turned to her. "I'm hoping the reason you made that decision is because of us."

"Maybe I just want to hang around Teo," she teased.

Slade rolled her on top of his body and lightly slapped one cheek of her ass. "I might have to punish you for that."

She gave a fake shiver. "Ooh! I'm so scared."

When he spoke again, his voice was husky, rough with his own need. "I just want you to know I never thought I'd find a woman like you. For a while I thought you might be too good to be true."

"And now?"

"I think you know the answer to that. I think we've done enough dancing around this issue. I love you. I told myself

I'd never say those words to a woman, but I also never thought I'd meet a woman like you."

She locked her gaze with his, seeing myriad emotions swirling in his eyes. "I love you too, Slade."

"If it's all the same to you, I'm turning off your phone until tomorrow. I talked to the guys when they all checked in to see how you were doing. They're taken care of, so I've turned my cell off already."

"Taken care of?" She lifted an eyebrow. "With their ladies, I hope?"

He nodded. "Marc got dropped off at Christy's. Man, I sure hope that's turning into something and that it works for him. He's been living in an emotional closet for a long time."

"What about her? I didn't really get to meet her."

"Me neither." He brushed the tips of his fingers down her cheek. "He's being very closemouthed about the whole thing. But he seems a little less closed in, so I'm hoping."

"And the others?"

"Megan's taking Beau to the basketball game tonight," he told her. "She's got courtside seats and he's about to wet himself."

Kari laughed. "And Trey?"

"Kenzi has to go to Corpus Christi for a couple of days for a client. He's going with."

"So everyone's set?"

"So it seems." He wove his fingers through her hair, holding her head in pace. "That leaves me free to devote every minute to you."

Yes, yes, yes!

His face was so close to hers that his breath, lightly scented from the mouthwash he'd used earlier, was a warm caress on her skin. His mouth was barely a whisper away from hers.

Kiss me! Kiss me!

Then he did, a light touch of lips at first, a soft brush. His tongue traced the outline of her mouth and licked the closed seam. Automatically she parted for him and his tongue slipped inside, softly invasive, tasting everywhere. It was a coaxing kiss more than a demanding one, and it made her weak in the knees. She clutched his arms to hold herself steady, her head swimming and her senses roaring to life.

"I meant what I said before." He lifted his head, his hazel eyes now darkened almost to a forest green. "For a man like me, the special woman to complete him can be almost nonexistent. My life is…different. I can be gone for weeks or even months then here for a long time. Even when I'm on base, if we're not training or planning a mission, I can at least come home for the weekends."

"I'll take it," she told him. "A little of you is better than a lot of someone else."

"I want us to plan a future together," he insisted. "My future is with you."

"Ditto. You got it, soldier."

"How about ordering in some dinner?" he asked. "You hungry?"

"Not for food." She placed a soft kiss on his lips. "I love you."

"I love you too. I don't know how I got so lucky with you."

"I think it was meant to be," she said in a whisper. "What were the chances we'd meet in Chicago and five years later end up in the same city? I always believe there's an invisible hand guiding us. Now I'm sure."

"It's guiding us in the right direction. That's for sure." He brushed his mouth over hers again. "I'd like to do some guiding with my own hands right now."

"Would you do something for me?" Her heart thudded a beat at what she was about to ask him.

"For you, anything."

"Let me freshen up a little. Then I want you to tie my hands when we make love. And blindfold me too."

He gave her a penetrating stare. "Are you sure, Kari? After this afternoon—"

"That's exactly why I want you to do it," she broke in. "I don't want to live with that image and that memory forever. When I think of restraint, I want it to be voluntary and with you."

He studied her face for so long she wondered if he was ever going to say anything. Then he gave a slow nod.

"I'd like that. In a way it's binding you to me."

She rolled off his body and slipped from the bed. "And don't forget to punish my impudent attitude," she teased.

His eyes darkened. "You liked it when I spanked you the other day."

She nodded. She'd more than liked it. It had made her hotter than hell. "Just like you did that night in Chicago."

She slipped into her bathroom, closed the door and stared at herself in the mirror.

Now or never, Kari. Show him how you feel. He said the words. Now it's time for you to take a chance.

Letting out a slow breath, she pushed away from the door and set about getting ready.

Slade had no idea what the hell Kari was doing, but her words kept echoing in his head. Tie her up? Blindfold her? Spank her? They'd already had a conversation about the appeal — or not — of BDSM and agreed for the most part it was a bit too extreme for both of them. But he knew of couples that introduced aspects of it into their sex lives and thrived on it. Just thinking about it made his cock swell even more and harden to painful attention.

Well, just lying here in bed like a lump wasn't getting him anywhere, so he pushed himself to his feet and set about straightening the bedclothes. He used the guest bathroom to do his own freshening up and was standing in the middle of the room when she walked back in. She had brushed her hair until it shone, letting it fall in thick auburn waves to her shoulders. The scent of the bubble bath still clung to her, a tantalizing fragrance that made him want to lick every inch of her skin. She wore no makeup except a touch of gloss on her lips and he thought she looked exquisite.

He watched her pull open a drawer in her dresser and take out two silk scarves, which she placed in his hands.

"I'm yours, Slade. Bind me to you. Let me feel your hands on me, everywhere on my body."

Jesus!

He used one of the scarves to blindfold her, then led her to the bed and helped her to lie on her stomach.

"I won't tie your hands to the headboard," he insisted. "That's way too much of a reminder of this afternoon and you don't need any flashbacks." He bent down and stroked his fingers along her cheek. "This will be special for us. Our own memories."

She nodded in agreement. He wrapped the silk around her wrists, crisscrossing them, and placing her bound hands on the pillow. Then he trailed his fingers down the length of her spine, pausing a moment to slide them into the hot crevice of her buttocks then down to nudge her thighs wide apart. He drew in a deep breath, let it out slowly and brought the flat of his hand down on her ass with a sharp *crack!*

Kari jerked in response but didn't make a sound. He did it again and again, the contact producing a dark shade of red that blossomed on her very delectable buttocks. When he slipped his fingers between her thighs seeking the entrance to her pussy, he found it to be soaked and very slick. He probed her wet channel and delivered another slap. Damn! Her inner walls clamped down at once and more juice coated his skin.

He slid out and placed his palm on one cheek of her buttocks. It still flamed with warmth, a heat that transferred itself to him. He couldn't begin to describe the feeling it gave him that after everything she'd been through today she was willing to submit to this. No, not submit. Participate. Share the pleasure. She'd told him on that long-ago night she'd never done this with anyone else or even wanted to. He'd been excited then, but now? Now he was humbled.

A rush of love for this woman surged through him like cascading rapids. All his reservations about leaving her waiting at home were nothing compared to her strength. He had been the weak one, unwilling to take a chance. Her strength made his heart swell. How many women would have survived today's chilling episode and not turned into a quivering mass?

They could play games later. Now he had something more important on his mind and he needed to be inside her to complete it. Yanking open the drawer to her nightstand, he then pulled out one of the condoms he kept there and rolled it on with hands that actually shook. In an instant he removed the scarves and turned her onto her back.

She stared at him, face flushed with passion, bewildered. "What—?"

"Ssh." He positioned himself between her thighs, let out a breath and drove into her with one, swift movement. "Later. We can play more later."

When she opened her mouth to say something else, he simply took it in a scorching kiss, licking her lips then thrusting his tongue inside to taste every surface. Her small, delicate tongue dueled with his in an erotic dance, sensation reaching every part of his body. As he swirled and tasted again and again, the rhythm increasing in tempo, he felt as if he were absorbing every part of this woman into his body.

He couldn't hang on to his control this time. Not when everything was suddenly so crystal clear to him. This was his present and his future, more than he'd ever expected from life. He slipped a hand between them, found her clit and massaged it with rapid strokes. They exploded together, the orgasm so intense it shook them. Everything else faded except the sensation and the feel of emptying himself into her body.

When the aftershocks subsided at last and she lay there, flushed, heart beating rapidly against his own, he smiled at her.

"I love you."

She grinned. "You told me. I love you too."

"Marry me. Now. Before I have to leave again." What if she said no? What if she wanted more time?

She wrinkled her forehead. "Slade? I don't understand. You've had so many reservations. I know you love me, but don't you need more time to sort everything out?"

"It's sorted. I could have lost you today if Glasgow had gotten it into his head to dispose of you. It scared the shit out of me. Nothing is worse than my fear of being without you. We can work out the rest of the details as we go along."

She blinked. "You'll shock the hell out of your men."

"Good," he told her. "Maybe it will give them ideas."

She laughed. "I wouldn't necessarily count on that, but we'll see." Then she sobered and such love bloomed in her eyes it humbled him. "Okay. Yes. I'll marry you."

"When?" he pushed.

"Whenever you want. We can get the license tomorrow if you like."

"I like and I want. Good. It's settled." He brushed his lips over hers. "And you know? It will be nice having you to come home to. Damn nice."

Epilogue

Kari Malone and Lt. Col. Slade Donovan were united in marriage on Sunday afternoon at the groom's ranch just south of San Antonio. Officiating was a friend of the groom, Colonel Paul Hutton, Army JAG officer. Sasha Crew and Sgt. Trey McIntyre served as honor attendants. The couple will make the ranch their primary residence but will continue to maintain an apartment in the city where the bride is a highly regarded assistant district attorney.

They spent their wedding night at a resort in Hill Country, just outside San Antonio, before leaving for their honeymoon to Hawaii the next day.

"I don't want to spend my wedding night traveling," Slade had insisted.

Now they sat at a table set for two on the balcony of the lavish suite Slade had reserved. The view was magnificent, rolling green pastures bathed in sunlight, a soft breeze whispering through the leaves on the trees.

"I'm going to have this laminated and frame it." Kari had the *San Antonio Express-News* newspaper that had been delivered along with their breakfast tray that morning on the table next to her, folded to their wedding announcement where she could keep looking at it. "Maybe I should also have it tattooed on your chest to warn off any other woman."

Slade chuckled. "I don't think you have to worry on that score, darlin'. There's not a woman in the world who could interest me anymore besides you."

She set the paper aside and picked up her coffee cup. "I

was glad your team members all brought someone to the wedding. It looks like we have some budding relationships."

"Hoorah to that," Slade agreed. "Megan certainly gives Beau more than he can handle. I never thought he'd stick to one woman for more than a week. It does my old heart good to see it."

"She hinted at a big story she's working on that hits all professional athletics. Sounds exciting."

Slade nodded. "She has to do some traveling in the next few days and Beau is going with her."

"And Trey with a corporate attorney?" She grinned. "They just seem so opposite."

"Not much different than you and me, darlin'." Slade lifted her free hand and placed a kiss on her knuckles.

"The biggest surprise was Marc," Kari mused.

He nodded. "I'm glad to see he's come out of the shadows, but I worried what kind of woman he'd hook up with."

"Christy seems very nice. Shy and quiet, and probably exactly what he needs. He certainly was solicitous of her."

Slade nodded. "There's definitely something good going on there. It'll be interesting to see where they all are when we get back." He pushed back from the table. "Speaking of getting back, we need to get crackin'. The airport limo will be here before long."

"Okay." Kari finished her last sip of coffee then rose. "Fine. I'm nearly all ready, anyway."

Slade pulled her into his arms. "I love you, Kari. You've become so much a part of my life I can't imagine it without you." He brushed a stray hair back from her forehead. "I want you to try not to worry while I'm gone. You know I'll text and Skype every chance I get."

"I'll worry," she told him, "but I trust you to come home safe and sound."

"Count on it," he told her.

He took her mouth in a scorching kiss, a promise of their life together and their future.

More books from
Totally Bound Publishing

Book one in the Deadly Intent series

She could never foresee the danger, death and desire that now surrounded her.

A cop with a mission. A woman with no memory. A killer who hunts them both.

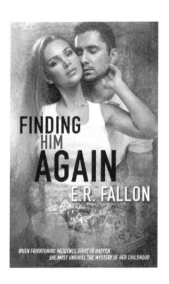

*She came home to find the one romance she always
regretted not having…*

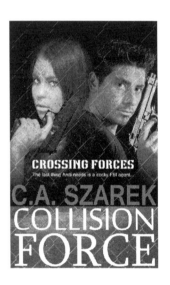

Book one in the Crossing Forces series

A bad boy FBI agent and a feisty widowed police detective collide pursuing a human trafficker in small-town Texas on their way to true love.

About the Author

Desiree Holt

A multi-published, award winning, Amazon and USA Today best-selling author, Desiree Holt has produced more than 200 titles and won many awards. She has received an EPIC E-Book Award, the Holt Medallion and many others including Author After Dark's Author of the Year. She has been featured on CBS Sunday Morning and in The Village Voice, The Daily Beast, USA Today, The Wall Street Journal, The London Daily Mail. She lives in Florida with her cats who insist they help her write her books, and is addicted to football.

Desiree Holt loves to hear from readers. You can find contact information, website details and an author profile page at https://www.totallybound.com/